The Photographer

Larissa
ENJOY & God Bless

Arleen Jennings

ARLEEN JENNINGS

 Books

THE PHOTOGRAPHER

Book Cover Photograph by Mohamed Nohassi
Cover design by Arleen Jennings
www.arleenjennings.com

For my Jayzel

Your compassionate heart for people
is an inspiration to me.

Chapter 1

NOT EVERYTHING IS BLACK AND WHITE

One more day. That was all Parker needed to complete his black and white photo collection of Philadelphia's Historic District. Inclement weather had hindered his progress and he was starting to feel the pressure of a time crunch. For him, getting the light right was just as important as the composition. His reputation as one of the best photographers in Philadelphia hung largely on his ability to capture the moment, the mood, and the energy that would bring his photographs to life.

With clear skies forecasted, Parker was out the door and reached the corner of 5th and Chestnut by daybreak. From this location, he could walk to all the landmarks still on his list.

A gust of cool autumn air tussled his black hair as he opened his door, causing him to shiver. Maybe he should have worn a light jacket, but it was too late for that now, he had work to do. After slipping on his Phillies baseball cap, he grabbed his camera bag off the back seat and started down the sleepy street lined with maple trees.

The Museum of the American Revolution was to be his first stop. When the sun rose over a distant building and light danced through the trees, Parker smiled at the prospect of a successful morning and hastened his pace.

Nearing the museum, Parker couldn't help but notice that the abandoned building on the opposite side of the street seemed to glow . . . almost luminous. He'd never seen anything like it and quickly grabbed his camera, hoping to capture its essence before the lighting changed.

Despite the obvious neglect, it was evident no expense had been spared when this four-story structure was built. Exquisitely carved molding framed the round-top windows and white pillars lined the façade. Ornate block molding ran the full length between the first and second floors. The forlorn building must have been a hundred fifty years old. Parker wondered what could have caused the building's demise. Though worn with time and a lack of upkeep, the windows were deliberately boarded over, even to the top floor. A heavy lock and chain protected the entrance, and the ground floor sported only small amounts of spray paint, suggesting even vandals dared not deface the building.

After taking several pictures, Parker turned his attention back to the museum and the other places still on his list. He made steady progress, but by 9:00, tourists had filled the streets and the historic buildings were swallowed up by large crowds. He decided to call it quits and head for home.

Of all the pictures Parker took that morning, he was most interested to see how the ones of the abandoned building turned out. If truth be told, the building was a real eyesore and a black spot on the Historic District, yet the extraordinary lighting was something he had never seen before. Then it hit him that in his haste he hadn't thought to switch out the black and white film for color. *Oh well, I can't change that now.*

It didn't take long to set things up and process the negatives in the darkroom Parker had built in his basement. Pleased with the light and quality of his photos, he used a 16 x 20 professional-grade paper. Once he was happy with his test sheet, he enlarged a picture of the abandoned building, slid it into the developer, and started gently rocking the tray. He mindlessly watched as the chemicals did their magic. The image began to appear, but something was wrong.

"What in the world?"

The red darkroom lighting made it difficult to determine exactly what was happening, but Parker thought he saw color in the black and white print. He leaned in, straining to see. More and more pigments filled the paper with what appeared to be a translucent image of the building when it was new. Using his tongs, he momentarily lifted the print and examined it more closely. Underneath the color, his original photo of the building was still visible in the background, boarded up and gray.

Then, as if touching a hot coal, Parker abruptly released the tongs that held the photo, dropping the paper back into the solution. He drew his tingling fingers to his mouth and whispered, "Impossible!"

Silence permeated the room until the timer reminded him to move the print into the next tray of chemicals. Parker continued the steps until the process was complete. Even after rinsing the print under cold water for a few minutes, the color remained perfectly intact.

He dried his hands and then began rubbing his bearded chin. "I don't see how this is possible."

More intrigued than stumped, he needed to know if it would happen again. Parker left the paper in a tub of water and hurried back to the enlarger. His hands trembled as he lined up a new piece of paper and transferred the next image. Sliding it into the solution, he watched intently. The result was exactly the same.

Realistically, if he had accidentally used a roll of colored film, it would be possible to have some interesting hues appear. But when he checked the discarded casement, the label confirmed the film was black and white. "Huh. Now what?"

Not wanting to waste chemicals, he chose a picture from his other roll of film and started the process for the third time. As the image came into view, there was no color, just a nice shot of Independence Hall. He did another, this time of the Liberty Bell. Again, a clean black-and-white photo, exactly as he would expect.

I guess the first two were flukes. Still curious, he went back to his original roll of film and did another print of the abandoned building. A full range of color appeared, exactly as it had before. Not wanting to give up on the entire roll, he developed a picture of the Museum of the American Revolution. It had no color in it. *Interesting. It's only happening with the pictures of the abandoned building . . . but why?*

He developed three more of them before finishing the photos of the historic sites. Once he had all the pictures he needed for the commission job, he hung the prints to dry on a line that ran the full length of the back wall. With his arms crossed, he leaned against the steel table. "This doesn't make any sense. The color is too consistent in all six photos to be by chance."

Not sure what to make of it, Parker put a fresh roll of film into his camera and drove back to Chestnut Street. The sun was high in the sky and people were everywhere, but he didn't care; he needed to see if the color would show again.

He had only taken a few pictures before his phone vibrated. In one quick motion, Parker slipped his camera under his left arm and got out his phone. He didn't recognize the number, but as a matter of business, he always answered. "Hello."

"Good afternoon, Parker, I watched you take pictures of the abandoned building on Chestnut Street this morning. How'd they turn out?"

"Who is this?"

"I'm a fan of your photography."

"So that gives you a right to stalk me?"

"I wasn't stalking. I enjoy the early morning light as much as you do, and I couldn't help but notice the abandoned building looked like it was wrapped in a blanket of transparent gold."

Parker whirled around to see if anyone was watching him. All the pedestrians were either preoccupied with area maps or were chatting about other things as they passed by. No one seemed to pay him any attention, so he crossed the street and took a seat on one of the marble benches.

"Hey, Parker, are you still there?" the man asked.

"Oh, uh, yeah. The lighting was mesmerizing for sure."

"Your prints must have turned out amazing."

"Actually, I'm not sure they did."

"But why not? Did you overexpose them or something?"

"No, it's just that, well, I had black and white film in my camera."

"Ah, so you didn't capture the color."

To Parker's surprise, disappointment salted the man's tone. Even though he didn't understand why it should matter, he felt compelled to explain. "But that's what's so confusing, color *did* fill the prints and I don't mean the golden glow. I've never seen anything like it."

"Perfect. That means the lighting worked and I got just what I wanted."

The man's abrupt optimism caused Parker to snap, "What do you mean—" Just then, an elderly couple walked by; the man narrowed his eyes as they both looked his way. With a nod and a small wave, he continued in a softer tone, "What do you mean you got what you wanted? I didn't take those pictures for you."

"Oh, but you did."

Because it was impossible, Parker had assumed the color would be gone by the time he got home. But now his mind raced, keeping beat with his pounding heart. "Who is this?"

"Calm down, son, and I'll explain."

"I'm not your son," Parker barked, no longer caring if anyone looked his way. "Why are you messing with me?"

"This is no laughing matter. To be clear, the color overlay became visible this morning because you took the photos of a specific place at a specific time."

"I didn't even know I was *supposed* to take those photos."

"Maybe not, but you will from now on if you accept my job offer."

Parker removed his Phillies cap and wiped sweat from his brow. "What job offer?"

"I need you to investigate a cold case for me. The consequences have gone further than the missing and justice must be served."

"I'm a photographer, not a private investigator."

"Yes, I know," the man said, "but that doesn't disqualify you from having the ability to solve this case. I chose you, in part, because of your photography skills; you have a great eye for seeing and capturing details. More importantly though, the unknown intrigues you and you appreciate a worthy challenge. This will come in handy if you accept my offer."

Instead of focusing on what he didn't understand, Parker asked about something he did. "Does this offer include getting paid?"

"Life is about more than money, but yes, you'll be paid—in more ways than you could ever imagine. However, first things first; are you interested in a change of pace that includes taking photos when and where I tell you, following leads, and deciphering clues? If yes, your payment will be the proceeds you make from selling the images you developed this morning. The next pictures you take, at my bidding, will include information that you'll have to figure out. When you have your answers, you'll need to act."

Parker didn't know what to think. He already made a good living as a professional photographer, but he never had extra images show up and these photos were definitely something he couldn't produce or replicate on his own. The payday would be substantial and that alone was enticing, but Parker couldn't understand the need for all this secrecy. "What's your name and when will we meet?"

"It's not like knowing my name will change anything and for now, we won't meet. Eventually you will understand, but in the meantime, I don't expect you to do this alone. Give your friend, Matt, a call and have him meet you at Chestnut Street at 6:00 tomorrow morning. Tell him to bring his 35mm, and this time I want you both to take pictures of the abandoned building. There will be different images and messages on each roll of film. Remember, you will need to take action on what you discover. You won't hear from me again until you solve your first mystery. Do we have a deal?"

The money would be nice, but Parker wasn't sure he was willing to give up his freedom, especially for a man who chose to remain anonymous. The knot in his stomach tightened as he considered the predicament. Still confused about the color and the improbability of this offer, he asked, "What's in this for you? And what's this about clues? It seems a bit childish, don't you think?"

"I'm confident that *childish* won't be the word you use if you give this a shot. Now, the only way for you to get the answer to your first question is to trust me and follow my leads."

"You should probably know that even if I'm willing to give this a shot, Matt won't be. He's the most pragmatic person I know, and he's getting married in less than two months."

"Matt will say yes because his fiancée, Haley, broke up with him earlier today. He will need the diversion."

Parker balked at this statement. *I know there's no way that's true, so how does this guy expect me to trust him?*

"If you choose not to accept my offer, the images you developed this morning, worth thousands of dollars each, will disappear. You'll be free from any obligation and I'll never contact you again. However, if you say yes, you'll find purpose far beyond the money."

Parker blew out a heavy breath and started walking back to his Jeep. Part of him wanted to say no, to stay with the status quo of making his own choices and being in control; yet a bigger part of him wanted to see what would happen next. "Okay, I'll do it . . . but only if Matt agrees to help."

"Perfect. Give him a call. I'll be in touch."

❑ ❑ ❑

Parker didn't know what to make of the day's events: the pictures, the caller, Matt . . . none of it made sense. Adding to his dilemma was the thought of calling Matt. How was he going to explain any of this, especially if Haley did end things? To clear his mind and avoid the call, he went for a run. Instead of taking his usual trek through the neighborhood, where everything would look familiar, he drove to the local high school.

He parked in the first open spot. From there he ran around the sports fields, up a bank, and through a paved wooded area that eventually reached several practice fields and a track. He continued along the perimeter of the fence where there was a well-worn path. Beyond the fence was a row of trees and beyond the trees, rows and rows of townhouses.

It didn't take Parker long to set a decent pace and forget about everything else. By the half-way point, though, he'd caught up to a young couple jogging on the same path ahead of him. As he approached, he could hear them flirting in between breaths. His thoughts immediately went to Matt and Haley. Any time he was with them, they always seemed happy and from what he knew, they had all the wedding details set.

The breakup can't be true but, even if it is, who is this nameless caller and what's his connection with Matt? Not wanting to think about the possibility of Haley breaking Matt's heart, Parker hurried past the couple and out of earshot.

Fifteen minutes later, he finished his run, returned home, and was doing stretches on the lawn in front of his townhouse when his phone rang.

It was Matt.

Before Parker answered, he pulled up the bottom of his T-shirt to wipe his face. "Hey, I was just about to call you. What's up?"

"Haley dumped me this afternoon." Matt groaned. "It's over!"

"No way. You're kidding, right?" Parker started to pace, as if this would help steady him for what was coming next.

"I wish I was kidding but I'm not. And get this—she didn't even have the guts to tell me in person. She sent an email."

Even though Parker had been forewarned, that didn't eliminate the ache he felt for his friend. "Wow. That was heartless."

"And devastating! I don't know what to do. It's not as simple as just breaking up. We already sent the invitations. We paid a deposit for the reception. We even booked our flights to Italy."

"I don't get it; you two seemed made for each other."

"That's what I thought, but apparently she met a guy at work and is willing to throw us away. No warning, no hint of discontentment, just bam, it's over. I guess love really is blind."

"Did she give you any other reason? Like an unresolved fight or something?"

"It wasn't a fight. Her email said I wasn't adventurous enough." Matt groaned. "She's just discovering this now? We've only been dating for like three years; it makes no sense."

"It sounds more like Haley got cold feet." Parker stopped pacing. "Maybe the thought of forever scared her. I'm sure she'll come to her senses."

"Not likely. She didn't ask to change the date; she had a friend stop by the office to give me the ring back. What am I going to do?"

"I have an idea. Meet me at the corner of 5th and Chestnut tomorrow morning at 6:00 and bring your film camera."

"Wait. What?"

"I have a new commission that you can help me with."

"Why Chestnut Street? And why so early?"

"There's a building I need to photograph, and the lighting is perfect at that hour."

"So much for a diversion. You realize my office is only a few blocks over, right?"

"Yeah. Is there a problem?"

"Haley and I would often have lunch at a café on the east end of Chestnut Street."

"Oh right. Sorry, that didn't cross my mind. I was thinking it'd be good for you to keep busy. I know I wouldn't want to be alone at a time like this. It would drive me crazy and I might do something stupid."

"Well, I don't have a death wish, if that's what you're implying."

"Not at all. I was thinking I'd be more apt to break something or say something I'd regret." Parker heard Matt let out a heavy sigh, but he didn't answer. "I could teach you more about aperture. We haven't done an early morning photo shoot together."

"I'm not really in the mood for a photography lesson."

"Didn't you just ask me what you were supposed to do? Well, I'm offering you an opportunity to be distracted. If you don't want to take me up on it, fine," Parker said, more sharply than he meant to.

"Fine."

Palpable tension filled the silence.

"Sorry, that wasn't fair. Will you come?"

Chapter 2

COLORFUL CLUES

Parker couldn't get to sleep so he wandered back to his dark room and picked up one of the prints. Maybe his mind was playing tricks on him. Lost in a whirl of frustration, he touched the surface, this time rubbing it with some force to see if the image would smudge or change. It didn't. There was no possible way for the color to show up, yet what confused him more was the fact that the color looked like a separate image hovering above the original photograph. He doubted that Matt, or anyone else for that matter, would be able to see the colorful overlay.

Then his mind began to race to other scenarios, like what if more images *did* show up? It would be fascinating, but what would they reveal and how committed would he have to be to this nameless caller?

He set down the print and went back to bed.

❑ ❑ ❑

Five o'clock came way too early. Parker felt as though he had just fallen asleep, but it was already time to face the uncertainty that lay ahead of him. Swinging his long legs off the bed, he sat on the edge and briskly rubbed his hands over the top of his head, leaving his hair a disheveled mess. Would extra images show up again? He had no reason to *believe* they would, yet with the photos in his darkroom and the unexpected reality that Matt's engagement was off, he supposed anything could be possible.

With a quick shake of his head, he wandered into the bathroom where he splashed cold water on his face and then stared blankly into the mirror. New places and new experiences were usually exciting. At the age of twenty-seven, he had already traveled to several places around the world and photographed a wide variety of things but never had any of his pictures contained extra images. Nor had a commission job come with a nameless client and a cold case to solve.

To set his mind at ease, he moved the colorful prints from his darkroom to his matting table at the far end of the basement where they would be out of sight. If nothing out of the ordinary happened, Matt would never need to know.

□ □ □

Matt arrived before Parker so he sat in his car and fished the engagement ring out of his pocket. He turned it this way and that. The movement made the ring sparkle, which only made his heart hurt worse. *This guy must be Superman amazing if Haley's willing to throw us away after three great years together.* His thoughts ran from one thing to the next, all ending with the same painful fact; he didn't get it.

Matt jumped when Parker rapped his knuckles on the car window. Quickly shoving the ring back into his pocket, he grabbed his camera bag and joined Parker on the sidewalk. "Uh, sorry, I didn't see you pull up."

"No worries, I'm not in a hurry."

Matt hadn't slept much. His round, baby face was red and swollen. His brown eyes were bloodshot. He hadn't shaved— not because of the hour or a lack of sleep. He simply didn't bother. The sweatpants he wore were baggy and the extra-large sweatshirt made his stocky frame look frumpy. Matt had lost thirty pounds in the last two months because his weight wasn't fair to Haley and he wanted to look sharp for the wedding. Today he didn't care.

"Rough night, huh?" Parker asked.

Matt pushed his wavy brown hair off his forehead and straightened his black-rimmed glasses. "Yeah, well, I'm here. Though I'm not seeing what's worth getting out of bed for."

The sun had lost its battle to a thick bank of clouds that rolled in during the night. Matt thought the subdued atmosphere seemed fitting, though he hoped the poor lighting wouldn't interfere with Parker's commission.

"The building's a few blocks that way." Parker nodded to his left and took off like a man on a mission.

Matt fell into stride beside him but said nothing. Parker either seemed to be clueless about his pain or very focused on his job. He wasn't sure which. *I guess I can't expect him to understand.*

When they reached the right spot, Parker pointed to the abandoned building across the street and said, "There it is; isn't she a beauty?"

"Yeah, like maybe a hundred years ago."

Parker slung his camera bag off his shoulder. "Do you want me to show you some different aperture settings?"

"No thanks," Matt said as he got out his camera. Normally, he would've looked forward to learning some new techniques. Parker was a good teacher, but today taking quality photos was the last thing on his mind.

"Suit yourself." Parker snapped a few shots before crossing the street.

They worked in silence as they photographed the old building. Each took several pictures, and for the time being Matt seemed distracted. He used a digital camera for work. Parker was the one who got him into film photography. He also taught him how to see the lines and shapes of architecture, which made his photos more artistic.

It didn't take long to get what they needed. While they packed up their equipment, Parker asked, "Do you know

17

anything about this building? It seems odd that such a prime piece of real estate would remain vacant."

"It's always been empty. Well, at least as long as I can remember."

"Interesting. We should check into it."

Matt shrugged. "Occasionally a new rumor would swirl, but the stories never matched, and I didn't care enough to find out the truth."

"If no one knows exactly what happened here, it sounds like it could be a mystery worth learning. Doesn't the writer in you want to know?"

"Not really. Do you care or are you just making small talk?"

"Both, but you're obviously not in the mood."

They walked back to their vehicles in silence, but before Matt could leave, Parker stopped him. "Want to come over and develop your film? We can grab some breakfast on the way."

It was a Saturday and Matt's plans to spend the day with Haley were canceled. "Sure, I'll come. If I go home, I'd probably give in to the temptation to stop to buy a dozen donuts and I wouldn't stop eating them until they were all gone."

"No offense, man, but that'd be stupid."

"You think?" Matt bobbed his head. "I said I would come."

❑ ❑ ❑

It was after 8:00 before they reached the house. Matt had used the darkroom before so he processed his roll of film and then helped set things up. When the negatives were ready, he chose the four he liked best and enlarged the first one.

Parker wiped the counters, even though they didn't need it. Then he stood across from Matt and watched him put his first print into the tray of developer.

To Matt's annoyance, Parker started drumming his fingers on the long, steel table. "Hey, is everything okay?"

"Yeah. Why?"

"I don't know; you just seem antsy."

Parker didn't answer or look up.

"Oh, I get it, you're afraid my photos will be better than yours, even though I didn't accept your help earlier."

"In your dreams," Parker said. He cracked a smile but kept his eyes on the developer.

"Fine, but can you please stop with the drumming?"

He did, but didn't leave the table.

When Matt's timer went off, he moved the print to the next tray, still confused as to why Parker watched with such interest. "Am I doing something wrong here? Your hovering is stressing me out."

"Just watching; is that a problem?"

"I guess not." Matt reset the timer. "It's just not normal, that's all."

Parker finally looked up and said, "Not bad for an amateur."

"Not bad? It's impressive and you know it. Now, don't you have your own film to get ready? I've got this."

Parker went to process his film while Matt went back to the enlarger to start his next picture.

They worked in silence. When Matt's third print was finished, Parker came to look. Matt expected a compliment but instead got no response at all. Parker only dropped his gaze and walked away. *Huh, what's with him?* He didn't bother to ask; he had his own life to worry about.

Matt started his last print, mindlessly rocking the tray of developer. His thoughts were on Haley and her infectious smile, and he smiled too. Then the unwelcome reality of her email flashed before his eyes and he began to shake his head. *But why—whoa* . . . He peered into the tray. *That's weird.*

Color spread across the image. The *black-and-white* image, he reminded himself.

"Uh, Parker? You need to come see this."

Parker turned so quickly that he ran his hip into the corner of the table, causing chemicals to slosh out of their trays. Ignoring the mess, he asked, "What is it?"

"I don't know." Matt didn't look up. "Hurry."

They both leaned over the tray and watched as the image continued to fill with color.

"Keep agitating it," Parker said.

"Oh, right."

When the color stopped, Parker muttered, "Huh, so it begins." Then louder, "How much time is left?"

Matt looked. "Not quite a minute, but the photo is ruined. I might as well throw it out and start over, right?"

"No. Finish the rest of the steps. I need to see it when it's dry."

"It's hard to tell in this lighting, but the color doesn't look like it's a part of my picture. What'd I do wrong?

"Nothing."

"How'd this happen, then?"

Parker shook his head. "I have no idea." He grabbed some paper towels and started to wipe up the spilled developer.

Matt had known something was off ever since they got home, but now Parker's reaction had him worried. "You don't even seem surprised. Has this happened before?"

Parker didn't reply.

With narrowed eyes, Matt crossed his arms and glared. "I'll take that as a yes. What's going on?"

The timer broke the silence, forcing Matt to turn his attention back to the print. Answers would have to wait.

He finished the next two steps and fished the print out of the tray of fixer. While he let the chemicals drip off, he tried to see if the color made sense. *Interesting. It looks like graffiti.* The next step was to rinse it, where he assumed the color would streak or stain or maybe even wash off.

In the meantime, Parker had enlarged his first print and dropped it into the developer. While he rocked the tray, he asked, "Is the color still there?"

"Yeah," Matt said, "it ruined my photo . . . and yet it looks deliberate. Can you please explain?"

"It's kind of a long story. Let's finish and I'll fill you in later."

Matt was too intrigued to argue. He left his photo in a tray of water and came to watch Parker. Two of his prints had some color, but they looked different from Matt's. The images gave the impression of paintings done in stipple; more gray than color.

"Interesting," Parker said. "I say we leave these images to dry." They hung them on the line along the back wall and left the darkroom.

Matt had waited long enough. "Okay, out with it. How's this happening?"

"Like I said, I don't know. But I have something to show you."

They walked to the other end of the basement.

Matt's mouth dropped open when he saw the prints spread out on the matting table. He picked up the one closest to him. "Wow, these are impressive."

Parker nodded. "Strangely enough, I'd have to agree."

Matt set the print down and leaned over another one. "These look too perfect to be by chance. Have you been experimenting with the chemicals? The ones we just did aren't nearly as impressive as these and they look like they were processed differently."

"I wish I could take credit, but I can't."

Matt straightened and turned his hands upward. "You're telling me this happened by chance?"

Parker tilted his head. "Um . . . yes and no. These look different because they're for a different purpose."

"What do you mean a different purpose? Can you please stop speaking in riddles and tell me what's going on?"

Now that all the photos were developed, Parker took time to share with Matt in detail the story about his photo shoot the day before. "The pictures of the abandoned building were the only ones I took that had extra images in them, so I figured they were a figment of my imagination.

"Anyway, I needed some fresh air. On a whim, I drove back to Chestnut Street with a new roll of film in my camera. While I was there, some guy called me and said he knew color had shown up in my black and white prints." Parker's voice intensified. "Then he said the extra images would provide information that could help solve a cold case. And he wants me to help!"

"Whoa! That's a jump. What does a cold case have to do with anything?"

"That's what I thought, and to make things even more awkward, the man wouldn't give me his name, but he did make me an offer."

"What kind of offer?"

Parker answered his question and finished the story. "There's one more thing you should probably know. This guy told me about your breakup with Haley before you called me last night."

"What?" Matt sprang forward. "You're telling me this guy has information on me?"

"Yeah, but he could have seen it on one of Haley's social media accounts. I wouldn't take it too much to heart."

"I didn't think she posted it, but then again, I haven't bothered to look. And no matter how you cut the pie, it's still none of this guy's business. If it weren't for these intriguing photos, I'd say I'm not a fan of your nameless caller."

"Well, you might need to give this some thought because he's the one who told me to ask you to come this morning. He wants you to help me."

Matt didn't even bother to pretend he was okay with this. He threw his hands toward Parker and started to leave the basement.

"Hey, where are you going?"

"Home, obviously. This is too creepy for me." He paused at the stairs. "Why does he want my help anyway?"

"He said you'd need a diversion." Parker walked toward Matt. "And that you'd be an asset."

"Me? An asset? That's laughable." He patted his chest. "I can't even figure out my own life. See you later."

"I know this is a lot to take in right now and—"

"And I'm leaving!"

Not willing to concede, Parker said, "The last thing he told me was that the proof we need would be in the photos we developed today. I say we give it a shot and see what happens. We can always bail at any time. I promise."

Matt had already pulled his keys from his pocket. He trained his eyes on the love knot pendant that Haley had given him at their college graduation.

"What do you think?" Parker dipped his head, trying to make eye contact. "You want to help. I know you do."

Matt spun the keychain around his index finger once and buried the pendant in his fist. "I'll probably end up regretting this, but a diversion does sound good."

"Okay, great. I need one more confirmation, though, before we commit. I'm supposed to sell these photos and the money that I make from them will be my payment to help this guy. So, here's what I'm thinking: if they sell for a reasonable price, we do this. If they don't, we walk away and forget it ever happened."

"What about the photos still in the darkroom?" Matt asked as they left the basement.

"I'd say that's a mystery for another day. I'll get these matted and take them to my gallery. If they sell, you'll be the first to know."

Chapter 3

DEFINING DETAILS

Monday morning Parker bagged up his new prints and took them to the Village Gallery. His stomach churned a little as he entered the showroom. Just because Matt could see the colorful overlay didn't guarantee anyone else would.

The owner, a stout man in his late fifties with a long graying beard and ponytail, came to say hello. "Hey, Parker, it's been a while. How've you been?"

"Hi, Bryce. I'm great. I was wondering if you'd look at my latest photos and see if they are something you'd be willing to sell for me."

"For you, absolutely. Your work is always impressive. Let's have a look."

He followed Bryce down the familiar hallway and into a large room. Some artwork hung on panels while other pieces leaned against the walls or lay on the table. Bryce cleared a space for Parker. "There. So, where have your adventures taken you recently?"

Parker opened his portfolio. "Actually, all I have is local stuff." He bit his lip as he pulled the first print from his bag and set it on the table.

Bryce bent over it to get a better look. His eyes went from the print to Parker and then back to the print. Without saying a word, he left the room.

Parker cringed, then called after him, "That bad, huh?"

A minute later he returned with a 10x loupe. "Not at all, I'm just confused." He looked at the other prints that Parker had set on the table. "Are these real?"

Parker cracked a smile. "Yes, of course. Why?"

"Well, for one, you always bring me black and white prints that you develop yourself. And for two, I can't imagine why you would bring me digital art with interesting overlays. It doesn't seem like your style."

"But they're not digital."

Bryce furrowed his brow. He leaned over the first image and carefully examined the print. Parker assumed he was looking for separations between the color and the black and white.

"Phenomenal. I've developed my own film for over thirty years. I've even kept up with the latest technical changes, but I've never seen anything like this before."

Because it took him so long, Parker wondered if Bryce could see something with the loupe that he couldn't see with the naked eye. It made him feel uneasy, and he clutched a handful of his button-down shirt and put pressure on his chest in hopes the pounding of his heartbeat wouldn't be heard from across the table.

Bryce finally straightened. "How were you able to use color photos that must have been taken fifty years ago and integrate them perfectly into your black and white photos?"

"You can't expect me to divulge my trade secrets now, can you?" Parker half laughed, but in the back of his mind he knew there was no way to explain the reality, or the mystery, of his most recent work. "How about we come up with a reasonable price and see what happens."

"Yeah, a price. I have no idea what a fair market value would be. Can you guarantee me that these were developed in your darkroom and you won't make any more?"

"I can."

"Good. By selling them as one of a kind, we can charge more."

"I won't argue with that." Parker smiled. "Do you need me to sign a legal form or something?"

Bryce ran his hand over his beard as he stared at Parker for a moment and then nodded. "Yes, I'll have you sign the form. It will give an added layer of confidence to our buyers. Not that it's needed. Your photography is highly regarded around here. To be honest, the paperwork will be for me. I can't risk losing my high-end clients over selling a digital knockoff."

Parker understood where Bryce was coming from and he couldn't blame him. "I have nothing to hide and you have nothing to fear. I'll stake my reputation on that!"

"Glad to hear it." Bryce nodded and started rubbing his hands together. "Now, because these are the abandoned building on Chestnut Street, they also have historical value. I say we start at no less than $3,500 each."

Parker whistled. "That's a bit high, don't you think?"

"Not at all. These are fantastic. The sheer fact that you were able to keep the reality of decay black and white and blend it with the beauty that once was by using color is incredible. If I can find the right buyer, you'll have a big payday coming."

"Thanks for your vote of confidence, but I can't afford to not have them sell because the price is too high."

"Realistically, we could probably get even more. I know a few historians who might be interested. I'll give them a call. Oh and while you're here, your last three photos sold over the weekend, so I owe you money."

"Sweet."

After signing the paperwork for the new photos and receiving payment for the old, Parker headed home. On his way, he found himself hoping his phone would ring. He wanted to talk to the man that set these events in motion. Then it dawned on him that he could just call the man back. As soon as he pulled into his parking spot, he got out his phone. To his chagrin, there were no numbers in his recent calls. "Huh? That's odd. I didn't clear them."

❏ ❏ ❏

Two days later his phone rang. It was Bryce. "Hey Parker, great news—your photos sold and for the price we asked. Two of the three historians I called came to look. They were so impressed with your work that neither of them tried to talk me down and between them, they bought all six."

"Interesting."

"Interesting? Are you *sick*? You should be elated!"

"I, I am. That's fantastic," Parker said as he heard, `but life is about more than money` echoing in his ears. His thoughts went to the photos still in his darkroom and he realized this commission was quickly becoming a reality.

Bryce didn't know about Parker's quandary, so he continued unabated. "I already have proof of payment, so you can get your money today. Oh, and I know you said these were one of a kind, but when can you bring me some *different* photos using the same technique? Everyone that saw them commented on how impressive they were."

"I can't. I mean, it's tricky and time-consuming."

"Well, that's too bad. For this price, it seems like it'd be worth perfecting your process so it's easier to achieve."

"True, but if I could easily produce them, it would lessen their value."

Bryce wouldn't let it go. "Would you be willing to teach me? I'd pay you for your time."

Parker chuckled at the thought, but only said, "How about we be thankful for this payday and not get too greedy?"

"Ouch, man." Bryce burst into a hearty laugh. "So when can you come? Because of the amount, I need you to sign some extra paperwork before I can transfer the money to your account."

"Okay, I'll be there within the hour." Parker hung up the phone but didn't move. He still had a hard time believing the photos were even real, let alone to have them sell so quickly and for so much. *Well, my mystery caller held up his end of the deal. Now, can I hold up mine?*

❑ ❑ ❑

Bryce had the paperwork ready by the time Parker arrived at the gallery. "Are you sure this payday won't change your mind about producing more of those incredible photos?"

"Ha, you're relentless. Maybe someday," Parker said as he reached to shake Bryce's hand. "Thanks for taking care of the business end of things for me."

"Anytime. I still say you should share your knowledge, though I can't blame you for keeping it a secret."

Parker didn't bother to reply.

As soon as he left the gallery, he called Matt and gave him the news.

"Wow. I knew the photos were impressive, but I didn't expect them to sell for that much."

"I know. It's amazing! So, are you going to help me?"

"Yeah. All of this is fascinating, and I want to see how it plays out."

Parker pumped his fist. "Glad to hear it. Now, the guy said we'd find clues in the photos that will require us to take action. I don't know what that means yet, but looking at the prints is our next step. When can you come?"

"I have to finish the article I'm writing. It's due by 4:00, but I'll work through lunch to save some time and come as soon as I can."

"Okay, see you in a bit."

❑ ❑ ❑

Matt had a rough few days. He hadn't heard a thing from Haley, and when he called her, it went to voicemail. After the third try, and not knowing what else to do, he left a message. "Uh, hi. I thought we should talk, seeing we have a wedding to call off." It was then that he lost control. His voice cracked as he blurted out, "Not that it matters now, but for the record, I'm still crazy in love with you." Quickly, he hung up so she wouldn't hear him cry.

Matt called in sick on Monday and missed a deadline on Tuesday, which didn't go over very well with his boss. Parker's call was just what he needed.

❑ ❑ ❑

Parker hadn't gone back into his darkroom since Saturday. The prints still hung on a string along the back wall where three of the ten photos had extra details. He took those down and then stepped back to look at the ones left on the line. *Hmm, Matt's becoming quite the photographer. I'll have to be sure to show him these later.*

Parker turned his attention to the image still in his hand. *Aren't these kinds of things only supposed to happen in dreams and fairy tales?* With a quick shake of the head, he picked up the other two prints, and brought them to his matting table where there was more room and better lighting.

❑ ❑ ❑

Matt arrived a little before 3:00 with two cups of black coffee. He let himself in and found Parker in his basement matting a print of the Grand Tetons. "Nice shot. I hadn't seen that one before." He held out one of the coffees.

"Oh, good call. Thanks." Parker took it and stepped back. "Yeah, Bryce is out of prints, so I went back through some old photos and found this one. Besides, I needed to keep myself busy, or I would've been tempted to look at the mysterious photos without you."

"Well, I'm here now, so let's get to it." Matt walked around the table and picked up his print. What appeared to be graffiti in the darkroom—now dry and in better lighting—was clearly a mural. "Hey, check this out. Isn't that the park where you sometimes go to run?"

"Could be. I hadn't looked that closely and, at first glance, I was distracted by the way the art weaves over the architecture of the building." A moment later he tapped the photo. "It sure is!

Here's the playground and there's the path that heads toward the river. And these two girls are sitting on my favorite bench. Sometimes I take my camera there to people watch and work on composition."

"That's it!" Matt pointed. "Those girls are the only people in the picture." The thought of finding something relevant caused him to perk up, his personal woes of Haley forgotten for the time being.

"Now that you mention it, I've never been at the park when there weren't a lot of people, so yeah, this could be our first clue."

"Do you have some paper and a pen handy? We should write down what we find. Then, when we see other things of interest, we can determine if they have anything to do with the park or these girls."

Parker found some paper and grabbed a pen off his desk. He scribbled down, 'two girls/park bench.' When nothing else stuck out to them, they set the mural print aside and started looking at the other two.

These photos were entirely different from the first one in that there wasn't much color at all. Initially, they looked like drawings done in stipple appearing exactly like the building, but upon closer inspection, they found that numbers and letters completely covered the images. A large variety of fonts were used. Some were bold and packed together, while others were thin and spread out. Each letter was either black, white, or a shade of gray, depending on the detail of the building. At first, they seemed random, but Parker and Matt soon noticed the letters weren't random at all. Mixed among the numbers were names; hundreds of them.

Matt adjusted his glasses. "This is getting weird. Are these names supposed to mean something or is it simply another artistic rendering of the building?"

"I'm sure they mean something."

"Maybe, but the stippling effect is cool. Do you think we should try to sell them?"

"No, we still have all the money we just made. I don't believe this is happening just so we can get rich. There has to be more to it." Parker ran his hand over the print closest to him. "I'm thinking we should see if any names stick out to us more than the rest." With that, he went back to his desk and found a magnifying glass and handed it to Matt. "See if this helps."

Matt began scanning one of the photos for clues. At first, nothing stuck out to him, so he kept moving across then down, back and forth. Meanwhile, Parker examined the other picture, wishing he knew what they were looking for.

"Matt, come check this out."

He brought the magnifying glass and looked where Parker was pointing.

"This name looks different. Can you see it?"

"Do you mean the name that appears to be highlighted?"

"Yeah, can you read it?"

"Yes. Mikayla Santos. I'll add it to our list."

"Okay, then keep looking to see if there are any more like it."

A few minutes passed before Matt found a second name with the same font and highlighting. "Samantha Ford." He wrote it down and then finished scouring the rest of the photo but found no others. Both were girl's names and simultaneously they wondered if the two names went with the two girls on the park bench.

"It's a start, but we still don't have a purpose. We have no reason to know the names of two random girls," Parker said. He turned to look at the last photo. "This one seems to have more numbers than names and the names sound more like street addresses."

"Here. Why don't you take a turn with the magnifying glass?" Matt held it out for Parker.

He took the glass and after a few minutes said, "These numbers remind me of something you'd see in a crime show; they're always talking about GPS coordinates. Do you know anything about that?"

"Ah, yes. Let me look. Last summer Haley and I got into geocaching. I even have the app!"

"I thought you said Haley didn't think you were adventurous enough. Don't you have to go places and try to find stuff for that?"

"Yeah, but we mostly did searches within a fifty-mile radius. I wouldn't say that was real adventurous. And, she's not the point—the numbers are."

Matt eagerly looked for number sequences that worked for latitude and longitude. Only one set of numbers matched and he punched them into his app. "We have a location, and look, it's just north of the city."

"Huh, so does that mean we're supposed to go find something?"

"Or someone—we have the names of two girls."

"Right, but why would we need to find them? That seems kind of odd."

Matt's eyes widened as he clasped his hands together. "I think I get it! Last night on the eleven o'clock news there was a report about two missing girls with their names and pictures. I don't remember the names because I wasn't paying attention, but I recall them saying something about the middle school and the last time they were seen."

"Do you think these clues are about those two girls?"

"It seems plausible. The park is only a few blocks from that middle school."

"We don't have any time to waste, then." Parker continued to study the photo. "We have the general vicinity, but we need more. A specific street, business, or house number, something."

"Wait, let me enlarge my map. It pinpoints the area and I can see what's there. The pin is on Washington Ave. See if you can find that in our image."

It took Parker a few minutes. "Look, 24 Washington Ave. We have our location." Parker grabbed his phone, found the number for the missing person's hotline and made the call.

"Hello. The two girls reported missing yesterday, have they been found?"

"No, sir, but please slow down; do you have information?"

"Maybe. Are their names Mikayla Santos and Samantha Ford?"

"I'll check, but first I need your name, address, and phone number to verify this isn't a prank."

Parker steadied his voice and gave the requested info.

Once the woman had what she needed, she said, "Yes, those are the girls reported to be missing. Have you seen them, or do you have a lead, Mr. Jackson?"

"I think they can be found at 24 Washington Ave in Northern Heights."

"And how have you acquired this information? Have you seen them?"

"It'd be hard to explain. Let's just say it's a hunch."

"Do you expect me to dispatch officers on a hunch?"

"I don't know. I guess I thought I should tell someone. It will take me forty-five minutes to get there and I don't know if the abductors will be armed or dangerous." His voice again began to tremble.

The operator paused a moment before answering. "That's a specific house number you just gave me. I will pass this information along to the police and see if they are willing to dispatch a unit to that address. If they find the girls, I'll have someone let you know. If not, you will have an officer on your doorstep. We don't take prank calls lightly."

Parker regained his composure and boldly said, "I understand. Please, make the call."

Chapter 4

LEARNING TO TRUST

"That was a bold move," Matt said when Parker got off the phone. "What if this location has nothing to do with those girls?"

"The names they had matched the names we found. We're at the beginning of a learning curve here and until we understand our purpose, I'd say we have to take some risks, make some calls, and get some answers."

"Yeah or end up in jail." A small laugh escaped Matt's lips. "What in the world have we gotten ourselves into?"

"I don't know." Parker followed Matt out of the basement. "At this point, all we can do is wait for news. My mystery caller told me that we wouldn't hear from him again until we solved our first case. It seems like we're heading in the right direction." He sat in the recliner, let his head fall back on the cushion, and closed his eyes. "Do you want to hang here, or do you want me to call you when I get the news?"

"I'll stay," Matt said as he stretched out on the couch. "There's no sense in leaving now. And anyway, I can't get Haley out of my mind when I'm home. I haven't slept much in days."

❏ ❏ ❏

About three hours later Parker woke to a knock at his door. He opened it to see two policemen in uniform. "Mr. Jackson?

34

I'm Officer Wilson. This is Officer Brown. We need to ask you a few questions about the lead you gave us."

"Did you find the missing girls? Are they safe?"

"I'll ask the questions," Wilson said.

"Um, okay. Do you want to come in?" Parker swung the door open and stepped back, making room for the officers to enter. In the meantime, he felt his phone vibrate so he gave it a quick look as he shut the door.

Matt had roused from his slumber and once he realized what was going on, he grabbed his glasses and came to listen.

"How did you know the girls were in that house?" Wilson asked.

"Earlier today I received an anonymous text with the names and location of two girls. My friend, Matt, here, saw the story on the news last night, so I figured it had to be legit and called the hotline."

"Let me see the text." He held out his hand.

Parker opened the text and gave him the phone.

"And you have no idea who sent this?"

"No, sir."

"We were concerned at first that you were a suspect who got cold feet, especially when your information was spot-on. But when we questioned the perps, it was clear that they had never heard of you," Brown said.

"So the girls are safe?" Matt blurted out.

"Yes, we've rescued them, and they weren't hurt."

"That's fantastic."

"It is," Wilson said, "but Parker, we'll need to take your phone so we can track the sender."

"You can't just take my phone."

"If you have nothing to hide, it'd be easier to consent." Wilson's voice was calm but forceful. "We can come back with a warrant, but then that just makes you look guilty."

"I'm not guilty!" Parker quickly looked from one officer to the other. "The girls are safe because of us."

"And we're grateful, but we can't leave any loose ends in this investigation. If others are involved, we need to know." He handed the phone to Brown.

Parker sighed. "Fine. But when will I get it back?"

"Give us a couple of hours and you can come to the station to retrieve it," Brown said.

"Can I give you my number?" Matt asked. "Then someone can call me when it's ready and I'll let Parker know."

"Sure, we can do that."

❑ ❑ ❑

When the officers were gone, Matt asked, "How'd you know a text was on your phone?"

"I got it just as they came in. It's a good thing too because I had no idea how to explain the truth."

"Yeah, about the truth, why didn't your guy just text in the first place? Or better yet, why didn't he call the police himself?"

"See, that's why you're a good reporter; you know the right questions to ask."

"But how do we find the answers?"

Parker lit up. "Maybe we just have. Now that the police have my phone, they should be able to track this guy down and discover his identity."

"That'd be nice. I don't like how he has an unfair advantage over us, even though I'm glad the girls are safe. For now, I guess the secrecy is worth it. What's next?"

"I suppose we wait for this guy to call."

"But the police have your phone."

"Hmm." Parker stepped to the window and watched as the cruiser pulled away. "Brown said it wouldn't take long."

"Unless they can't find any information on this guy; he probably used a burner phone."

"I didn't think of that, but we can hope, right?"

"Right. Hey, you know what would be funny? If we could find out who this guy is without him knowing we know."

Parker stifled a laugh. "Am I detecting the mystery writer in you looking for a plot?"

"Maybe." Matt's smile didn't reach his eyes. "Thinking about stuff like this helps me keep my mind off Haley."

"You could always think about how cool it was to discover the names and location of those girls. I wouldn't have found them without you."

"That was incredible for sure, even though it wasn't the most logical way to get us information. I mean, what would've happened if we didn't figure it out?"

"Hopefully, the guy would've called the hotline himself. I'm still baffled as to why he even bothered to waste our time, especially when he already had the answer. So at this point, it's hard to know what he'd do or why he said he needed our help in the first place."

"It makes no sense to me either." Matt started for the door but then turned back. "Hey, do you mind if I take the photo with all the names on it? I think it's a neat piece of art."

"Absolutely. A souvenir of our first success story and a good reminder of how this all started. I'll keep the one with the numbers."

Matt followed Parker back to the basement and when they reached the matting table, he said, "What the—"

"No way!"

All three pictures had changed. The first still had the old building in the background, but it appeared to have a new message. In the other two photos, the building had disappeared completely. In its place was what looked like parchment paper covered with beautiful, handwritten calligraphy.

Parker quickly scanned the room, looking for an intruder. It was one thing to have the chemicals mess with his photos, but it seemed a bit extreme to have the photo paper change to real parchment.

One parchment had Parker's name at the top; the other had Matt's.

Parker picked his up. "Huh, I didn't see this coming."

Matt didn't answer. He'd already dropped onto the sofa that backed against the darkroom wall and buried his face in his hands.

Parker knew Matt was shaken, but without his phone, he figured this was the guy's way to get them a message. He read his aloud.

Parker Jackson ~ After your dad left when you were ten, your mom sent you to spend your summers with her brother's family. It was your Uncle Steve who first noticed you were floundering in your early teens. He tried to be a dad to you the best he could, but it wasn't enough to help you through the school year. He was the one who bought you your first camera, hoping it would give you a constructive outlet and help you cope. It worked. You took that camera with you everywhere and you've become a very talented photographer. Your specialty is · seeing and capturing the details often overlooked by your peers.

You love hiking and your photos of nature are impressive, as well. You moved to Philadelphia fourteen months ago and make your living as a freelance photographer. Along with your photography skills, you have a strong and outgoing personality, which will be helpful in the days to come.

Moving forward, everything I show you is for a purpose; don't overlook what seems to be irrelevant. Keep all the photos, even ones that don't have clues. When situations become difficult, don't quit.

Parker stared at the parchment for a minute before setting it down. "This is . . . just . . . wow." He rubbed his chin, not knowing what else to say.

Then he picked up Matt's parchment and brought it to him.

Matt shook his head and pushed it away. "I can't."

"Well, you need to at least listen, then," Parker said.

Matt Howard ~ When you were in eighth grade, you enjoyed reading adventure novels, especially ones written by Robert Louis Stevenson. You entered an essay contest and wrote a short story about finding a hidden treasure. Though you didn't win the contest, your teacher said you had potential. It was at that point you decided to become a writer and over the years you've submitted other stories to online contests. You majored in English and got a job as a journalist, but recently you've felt confined, writing less-than-thrilling articles for the business section of the newspaper. You keep with it because at least your work includes writing, but your true passion is to write novels. Currently, you have three different stories started on your computer but haven't put the effort into completing any of them.

You met Parker three years ago when you wrote an article on the opening of his exhibit at the Village Gallery. You became fast friends and you are my choice to help Parker with this mission.

Moving forward, pay attention to details and write things down. I want you to include what you learn from the clues, what you learn from and about others, and what you learn about yourself. Someday you'll write this story.

Matt sat back on the sofa, momentarily mute. Then, as if waking from a disturbing dream—his eyes wild with fear—he found his voice. "I want out. I don't want anything to do with this. Ten minutes ago, yes, but not now. Not anymore . . ."

"Come on, Matt—"

"Don't," he snapped. "Just don't. How are the pictures changing? How does this guy know so much about us? And why does he feel it's his job to invade our lives? I was joking about finding him, but that was before I realized how much he knows about us." Beads of perspiration dotted Matt's forehead. "Am I supposed to quit my job to follow leads on pictures that mysteriously appear and then magically change? We've never met this guy and know nothing about him. How do we know he won't leave us stranded halfway around the world? Or even worse?"

Parker set Matt's parchment on the table and then gently ran a finger over his. Taking in a deep breath, he let it out slowly, laboring to maintain his own composure. The wrong answer would send Matt packing and he couldn't afford that. Slowly, he turned. They locked eyes. "This is undoubtedly creepy, and you have every right to be freaked out." Parker patted his chest. "My heart's pounding too. My instincts say run! But for reasons I can't explain, I don't think we should."

Matt leaned back and locked his fingers behind his head. "You're serious, aren't you?"

"I am. He told me that he needed help with a cold case. I think he let us find the girls rather quickly, kind of like a test, so we would learn to trust him."

Matt scoffed. "Then you're crazier than I thought. I don't trust any of this." He got to his feet.

"I know it's a lot to take in. I say we call it a day."

"I say we call it quits." Matt started for the door.

"Fine. Go ahead and quit." He flopped onto the couch that Matt had just vacated. *Now what am I supposed to do?*

❑ ❑ ❑

A few hours later Matt showed up on Parker's doorstep. "Hey, uh, sorry I acted like such an idiot earlier."

Parker joined him on the porch, looking equally drained. "Yeah, well, it's not like I handled the situation any better. I guess we both need to get used to strange and unexpected things happening."

"I hope you realize that's going to be harder than it sounds."

"You're probably right." Parker nodded empathetically. "But hopefully it'll be worth it. I'm not going to look at the other picture until tomorrow—so if this is your way of saying that you want to help, come over after work, okay?"

"Sure, but first, they called from the police station and said you could come to get your phone."

"Sweet. It'll be fun to find out who sent the text. Want to come along?"

"Not really. You can fill me in tomorrow."

❑ ❑ ❑

Matt didn't have set work hours because he often had to cover an event either in the evening or on the weekend. On the days he didn't have a late appointment, he would get to the office early and was usually able to leave by midafternoon. Parker assumed he'd show up around 4:00.

By 6:00 Parker was getting restless and finally gave Matt a call. "Hey, I thought you were coming over to help me figure out our new image. What's the holdup?"

"I changed my mind. I'm not coming," Matt grumbled. "Do I need to explain why?"

"That'd be helpful."

"You know what? It doesn't matter because I'm not coming."

"Quit screwing around. We've got work to do."

"Screwing around? No, that's what you're doing."

"What's that supposed to mean?" Parker snapped, his patience now wearing thin.

"I can't believe you've committed to this ludicrous scheme."

"Why wouldn't I commit? It's fascinating."

"So that's your choice, but how did I get pulled into this mess?"

"Seriously? We've been through this already."

"I don't care. Our personal lives are none of this guy's business. Why'd he have to tell you about Haley? That was just wrong!"

"Yes, I agree that was rather heartless, but then again, I would never have thought to ask you to help if it wasn't for him."

"Like that's supposed to be comforting. How'd he even find out? It's not like we had it blasted all over social media."

"I have no idea, but you're stuck on the wrong details. This is about helping people, remember?"

"Well, I'm people and he's *not* helping me. He's invaded our lives and then expects us to drop everything without so much as a name. I won't help."

"I get it, but don't forget, we got paid in advance. I feel like we owe—"

"You got paid in advance," Matt barked. "There is no we!" After a short pause, he added, "Do you want to know what pushed me over the edge?"

Parker didn't bother to reply.

"Having those photos change the second time."

"Yeah, well, how about you tell me something I don't know."

There was an awkward silence, so Parker started pacing the length of his basement.

Then, out of the blue, Matt blurted out, "Ha, good one, Parker. You got me." Even though he laughed, he sounded angry.

Parker stopped in his tracks. "What are you talking about?"

"I finally get it. You switched the prints out after I fell asleep, didn't you?"

"Wait, what?"

"Pretending the parchments were legit was how you could keep this absurd scheme going. What, did you figure I'd be extra gullible right now because of Haley?"

"Wow." Parker raked his free hand through his hair, trying not to lose his cool. "How'd you come to that conclusion?"

"Because there's no other logical explanation and you can be a real jerk sometimes."

"Thanks for your vote of confidence. I guess I'll see you around." Parker hung up before Matt could reply. It wasn't worth losing his best friend over it, and he knew they'd both have regrets if the conversation continued.

Chapter 5

LISTEN AND OBEY

Matt flung himself onto his bed. More than the crazy, inexplicable events of the last few days, the breakup had finally gotten the best of him. His heart hurt. He couldn't think straight.

Was there anything that could fill the void or make the pain disappear? If there was, he didn't know how or where to find it. Empty and at a loss, he pulled the covers over his head and cried for a long time. Eventually, sleep came.

It wasn't quite dark out when Matt woke to the sound of a text. Kicking off the blankets, he reached for his glasses and opened his phone. The text read, 'Go to Parker's house. You have work to do.'

He crawled out of bed and went to wash his face. As he stared into the mirror, he didn't recognize himself. The once happy-go-lucky guy that was full of life had become broken and petty.

The more he thought about what he said to Parker, the more he realized blaming him was foolish. Just because he was sad and afraid didn't mean he should take his frustrations out on him. And anyway, Parker was too sensible to chase after a phantom or a myth. *Ugh, I'm the one that can be a real jerk.*

He knew he needed to apologize but couldn't bring himself to make the call.

Matt's phone vibrated again, but when he saw it was from the same guy, he threw it across the room and started screaming, "I know I need to apologize to Parker, but I didn't say I was going to help you! Geez, give it a rest and find someone else."

The phone hit an overflowing basket of laundry. Instead of retrieving it, he went to get changed, and then to the kitchen to find something to eat. Twenty minutes passed before he came to retrieve his phone and read the text.

'You are my choice. Go now.'

"Alright already!" In a huff, he rushed out, slamming the solid wood door behind him. The thud was so severe that it reverberated down the hall of his third-story apartment, but he didn't care.

Because the traffic was thin at that hour, he was able to reach Parker's townhouse in less than fifteen minutes. Parker must not have heard the doorbell so, after a few more tries, Matt called him. "Hey, can you let me in?"

"You're here? I thought you weren't coming."

"Just open the door already!"

"Okay, but I just dropped a print into the developer. Hang tight; I'll come as soon as it's finished."

Matt took a seat on the porch and breathed a sigh of relief. He was glad Parker didn't sound angry.

It took Parker about five minutes before he joined Matt. "So, what changed your mind?"

"I got a text, presumably from your mystery caller. It said, 'Go to Parker's house. You have work to do.' It's the only reason I'm here."

"You got a text?" Parker stepped forward and put out his hand. "Here, let me see."

"Two, actually." Matt handed him his phone.

Parker started scrolling through the text messages. "Just as I suspected, there's no text here from anyone you don't know."

"Quit messing with me. I'm not in the mood for a prank."

"Seriously? After your accusation earlier this evening, why would I even risk trying to be funny?"

"Yeah, about that, sorry. I know you're good at your job, but not that good." For the first time that evening, Matt cracked a smile.

"Nice, sarcasm; it suits you." Parker returned the smile. "Here, look for yourself."

Matt took his phone and when he found no text, he said, "Well, I guess I shouldn't be surprised." He slipped the phone into his pocket, cupped his hands behind his head, and looked at Parker. "How'd you know the text wouldn't be there?"

"That'd be because I actually tried to call this guy the other day and there was no evidence of any calls on my phone . . . blocked or otherwise. The text the police needed is still there, but when I tried to reply to that text, it came back as undeliverable."

"Oh yeah. Did the police find our guy?"

"If they did, they didn't tell me."

Matt dropped his hands over his knees and sat forward. "Can you give me one good reason why we should continue? Think about it, you have a dream job and make good money. You're not tied down to anyone or anything. To be honest, I'm amazed you're willing to take orders from someone you've never met and know nothing about."

Parker leaned against the porch railing and crossed his legs. "Did I ever mention my uncle was career military?"

Matt shook his head.

"Well, I stayed with his family during my summer vacations. When he was stationed stateside, I spent a lot of time with him and he often told me stories of deployments and different situations that made it hard on his family. There were places he didn't want to go and places it wasn't safe for his family to join him, but that's the life he chose. Obeying his commanding officer was all part of the job. He never complained, even when my aunt would cry. As I got older, he became a father figure to me and taught me to respect authority."

"There's a major difference though, he knew who his authority was," Matt interrupted.

"True, but I understand the principle and it seems appropriate to apply a cautious compliance toward our mystery guy until he gives us a reason to doubt. I'm not sure why, but I feel like we'll be a part of something pretty important if we see this through."

"Well, on that point, we already have," Matt said. He straightened his glasses and stood. "Playing a part in saving those girls was incredibly important. I say we look at our new image."

Parker pumped his fists. "Finally."

Matt rolled his eyes as he took the lead and went inside. Once they got to the basement, he asked, "Do you have any idea what to expect next?"

"Not a clue."

The new image showed three small ships sailing across the old building. Not a colorful mural, like the image of the park, but gray and engraved.

Matt shoved his hands into his pockets. "What are we supposed to do with this?"

"Think. Maybe the ships are symbolic or something." Parker took Matt's place, leaned over the image, and started drumming his fingers on the table. "I suppose they could represent another era, but I'd sooner think they mean travel."

"Travel to where?"

Parker straightened and shrugged. "I don't know. You're the writer and a pretty good storyteller."

Matt raised an eyebrow. "Are you saying that you want me to make something up?"

"No, I want you to get creative. If this is the only clue we have, we've got to start thinking outside the box."

Matt caught the compliment, but he didn't see how turning this into story time was going to help. He also knew he wasn't fully committed, which was reflected in his half-hearted attitude.

Did he want to help or not? He needed to decide and do it soon.

Mustering just enough resolve to see what would happen next, he came back to the table.

Parker looked relieved as he stepped aside.

Matt picked up the print and with a glint in his eye, said, "How about time-travel?"

"Why not? That'd be cool."

"And it'd fit right into this already implausible scenario."

"True, but seriously—"

"Hang on a second. This looks like an image you'd see on a quarter."

"Now you're thinking. I'll look." Parker grabbed his phone and found it on a website. "Look, the state quarter of Virginia."

"Okay, but Virginia is a big state, so now what?"

Matt set the print down and they both looked again at the image, hoping there was something they missed.

Without warning, the image began to change.

Matt flinched and grabbed the table to steady himself.

Parker's eyes widened. "Whoa . . ."

Once things stopped moving, the image on the coin showed three massive warships. Though they were still embossed like the smaller ships, the building on Chestnut Street had vanished altogether and a city skyline appeared behind the ships.

"I guess this should help you believe that I wasn't the one making the images change."

"Ha, I guess so." Matt let go of the table and clasped his hands together. "That was cool and if I'm not mistaken, there's a Naval Base in Norfolk."

"Yeah, there is. I went there once with my uncle when I was a kid. But seriously, it'd be a lot easier if this guy would simply call or text and say, 'Go to Norfolk, Virginia.'"

"Where's the fun in that? I'll make a note of it."

With the location the only clue they could find, they decided to drive to Virginia. They assumed they'd receive more information when they got there.

"I have to cover the grand opening of a fitness center on Saturday. Can we wait and leave on Sunday?" Matt asked.

"Sunday works."

❑ ❑ ❑

They reached the outskirts of Norfolk by 12:30. Not sure where to go or what to do next, they found a diner. It was a beautiful September day so their conversation turned to what they should do after lunch. That took all of three seconds to decide. The beach.

As soon as they finished eating, Parker got a text.

'Take a photo of the menu.'

He used his phone, saw the picture was legible, and slipped it back into his pocket.

"To the beach then?" Matt asked as he stood. "We might as well enjoy some waves while we wait for our next message."

Parker put some cash on the table, and they left the diner. "Here." He tossed his keys to Matt. "You can drive. I'm going to look for a hotel."

Matt had found directions to the beach while they ate, so he punched the address into Parker's GPS and then started backing out.

In the meantime, Parker got out his phone. The picture of the menu was still opened. "Hey, hold up—check this out. My picture changed to look like classified ads from a newspaper."

Matt made sure no one was coming and then looked at Parker's phone. "That's interesting."

"Yeah, we should probably check it out before leaving."

Matt agreed and pulled back into his parking spot.

In the bottom right corner, there was an ad circled in red. Parker stretched the image to make the words big enough to read. 'Rooms for Rent. No Minimum Stay.'

Without consulting Matt, he grabbed a pen out of the glove box, wrote down the number, and made the call. "Hello, Ma'am. I just found your ad; do you happen to have rooms available for tonight?"

"Yes, I have two. Would you like one?"

"I'll take them both. I'm in town with a friend and we were looking for two rooms."

"Even better."

"Where are you located? I don't see an address."

"The ad doesn't have my address. I meet possible tenants first before bringing anyone to my house. It's a dangerous world out there; I hope you understand."

"Oh, for sure. Not a problem."

"Good. I'm spending the afternoon with friends, do you mind if we meet later, say 5:30?"

"That works."

"Okay, I'll meet you at Casey's Café. My name's Anna."

"I'm Parker. My friend is Matt. How will we recognize you?"

"I'll be wearing a Philadelphia Phillies T-shirt and baseball cap. There won't be a lot of middle-aged women dressed like that."

"We'll be there." Parker hung up and turned to Matt. "We're good to go to the beach. We can't meet about the rooms until 5:30."

Matt started the Jeep again and sped out of the parking lot without saying a word.

Parker banged against the door. "Hey, dude?"

"What?" Matt snapped.

"What's with the lead foot? And you're crushing my steering wheel."

"Oh." He loosened his grip, allowing the color to rush back into his knuckles.

"What's wrong?"

"Nothing."

"Matt?"

"Fine. Why does this guy have to control where we sleep? What's the big deal if we stay at a hotel?"

"I don't get it. Two minutes ago, you were fine."

"Are you sure it's okay with this *guy* if we go to the beach right now? Don't we need to get permission first?"

"Wow."

"Come on, Parker. You didn't even ask if I was okay with this. You see a sign and then make plans like we don't have a choice in the matter."

"Well, do we? The text came, I took the picture, and the info we needed was right there. Why wouldn't I follow the lead?"

"It just feels like we've become puppets acting out a play in another man's theater. It's like this guy sees our every move, or worse—tells us what our move should be. You don't find this all a bit disturbing?"

"To be honest, I find it invigorating. Until he gives us a reason not to, I say we trust him."

"I didn't say I don't trust him. I'm saying he could lighten up on the micromanaging. What if I don't want to stay at some old lady's house?"

"What if she's a part of our purpose for being here? Ever think of that?"

"No." Matt merged onto the highway and gunned the Jeep up to speed.

"And, even if she's not," Parker continued, "the fact that we got a new message is exciting. If the messages stop coming or the images quit showing up, we have no direction. Then what? We might as well part ways and go back to our day jobs. Just to know we're helping people and that there is a purpose for all this craziness is worth the inconvenience to me."

"Thanks for the speech. It was quite touching."

"What?" Parker barked. "Do you want me to treat you like you're my mother? I'll be sure to ask you for permission next time I get a message."

Matt wisely held his tongue, knowing his previous retort was uncalled for.

Parker sighed. "Fine, have it your way." He got out his phone and started answering customer emails.

Though Matt shifted in his seat and slowed the Jeep to a reasonable speed, all he could think about was Haley and what went wrong. He initially thought if he helped Parker and kept busy, it would help neutralize his mood swings, but all the uncertainty ahead of them seemed to make things worse.

They rode the rest of the way to the beach in silence.

Parker was still replying to an email when Matt found a place to park, so he left the Jeep running with the AC on and fished Haley's ring out of his pocket. He held it above the steering wheel and watched it glisten in the sunlight.

"So, this is actually about Haley, huh?" Parker asked after he finished with the last email.

Matt pinched his lips and nodded. "Mostly." He shoved the ring back into his pocket. "I'm not even close to being over her, so the thought of having to stay with a stranger isn't something I want to do right now."

"I get that, but Haley can't be a reason not to follow the leads."

"I know and yet the leads are a part of my problem."

"How so?"

"I need space. Time to think. Room to breathe. I still feel like I'm the wrong guy to be helping you right now."

"Well, you're the right guy, so you're going to have to get over that. I'm sure once we have a specific lead to follow, you'll be ready and even want to help." Parker opened his door. "In the meantime, I say we go catch some waves."

Matt turned off the Jeep and handed Parker his keys. "Hey, I hope this doesn't turn into an apology tour, but thanks for not staying mad at me."

"Ha, well you do know how to test my patience. Though I can't say I blame you."

"I wish it were as easy as, out of sight, out of mind, but—"

"But you'll get there."

Some time at the beach was just what they needed. The afternoon passed much too quickly.

Then, noticing the time, Matt asked, "Who are we meeting and where?"

"The woman's name is Anna. She wants us to meet her at Casey's Café." Parker got out his phone and found it. "It's about twenty minutes from here. We should probably get going."

Chapter 6

FOLLOWING THE LEADS

The directions to Casey's Café took them west, away from the hubbub of tourists and traffic. Large colonial houses lined the streets, each in pristine condition with immaculate lawns and gardens.

"We probably wouldn't have come to this part of town if you didn't make that call." Matt put down his window and leaned out. "These houses must date back to the early eighteen hundreds. They're beautiful."

Parker nodded with a relieved smile.

A few minutes later, they found Casey's Café. It looked similar to the rest of the houses in this area, but the owners had converted the first floor into a coffee shop. People gathered here and there on the wide wraparound porch. Some were standing or leaning against the railing, while others sat in Adirondack chairs.

"Popular place," Parker said as they started up the long walk.

They were a bit early. Since the ocean sun had taken its toll on their bodies, they decided to wait inside. The café was cozy, sporting colors of sea greens and blues with touches of ocean décor; appropriate for the area, but not overdone. After ordering iced coffees, they found a free table by a window that overlooked the street. The air conditioning felt good on their sunburned skin.

It wasn't long before a slender, middle-aged woman came in. She stood about 5'7" and wore dark blue capris and a white Phillies T-shirt. Her short, blonde hair was tucked neatly behind her ears and underneath a Philadelphia Phillies baseball cap. Parker gave a low wave to let her know they were there. She acknowledged the gesture and then ordered a strawberry smoothie before joining them.

"Hi, I'm Anna. I trust you are Parker and Matt." Each man nodded as she mentioned their names.

This woman looked nothing like what either of them expected. Though older, she was vibrant, and her hazel eyes sparkled. She had high cheekbones, a narrow nose, and a pleasant smile. Taking a seat at the end of the table, she said, "Sorry for the inconvenience. The extra income is nice, but years ago I had something very valuable stolen from me and I can't afford any more losses. I feel more comfortable screening possible houseguests first."

"Makes sense. So, what do you want to know about us?" Parker asked.

"Well for starters, where are you boys from?"

"Philadelphia," Matt answered. "I write for a newspaper."

"Yeah, and I'm a professional photographer. We're in town on business."

"Small world, I'm from Philadelphia, too." She grinned, pointing to her shirt and cap. "Still rooting for the hometown team."

"Oh yeah? Where'd you live?" Parker asked.

"Right in the city, but that was a lifetime ago." Anna's voice trailed off as she stirred her smoothie and took a drink.

Parker noticed she shook her head as if trying to clear a distant memory. He changed the subject. "How long have you lived in Virginia Beach?"

"It's not a date I put on my calendar, but it's been well over a decade. What kind of photography do you do?"

"A variety of things, but mostly architecture and landscapes." Parker grabbed his wallet and pulled out a business card. "Here's a sample of my work. If you want to see more, you can check out my website. The address is on the bottom."

"Impressive. I'll definitely look later. Maybe this year I can surprise my son and his wife with a new piece of artwork for Christmas. They love art and photography; this would be perfect." Her smile widened. "Especially when I can say I know the photographer."

"I'll tell you what, if there's something in this area that they would specifically like, I'll take some photos while we're here and you can choose the one you like best."

"Seriously? That would be wonderful." Anna rubbed her hands together as she considered her options. "How about a photo of the aircraft carriers? My son, Owen, works in Norfolk at one of the shipping yards, but not at the Naval Base. He says the navy ships are not only massive but they also project strength and a sense of security. That would look impressive above their couch."

"Sounds like the perfect gift. I have a client who asked me to take an assortment of photos in and around Norfolk and Virginia Beach. I'm sure we can fit this into our schedule. Is there a place where civilians can get a good look at the ships?"

"You can't get onto the base without a clearance and I'm not sure where a good place to see the ships would be. There are boat tours; we took one a few years ago. If you like being on the water, that'd be a fun place to try."

"We'll check it out and see what's available," Parker said.

"Wait!" Anna's eyes beamed with excitement. "My office is in a twenty-six-story building on the bay. I could get permission for you to go to the roof. I bet you could get some amazing shots from up there—guaranteed to be photos you won't see on the local postcards."

"Thanks, Anna. That sounds like a great idea."

"They might even be good enough that you can sell some of them for your business. I'll ask my boss tomorrow to make sure it's okay."

He smiled at her enthusiasm. "When you ask, see if we can come either first thing in the morning or late afternoon. The right lighting is just as important as the subject matter."

"That's good to know."

"And if the rooftop view turns out to be as good as you say, I'll give you a deal on the price."

"That's very kind of you, but it wasn't why I offered."

"I know. That's why *I did*." Parker tipped his iced coffee at her before taking a drink.

Anna hadn't stopped grinning since she thought of the idea. "I'll see what I can do."

"Great. Matt and I have other commitments for a few days so if you can't get permission for tomorrow, Tuesday would work."

"Oh snap, thanks for reminding me why we're here." A nervous laugh escaped Anna's lips as she looked at her watch. "Sorry for taking up so much of your time. The prospect of surprising Owen distracted me."

"No worries, we're not in a hurry," Matt said. "And I was hoping we could see the ships while we're in town."

"Nice." Anna pulled a small planner from her purse. "Now, how long do you plan on staying?"

"I'm thinking only a few days, but maybe longer," Parker said.

"Yeah, unfortunately, we're not exactly sure," Matt chimed in. "Is that going to be a problem?"

She flipped open the planner. "Actually, the rooms are available for the next two weeks. If I get another call while you're still here, at that point, I'd need a commitment or an end date."

Anna's laid-back approach to screening tenants surprised Parker. *Must be she figures she's a good judge of character and can detect a possible risk through conversation.* "Perfect, that gives us some leeway. Thanks."

"I do have a few ground rules. I don't have a curfew—that would be ridiculous—but I do ask that you be quiet if you come in after 11:00. Also, you have full use of the kitchen; just make sure you clean up when you're done." Nods were enough and Anna concluded. "I have a contract for you to sign and I'll need to take a picture of both your driver's licenses before bringing you to my house." She blushed and quickly added, "It's no different than if you stayed at a hotel."

This seemed fair, so they handed over their licenses and signed the paperwork.

While they finished their drinks, they talked baseball and bemoaned how bad the Phillies were doing. Then Anna had them follow her to the house.

The houses were not as big or as expensive as the ones they passed on the way to the café, but it was still a nice neighborhood. Finally, Anna pulled in front of a sage green craftsman style home with a burgundy door. Hanging flower baskets adorned a porch supported by stone pillars, and an American flag flapped gently in the evening breeze. She parked on the street and Parker pulled in behind her.

When they congregated on the sidewalk, Anna said, "I hope you're not disappointed that I don't live in one of those fancy mansions."

"This is perfect," Matt said. "I have an article that I need to finish in the morning, so the peaceful surroundings will make it easier to focus."

"Great. Let me give you a quick tour of the areas of the house you can use and then I'll show you to your rooms; they're on the second floor."

When Anna saw all the camera equipment and laptops that they brought in with their luggage, she told them they could use her office.

"That won't be necessary. We have no intentions of invading your personal space," Parker said.

"Oh, don't be silly. I offered, and you'll gladly accept." Anna's smile brightened the whole room.

"Alright then, we accept." He knew the extra room would come in handy when they looked at their new images and it would also give them privacy as they hashed out possible scenarios, depending upon what showed up in their next photos. "Thanks for making us feel so welcomed."

"No problem, I want to make sure you're comfortable. Oh, I almost forgot; here's the temporary code for the house." She handed Parker a small piece of paper. "It only opens the back door, but you can pull your Jeep into the driveway."

Just then, Matt's phone rang. He excused himself and stepped outside before answering.

"How do you like your living arrangements?" the caller asked.

Matt blushed to think how ungrateful he had seemed only hours earlier. Then suddenly it hit him that he was talking to their mystery guy. This was the first time he had heard his voice. Here was his opportunity to ask him how he made the images appear. But when he answered, all he said was, "Very nice, sir. Thanks for the lead."

"You're welcome, but now to business. I need you and Parker to head into the heart of the city. Find a mission, and from there, head toward the beach and find an art gallery."

"Any one in particular?" Matt asked. He thought it was odd that the man wasn't more specific.

"No, I trust you'll find what you need. You know the drill; take several photos at both places. Keep all the pictures, even if they don't seem relevant. When you're finished with the photo shoots, head to the north end of the boardwalk. The restaurant there is nice, and you can get your favorite dish." Without waiting for a reply, the call ended.

Matt's expression soured as he stared at his phone. *Why does he do that? Oh well, I guess I should go tell Parker.*

He found him sitting at the kitchen island with a glass of iced tea, chatting with Anna. "Who was that, Haley?"

"No. It was our mystery—I mean our client."

Anna must have noticed the catch because she nodded to Parker and left the room.

Not wanting to make the gaffe too obvious, Matt continued before she was out of earshot. "He wants us to head downtown and gave me some instructions on where to take pictures.

Chapter 7

THE RIGHT MISSION

Parker did a quick web search of the area. Several missions popped up around the city, so they drove to the closest one from Anna's house. Neither of them felt inspired by this place, but then they figured it wouldn't matter. The guy said any mission would do.

Each took a few pictures and, without much conversation got back into the Jeep and started toward the art gallery. To their surprise, there was another mission only a few blocks away. Feeling compelled, they stopped. Sandwiched between several run-down buildings, an equally worn structure emanated hope against the odds in this neglected part of the city. Maybe it was the words New Beginnings brightly painted on the large storefront window and the impressive mural of the beach with children playing. Or maybe it was the strategically placed lamp lighting the interior, which created a warm and inviting glow.

The people who lingered on the street looked at them suspiciously as they got out of the Jeep wearing touristy clothing and toting expensive cameras. Parker ignored them and started taking pictures. His focus was on the significance of this building and why he felt drawn to it.

Matt, on the other hand, only took a few pictures before striking up a conversation with an elderly couple who had stopped to watch.

"Why are you taking pictures of this building? It's not exactly a tourist destination," the woman said coldly.

"I'm a reporter and I'm doing research for a story about local missions."

The gentleman gave Matt a quizzical look, not content with his answer. "Why didn't you come during the day, when the mission was open?"

"Fair enough. We were delayed earlier and came as soon as we could. Do you know anything about this mission that could help me make up for lost time?"

"Not really, but during the day there's always a buzz of activity here. You should stop back tomorrow."

"Okay. Thanks," Matt said.

The couple gave weak nods, crossed the street, and disappeared into one of the apartment buildings. Matt shook his head as he walked back to the Jeep. Leaning against it, he crossed his legs and started looking through his camera's viewfinder.

"I only got two pictures before talking with those people. They didn't believe my story. I don't see what's the big deal . . . It's not like taking pictures is a crime."

Parker looked over his camera. "No, but you weren't exactly honest with them, either."

Matt cringed. "Point taken. I guess the reporter in me is always looking for a story. Besides, it seemed more believable than the truth. I suppose I could've said, 'Well actually, we have this nameless, faceless, cryptic caller who tells us to take pictures of random buildings in different cities and then magical clues appear in the photos. And get this, we're gullible enough to follow his leads. That's why we're here. Make sense? I didn't think so. Now, if you will excuse me, I have more pictures to take.'"

"Wow, that's hilarious. What happened to my friend? The guy I knew before this started was extremely rational and undeniably boring."

"Oh snap. That was harsh." Matt laughed. "Well, I'm glad you appreciate the humor in the complexity of our present situation. And boring? You can't be talking about me."

"You're crazy," Parker said, as he started to bag up his camera. "I'm glad you find this funny though." He was thankful Matt was in a good mood. After their rift earlier, he wasn't sure how long it would be before Matt crashed again.

Still laughing—more from too much sun and not enough sleep—Matt asked, "Do you think if I become a crazed lunatic, Haley will want me back?"

"No. No one wants a crazed lunatic. But truthfully, some added flare and fresh enthusiasm might remind her of why she loved you. Well, once her infatuation with what's-his-face is over, that is."

"Yeah, well, I don't want to talk about what's-his-face." Matt stepped away from the Jeep and shoved his hands into his pockets. "No matter how implausible this adventure is, I'm glad Haley's out of the picture." The pain in his eyes betrayed him. He dropped his gaze before adding, "At least for now. Are you ready to go?"

"Sure." As they drove toward the art gallery, Parker left Matt to his own thoughts. He was preoccupied with the contrasts between the two missions and how they made him feel. Finally, he said, "Not to get all philosophical, but it'll be interesting to see if we get extra images from both missions. Did you notice a difference?"

Matt cleared his throat before answering. "Absolutely. Our guy told me that he trusted we would find what we needed. Did that mean any mission would do or were we drawn to the second one? I say it was the latter."

"Me too. I guess we'll have to wait and see. I hope we find the right art gallery on our first try, I'm hungry." Parker's stomach growled and they both laughed.

"Well it *is* on our way to the restaurant and—"

"And our guy knows so much about us, I'm sure he picked the restaurant so that we would drive past the right gallery. He's clever like that, making us *feel* like we have a choice, but subconsciously controlling us."

Matt laughed again. "When did you become so cynical?"

"It's all your fault."

"My fault? How's that?"

"Remember how you threw a fit about this guy 'controlling everything' earlier today?"

"Yeah." Matt sobered. "Your point?"

"Well, I got to thinking about it. This would be a perfect way to make us feel like we're in control when we're not." Parker tried to keep a straight face.

"Oh, I see, subliminal messaging to get us to do his bidding," Matt quipped. "You might be onto something."

"I am and you know it." Parker grinned as he looked out both windows. "Hey, help me find a parking spot; this place is a zoo."

It was a beautiful evening and tourism in Virginia Beach kept vendors and shops open well into the evening. People were everywhere. To extend the gallery's display area, artwork hung on fishing nets under a well-lit canopy. Nautical crafts, including wood and wire work, decorated the building's façade. Pottery stands accentuated the perimeter.

Pleased with the ambiance and artistic display, they both started taking pictures. They weren't concerned with all the people; for all they knew, one or more of them could be a part of their guy's plan.

❑ ❑ ❑

It was after 11:00 by the time they reached the house. Sunburnt and exhausted, they decided the photos could wait until morning.

Anna had left a note on the kitchen counter. 'If I don't see you before I leave for work, there is a variety of breakfast foods, juice, and coffee in the kitchen. Please help yourselves.'

Matt was the first to rise, though neither woke very early. He got a cup of coffee and began working on his story about the fitness center's grand opening. He had all the pictures and interviews from Saturday and now he had to get the article written and sent to the paper. His boss didn't care if he was out of town as long as he got his work submitted before the deadline.

When Parker got up, he went for a run and then took a shower before coming to see how Matt was doing. "Are you almost done with your article?"

"It shouldn't take too much longer."

"Okay. I'll get some breakfast first, but then we should look at the photos."

"Sounds good."

There was a local newspaper on the kitchen table, so Parker flipped through it while he ate. An article about the New Beginnings Mission, complete with pictures, caught his attention. A twenty-fifth-anniversary celebration was held there on Saturday. *Hmm, now it makes sense why that couple didn't believe Matt.* He read the article before bringing the paper with him to the office.

Initially, Parker wasn't sure if images would appear using his digital camera—before yesterday all their information came from film developed in his darkroom—but after having the photo of the menu change on his phone, he knew that wouldn't be an issue. He sat at the desk and slipped the camera's SD card into the laptop.

Nothing extra showed up in the photos from the first mission. Not surprised or worried that maybe nothing would show up in any of the photos, Parker continued to the pictures of the second mission. His eyes widened as he saw people of varying ages and ethnicities standing in front of the building and by the entrance. *Oh wow, this is different.* "Hey Matt, come check this out."

"Starting without me?" Matt saved his article and set his laptop on the couch.

"Yeah, yeah. You were working, and I didn't want to wait any longer." He pointed to the screen. "Look, our new message is people. No one was in front of the mission last night and the lighting suggests midmorning."

Matt looked over Parker's shoulder and said, "This is definitely cool, but what are we looking for?"

"Your guess is as good as mine." Parker took the six photos that had people in them and put them in two rows of three on the same screen. "There, that should help. I say we look for similarities."

Matt leaned closer and, for a moment, focused on each photo. Then he stepped back so he could see them all at once. "Look. There's a girl with red hair in every picture."

"I see her too, and though it's hard to tell in the ones where she's wearing a baseball cap and sunglasses, I think it's the same girl."

"It is, look." Matt pointed. "See, she's wearing the same ripped outfit in a few of the pictures."

"Let's not get ahead of ourselves. We should make sure there aren't multiple pictures of anyone else." Parker made each of the images bigger and they looked again.

After a bit, Matt said, "This is so weird, none of the other people are in more than one picture."

"I'm not seeing any other matches either. I'd say that makes the girl our first lead. How old do you think she is?"

"I'd say, mid to late teens." Matt left the table to get his notebook. On the way back, he grabbed an extra chair and took a seat next to Parker before adding, "I hope the mission was able to help her. She looks like she hasn't eaten in weeks and is in desperate need of a shower."

It was then that Parker remembered the newspaper article. "Oh, Matt, look at this." Parker handed him the paper. "There's a story about this mission. Now it makes sense why that couple

66

questioned your explanation last night; reporters had already been there to take pictures and do interviews."

"Does the article have pictures?" Matt's eyes widened with expectation.

Parker caught his meaning. "It does. It would be sweet if we could find her."

Matt opened the paper and searched for the redheaded girl. She wasn't in any of the pictures. "Oh well, it was worth a try."

"You know," Parker said as he spun his chair toward Matt, "because we solved our first case so quickly, I think we've forgotten that our guy told me he needed help with a cold case. I'm guessing that the mission wasn't able to help her."

"Right, a cold case. I don't like the sounds of that, especially after seeing these photos." With a heavy sigh, he started writing a description of the girl. "What showed at the gallery?"

"I haven't looked at those yet."

Parker saved the mission photos before scrolling to the ones from the gallery. They looked pretty much the same as when they took them the night before, except neither of them remembered seeing a redheaded girl. In the first picture, she looked to be eight or nine. Her long, wavy, red hair was tied back into a ponytail with a light-blue bow.

She would've simply been another face in the crowd if it weren't for her hair. Parker reopened one of the photos from the mission and enlarged the girl's face in both. "It's the same girl, isn't it?"

"Could be."

The next picture showed the same girl excitedly pointing at a painting of the ocean while pulling her mother toward it.

"Well, the girl is obviously relevant." Parker started tapping his fingers on the edge of his laptop before adding, "But I don't understand how having a picture of her when she's young and healthy helps us any."

"Hold up." Matt jumped to his feet and went to get his SD card. "Here, hopefully my pictures will fill in the blanks."

Parker eagerly took the card and slipped it into his computer. A few clicks later, he said, "Huh, what do we have here?"

None of Matt's photos had any hint of a mission or the gallery in them. The first one had the same coin effect as the photo that brought them to Virginia, but the image was different. It showed three musical instruments: a guitar, a violin, and a trumpet. There were also three stars.

"I'm guessing it would be safe to say this represents another state," Matt suggested.

"I still have that site open on my phone. I'll look." Parker found the coin in no time. "Here it is. Three instruments and three stars. Tennessee." Then his excitement abruptly disappeared. "If our next destination is somewhere in Tennessee, why'd we need to come to Virginia Beach?"

"For real, Parker? Now, who's whining? I hope our guy calls you and sets you straight." Matt's grin was priceless.

"Touché. I guess I deserved that."

"You did! Seriously, though, remember our parchments? Yours said to keep all the pictures and mine said to keep a journal of all the clues, even the ones that *don't seem relevant* at the time. I'm sure this will eventually make sense."

"I hope so." Parker scrolled to the next photo. It showed a two-story, brick building lined with solid rows of windows and surrounded by sports fields. A large, neon sign, adorned with purple irises, stood proudly on the front lawn.

"This must be a school. Can you zoom in?"

Parker enlarged the sign and was able to make out the name "Redford High School, Home of the Badgers."

Within seconds, Matt found the school on his phone. "It's in a suburb north of Memphis. Does this mean we head home and book flights, or do we drive? According to my app, it's a little over fourteen hours from here."

"Maybe, but hold up—let's see what's in your last photo before we start making plans."

There she was again; a portrait of the redheaded girl. This time, her age was somewhere in between the other photos they already had. Parker scrolled back to the picture of the school.

"A yearbook picture and a school. I think it'd be safe to say we need to go to Memphis."

The door to the office was open and Anna walked in without hesitation. "Oh, sorry to intrude. I didn't realize you guys were still here."

Parker stood. "We were hoping to leave soon, but we had some business to take care of first."

"Please don't feel rushed on my account. The sweater I want happens to be in that closet." She pointed and then walked past them.

Matt shifted in his seat, so he'd be facing her when she turned. "Thanks again for letting us use this room. It's a great place to work."

"Well good. That makes me happy." She slipped on the sweater and started to leave.

Parker stopped her. "Anna, wait. I tend to notice photos no matter where I am, but especially if they're done in black and white. So, if you don't mind me asking, who are the people in the pictures on your desk? I assume this one is of Owen and his family, right?"

Anna nodded.

"Good looking family. And the photo of the little girl? She looks a lot like you."

Anna walked to the desk and picked up the picture. She ran her fingers over the glass before saying, "This is my daughter, Nora."

Parker didn't notice that Anna's eyes welled with tears. "Cute little thing. Where are the current photos of her?"

Chapter 8

ANNA'S STORY

Anna blinked hard. Her tears spilled over and hit the glass. With a shudder, she set the picture back in its place on the desk and quickly dried her eyes. "Um, sorry."

"Wait, did I say something wrong?" Parker gently touched her arm. "I didn't mean to upset you."

Anna winced as if a shot of pain ran through her. "No, it's not you. It's just that I would love to have a current picture of Nora. This is the last one I have of her." Her hand visibly shook when she covered her lips. "Ahem, excuse me. I . . . I've got to go."

Parker didn't know what to do. Matt must have caught the bewildered look on his face because he jumped to his feet and followed her out of the room. "Anna, wait . . . do you want to talk about it?"

With fresh tears running down her cheeks, she turned to face him. Through uncontrollable heaves, she pushed out the words, "There's nothing to talk about. Nora's gone." To Matt's surprise, she buried her face in his chest and cried, "Someone stole her from us!"

Tentatively, he put his arms around her and let her cry.

After a bit, she pulled away. Her mascara was smudged, and her cheeks were red and swollen. "Oh, Matt, I'm so sorry. I don't know what's come over me." She hurried toward the kitchen.

"Anna, please don't go. We want to know what happened."

She turned on a dime and stared. "Why in the world would you want to hear my story?"

"Because you're obviously hurting and sometimes it helps to get things off our chests."

She shook her head. "I haven't had an outburst like that in years. There's no need for you to concern yourselves; I'll get over it soon enough. And anyway, I don't want to keep you from your responsibilities."

"Actually, you might be able to help us," Matt said. "Last week we received information that led to the rescue of two eighth-grade girls that had been abducted. Thankfully, the police arrived before any harm came to them, but from the sound of it, you didn't get the help you needed to save your little girl."

"Right." Anna crossed her arms, now looking more angry than sad.

"Well, recently we obtained new information about another teenaged girl who looks in desperate need of help. The details aren't clear enough to—"

Anna held up a hand and cut Matt off. "Wait, I thought you said you were a writer, not a private investigator?"

"I *am* a writer, and Parker *is* a photographer, but when we uncovered information about those girls, we felt it was our duty to go to the authorities."

"Wow, that's wonderful that you were willing to get involved, but I don't see how my story can help you, especially when it happened twenty years ago."

"I'm curious; since then have you learned anything about the abduction of your daughter that might have helped you find her, had you known about it earlier?"

Anna shook her head. "To this day it grieves me how little people care or dare to engage. You two are an anomaly." She cracked a weak smile. "Well anyway, at first we hoped and prayed that we'd get a ransom note, a chance to buy our baby back, but *no*, Nora was gone. We've not heard a thing about her since."

"I'm so sorry. Neither of us have children, so there's no way we can relate to the horror of such a loss. If we don't find any more information about this girl, it will be easy to quit."

"Oh, please don't quit. Whatever you do, don't quit." Anna stepped forward and put her hand on Matt's arm. "One of the hardest things we went through was feeling like our loss didn't matter to anyone else. It's a heavy burden to bear. Couple that with the guilt and shame that comes with *losing* a child. How irresponsible is that?"

Parker joined them. "That's a burden no one should have to bear. I'm sorry I mentioned the picture on your desk. We obviously didn't know about your daughter."

"And why would you? I'm not upset because you asked; it's simply a wound that never heals, that's all." Anna closed her eyes and rubbed her temples.

Parker nodded to Matt and whispered, "Let's give her some space." He didn't feel it was their place to press her any further.

It was then that Anna opened her eyes and said, "If you two truly want to hear my story, I'll tell you, because the thought of another abducted girl not getting the help she needs makes me sick."

"Shall we?" Matt gestured with his hands toward the office and started walking that way. Parker and Anna followed him.

Anna went to the desk and picked up Nora's picture. As she looked at it, she said, "Parker, I must agree with you; she *was* a cute little thing. I'm glad I have this memory of her."

Parker came and looked at the picture. "I don't even know what to say, except that if it's still too painful to talk about, we don't expect you to."

"No, I want to. It's been years since I've told anyone about this. Maybe it'll do me some good." Anna still held the picture of Nora in her hands, so she looked at it for a moment longer. "Wow. This is going to be harder than I thought." She took a deep breath before starting. "Twenty years ago, we lived in

Philadelphia. When the weather was nice, I took Owen and Nora to a park near our home. He was four at the time, and she was a few months shy of two. They loved the park and I enjoyed getting out of our small apartment.

"On this particular day, Owen played on the monkey bars and Nora ran from one thing to the next, so I occupied myself with chasing her. We were carefree and happy. Then Owen's cry caught my attention and for a moment I took my eye off Nora and went to make sure he was okay. He had fallen and scraped his knee. When I looked up, Nora was missing. I got Owen to his feet and we went to look for her but couldn't find her anywhere. Suddenly a sick, overwhelming feeling hit me, and I panicked. I started frantically running around the playground calling Nora's name while looking in all the tunnels and under the slides. Fear gripped my heart and I yelled louder. I begged those who were there to help me find my little girl.

"A few of the moms who had seen Nora with me only minutes earlier turned their focus to making sure their own children were safe. At the time I was too desperate to care that none of them came to help me. I continued to call her name but to no avail. Then I quickly searched the perimeter of the park to see if anyone had a little girl in tow. Buildings and the street were close. A planned abduction was certainly possible, but I didn't think that was what actually happened.

"I screamed louder, again begging those who stood by to help. But Nora was gone." As she talked, the horror of that dreadful day overwhelmed her. She collapsed into the empty chair, buried her face in her hands, and wept.

Matt removed his glasses and wiped a tear from his cheek, while Parker sat there rubbing his chin. Neither could imagine the gut-wrenching trauma of such a loss.

The gravity of Anna's reality engulfed the room and for a bit no one stirred.

Eventually, she reached for a tissue and blew her nose. "Huh. Well, finally a young couple with no children approached me to see if there was anything they could do to help. I remember saying, 'Call the police! My little girl is missing!' Keep in mind, this was before the age of cell phones. The man left immediately to get help and the woman stayed with me. I cried, 'I need my baby. Oh God, where is my baby?' We both called her name and kept looking while we waited. I hoped something had caught Nora's eye or that she was playing in one of the tunnels and too preoccupied to answer."

She shook her head and covered her mouth to squelch another bout of hysteria. It took a moment before she could continue. "Once the police arrived, they questioned everyone who was still in the park. Several of the moms had already gathered up their children and left. I pleaded for help. No one came forward saying they saw anyone take her. It was like she just disappeared. I was so overwhelmed that I fell to the ground, trembling, and crying hysterically. Poor Owen didn't understand. He started shaking my arm. 'Mommy, Mommy, why are you crying?' Then he must have realized his little sister wasn't with me. 'Mommy, where's Nora? Why can't you find Nora?' His small, concerned voice broke my heart even more. I would've gladly given my life in exchange for Nora's. Living without her was unbearable.

"When a few weeks had passed and no information of Nora surfaced, we lost all hope. That wasn't the end of it, though. The police came to our apartment and started interrogating me like I had something to do with it. They asked if we were in financial trouble, even questioning if we'd sold Nora and tried to make it look like she was abducted. I couldn't believe my ears. We weren't in financial trouble. I told them they could check. All our bills were paid."

Matt looked up from his notes and said, "I know that seemed calloused, but unfortunately it's happened before."

"I suppose, but because we didn't sell our child, it frayed my nerves even more. It seemed like more focus was put on us than finding Nora. Our family was under investigation for months. Our bank records were seized, and our every move watched. I pleaded for help. 'We didn't sell our baby. Why won't you help us find her?'"

She leaned forward and picked up the picture again. "Unfortunately, no help came, no information was found and like I said, we've never seen or heard from Nora since.

"Eventually our names were cleared of all wrongdoing, but our lives were ruined. I fell into a deep depression and couldn't cope. My once loving and honorable husband, Quinn, started drinking in excess and became verbally abusive. He said Nora's disappearance was my fault and he hated me for it. He could no longer speak civilly to me and threw it in my face every opportunity he could." Anna sighed. "This took its toll on my already weakened state. Occasionally, when he was extra mad, he'd hit me. Now I not only had to deal with the loss of a missing child, our marriage was on the rocks."

"Is that how you got the scar on your right cheek?" Matt asked.

"Yes, one time he hit me so hard that I blacked out and fell into the coffee table. I needed six stitches."

Neither Anna nor Matt noticed Parker's clenched fists.

She continued unabated. "My mother encouraged me to get an order of protection or to move out. She told me it was no environment to raise my son. Things got worse and with my parents' help, I finally got my own place and a job.

"Quinn never hit Owen or hurt him in any way, so we worked out visitation and my dad would drop him off and pick him up.

"Then the craziest thing happened; his parents walked away from a successful business and left the area. Quinn went with them. Money was wired to my account each month for Owen and there was no custody battle. I did have an email address so I sent pictures of Owen with an update every month so Quinn and my in-laws could watch him grow.

"Quinn never replied, but his mother acknowledged they got the emails and thanked me. About six months after they moved, she sent me a long email saying she was sorry. She loved me and knew I was a good wife and mother. She encouraged me not to blame myself because it wasn't my fault—but Quinn needed help. They felt a fresh start somewhere else might bring their son back from the abyss. The pictures of Owen only reminded him of his loss.

"Understanding, but not understanding, I asked if I should keep sending pictures. She requested that I send them to her and when the time was right, she would show them to Quinn. We've kept in touch all these years and invited them to Owen's wedding. They didn't come. Even that breaks my heart, but then you don't need to know every detail. Sorry—"

"You have no reason to apologize, Anna. We asked," Matt said, "and now we realize how difficult it was for you to tell us your story. We're so sorry for your loss."

"Me, too. Oh, look at the time! Please excuse me; I need to get back to work." She stood and put the picture next to the one of Owen. "If you ever find the girl you're looking for, maybe you could let me know her story."

"We will," Parker said. "We most certainly will."

With a tired smile, Anna nodded and left the room.

Chapter 9

ROAD TRIP

They heard the front door shut. This seemed to wake Parker from his stupor. He walked to the front window and with the back of his hand, moved the sheer curtain just far enough to see Anna climb into her Mini Cooper. From there, he could see that she buried her face in her hands; her shoulders rose and fell. A twinge of pain shot through Parker's heart and his whole body shuddered. Before he had time to regain his own composure, she started the car and sped away. Parker remained at the window until she was out of sight.

Matt had turned back to his notebook and was adding a few more details. He looked up when Parker approached the desk. "I was surprised by Anna's initial response. Her pain was so raw like one would react to a fresh gash, yet it oozed with years of regret."

"The story is devastating, for sure." Parker briskly rubbed his hands together. "I can see how it would be like a wound that never heals."

"She certainly threw me for a loop when she fell into my arms. I wasn't even sure if holding her was the right thing to do, but then she didn't exactly give me a choice."

"I thought you handled it well." Parker spun the chair toward Matt and took a seat. "Why do you think she had such a strong reaction? It's not like she doesn't see that picture every time she comes in here."

"My guess would be because it matters."

"But how? We can't change her past or bring healing to her broken heart."

"I know, but now I feel more inclined to find out what's going on with the girl in our photos. The ones at the mission were disturbing."

"That's for sure," Parker said. "The thing that bothered me the most about Anna's story is the fact that someone must have seen the perps take Nora, so why didn't they try to stop them?"

"Or at least yell for help." Matt rapidly tapped his pen on his notebook. "And if nothing else, stay to describe the perps to the police."

"But see, that's my point exactly. I don't want to be guilty of not helping the redheaded girl. She's in our photos, so there has to be more to it, and we need to find out what." Parker turned back to his laptop and reopened the mission photos. "Her eyes are so dark in these ones that I didn't even notice they were green."

Matt came to the desk so he could look. "You know, this could've been the plight of our first two girls if the police didn't find them when they did."

"Yeah or worse . . . in the sex-trafficking world they don't usually live to tell their stories."

"Maybe this girl escaped."

Parker raised an eyebrow.

"What? You said to get creative. This girl looks more scared than strung out on drugs or something. We need to find her."

"I agree, but there's nothing we can do about it right now. How about finishing your article so we can go out?"

"Oh, man, I forgot about that. Thanks." Matt hurried to the couch and opened his laptop. After a minute, he said, "I have the article written. It won't take me long now to proof it and get it sent."

"Great. While you do that, I'll get these photos saved to the cloud." When he was done, Parker put his SD Card back into his digital camera and then loaded a new roll of black and white film into his 35mm. It was his camera of choice for commission jobs.

Matt hit the send button and closed his computer. "There. I'm happy to have that out of the way; now we can focus on finding the girl."

"And taking some pictures of the ships for Anna," Parker added. He slung his camera bag over his shoulder and grabbed his keys. "Are you ready?"

"Almost. Hand me my SD Card. I'd like to take some pictures, too."

While Matt bagged up his camera, Parker looked for directions to the naval base.

"Do you mind if we stop to get some lunch first?" Matt asked. "I didn't have breakfast."

"Sure, we can look for a place on the way."

They found a quaint little diner with a self-serve coffee bar and a lounge area with a couch and a few cushioned chairs. A chalkboard menu filled one wall. After ordering, they got themselves some coffee and sat in one of the booths near the front window. Their conversation turned back to Anna's story.

"You'd never know by looking at Anna or hearing her talk that she's suffered such a devastating blow," Parker said.

"Well, it did happen two decades ago—"

"Which makes it all the more surprising that she reacted the way she did."

"True, but if she didn't have that reaction, we wouldn't have pressed for information and her story wouldn't be pushing us to find the redheaded girl." Matt took a sip of coffee and then set it to the side, giving the waitress room to set down his food. "Thank you."

They started eating before Parker said, "I think we should go back to the mission. We can show them our pictures; maybe someone there will recognize her."

"Sure, we can do that, but if she's here, why would we need the photos in Memphis?"

"You have a point, but if that's the case, why would we need photos of the mission here? Or better yet, why'd we need to come here at all?" Parker shook his head and took another bite of his burger.

"I didn't say we shouldn't go to the mission. I just don't think we'll find what we need there, that's all."

They realized the conversation was getting a bit testy, so they finished their lunch in silence.

A few minutes later, their phones vibrated, and they both hurried to open their respective text. Neither had words, only the picture from the yearbook and the one of the high school.

Matt showed Parker his phone.

"Yeah, I got the same text. Does this mean we're off to Memphis?" Parker asked with a sheepish grin.

Matt perked up and smiled. "Absolutely. Are we flying or driving, and when do we leave?"

Parker was surprised by Matt's enthusiasm, so he tried to temper it. "Well, we still need to get photos of the ships and I don't feel rushed to react as I did with the info we found in Philly. Are you up for a road trip?"

"Sure. I need to call my boss first, though, to confirm that it's okay to use some of my vacation. It's not like I need to save it for my honeymoon anymore."

Parker breathed a sigh of relief when Matt mentioned his honeymoon and it didn't send him into a tailspin. "Perfect, that way we can take the time to figure out who this girl is and why she needs our help. But if you don't mind, I'd rather leave in the morning."

"Morning works," Matt said. "I say we start looking for a boat tour. From what I found on the web, that's the best way for civilians to see the ships."

"I'll help. Let's try to find one that focuses on the ships, without it being a tour of the whole harbor." After checking out a few different sites, Parker said, "Here's one. A tour starts at 2:00."

Matt looked at his watch. "If we leave now, we should be able to make it in time."

The weather was overcast but not raining. As a photographer, Parker liked the feel of the subdued lighting. He thought it would make the ships seem even more foreboding, especially in the photos he planned to shoot in black and white.

They made it to the pier on time, boarded the boat, and found an open spot by the railing on the upper deck.

"Are you excited about taking pictures for your real job?" Matt asked.

"Ha, the job we're on now seems real enough. I have money in the bank to prove it." Parker grinned. He got out his 35mm and put on a wide-angle lens. He wanted to be sure he could get some pictures of an entire ship.

Matt leaned against the railing. "You know what I mean. The pictures you get to take now are for a commission, not because some mysterious guy told you to."

Parker became serious. "I knew what you meant, and yet, the more we take pictures that change, the more I see there's a purpose beyond the money. So, in truth, this will be fun, but it won't be nearly as important."

"There, you're doing it again."

"Doing what again?

"Caring," Matt said. "This is the first time, at least since I've known you, that you've committed to something outside of your control."

A small smile crept into the corner of Parker's lips as he looked through his viewfinder to make sure he had on the lens he wanted. Then he turned to Matt. "Well, I got to thinking about what you said earlier. This is the first time there could be negative consequences if we don't see this through."

Matt nodded thoughtfully. The boat started to move, so he quickly got out his own camera and spun toward the water.

They fell silent.

Parker's musings took him back to the mission photos and the improbability of how they got their information. He knew his strengths: adventurous, quick to act, and good at his job. The thing that was new to him was the fact that he did care about the welfare of this girl. That, combined with the guesswork of finding her, was enough to perplex him. Lost in thought, he wasn't paying attention when the ships came into view.

Matt nudged his arm. "Hey man, wake up. You have work to do."

"Oh, wow. I forgot how big these aircraft carriers are."

"No wonder Owen feels a sense of security about them."

The ships were so big that Parker had time to switch between cameras and he still used a whole roll of film.

On their way back to the dock, Matt started looking at his photos. "I should get one of these framed for my office. Maybe it will remind me to be more assertive and adventurous."

Parker winced at the underlying purpose for that remark. The last thing they needed was for Matt to fall back into a funk about Haley. He acknowledged the comment with a nod but quickly moved the conversation forward. "I know we got some amazing shots, but if you don't mind, I'd still like to see the view from Anna's building."

Matt powered down his camera. "I'm game, but it's getting late, so we better get going."

◻ ◻ ◻

By the time they finished the boat tour and had taken photos from Anna's building, it was almost 5:00 and too late to stop back at the mission. The clouds had given way to sunshine and because there was no pressing need to look at the photos, they decided to do some sightseeing. They walked the boardwalk, got dinner and were back to Anna's house by 9:00.

She sat curled up on the couch with a cup of tea and a book. When they came in, she inquired about their evening and seemed her pleasant self, although her eyes were swollen, and her cheeks and nose were red.

Matt offered a brief rundown of their evening and then asked, "How about you?"

"Well, as you can probably see, I spent most of the evening crying, but I feel better now. I don't know why I got so emotional earlier when Parker asked about the picture of Nora and then again tonight when I got home." She shook her head as if trying not to let those thoughts overtake her for the third time.

"We didn't think you were too emotional at all." Matt gave a reassuring smile. "Getting a glimpse into the devastating reality of your past is actually what's pushing us to pursue our latest leads. All we have is the location of a high school north of Memphis and a picture of a girl. We're not sure what kind of trouble she's in or what we can do to help, but we're going to find out."

"Yeah," Parker said. "The one thing we know for sure is that we don't want another family to feel like help never came."

"It's very sweet of you guys to care about the welfare of a girl you've never met."

"And also, kind of weird," Parker said. "Following snippets of information isn't exactly easy. I'm ashamed to admit it, but we don't exactly know what we're doing."

"I have total confidence in you. Two girls have already been saved and their families will never have to endure the pain that I've had to live with. I'm sorry to see you go, but good luck with your search."

"Thanks. I'll email you the proofs of the ships when I have them ready. In the meantime, I'll need you to send me the dimensions of the space so I can custom-size the photo for you."

"I will. I'll even take a few pictures of the room to help you decide which of the photos would be a good fit," Anna said.

"Perfect, thanks."

"Oh, I'm planning a trip to Philadelphia in a few weeks with Owen and his family. Would you guys be interested in catching a baseball game with us while we're there?"

"We'd love to catch a game with you. Just let us know when."

Chapter 10

A NIGHT TERROR

That night Parker had a night terror. The room closed in around him, horror consumed his dreams. His sheets were wet with sweat as he thrashed and swung at the air. Then, loud enough to wake the others, he started screaming, "Stop! You're going to kill her! Don't kill her. No, stop, stop . . ."

Matt bolted out of bed and ran into Parker's room. Forcefully, he shook his shoulder. "Parker, wake up. It's only a drea—"

Parker swung him to the floor, straddled his body, and started hitting him as hard as he could. Though he appeared to be awake, the dream remained vivid in his mind. "You'll never hurt her again! Never! You beast!"

Matt's pleas for Parker to stop went unheeded. He only blocked a few blows before blacking out. Punch after punch brutally landed on Matt's face.

Anna had barely reached the doorway before changing course. She quickly grabbed a broom from the hall closet and rushed into the room. With all her might, she leveled a severe blow to the middle of Parker's back.

This seemed to get his attention because even though the flames of rage still filled his eyes, he quit swinging. Suddenly, the room came into focus. When he saw Matt's bloodied face and lifeless body, he scrambled off him. In horror, he looked at

85

his hands. "Oh God, what have I done? Help! Somebody, help!"

Anna had run out of the room and was returning now with a bowl of water and clean towels. Blood gushed from around Matt's left eye, ran past his ear, and was dripping onto the carpet. She quickly wet a towel and covered the gashes. When she lifted the cloth, blood still gushed from the wounds. A cut was above his eye and an even longer one along his cheekbone. "He's going to need stitches."

Parker pulled himself to his feet. "Can I drive, or should we call an ambulance?"

"You can drive, but we need gauze first. There's some in the bathroom cupboard on the top right shelf. Go get it. Hurry!"

She placed a fresh towel over Matt's eye. The smaller cuts would have to wait.

Matt had regained consciousness and tried to get up. "Not yet, Matt." She rested her free hand on his chest. "Try to relax."

Parker ran back in with the gauze and medical tape and kneeled next to Anna. "Here, what can I do to help?"

"Go pull your Jeep closer to the door."

Parker threw on a pair of jeans and sneakers, grabbed his keys, and raced down the stairs. He was back before Anna finished putting gauze on the gash.

"Matt, we need you to sit up before we have you stand. Okay?"

"Uh-huh."

"Parker, can you put a hand under Matt's back and help lift him? I'll take his hands to keep him steady."

As soon as he sat up, Matt's head bobbed forward. He went limp.

"Whoa!" Parker grabbed his shoulders. "He's blacking out again. Now what?"

"Let's wait a minute and see if he gets his bearings. If not, I'll call for an ambulance. Matt, can you hear me?" Anna asked.

It took a few seconds for his good eye to come into focus. "What happened?" He reached for his eye.

"You're hurt." Anna stopped his hand. "We need to get you to the hospital."

His head bobbed. "Wow, I'm so dizzy."

"We can wait a minute, but you're bleeding badly. You need to see a doctor."

They couldn't afford to wait long so Parker knelt beside him. "Here, put your arm around my shoulder."

Anna got on the other side and they lifted him to his feet. "Steady now. Do you think you can walk?"

"I'll try."

Slowly, they made their way out of the room and down the stairs. By the time they got outside, Matt was stable enough to climb into the back seat of Parker's Jeep. Anna ran around to the other side, got in, and had Matt lay his head in her lap. Fresh blood had already seeped through the gauze.

"No, Anna, you're not coming. I'll take Matt to the hospital and then find a room somewhere else. I don't want you afraid to sleep in your own house."

"I'm coming. Now shut up and drive!" Her tone immediately silenced him.

When they reached the hospital, Parker ran inside to get help. Within minutes a wheelchair was beside the Jeep and Matt was whisked away. Anna followed while Parker moved his vehicle. Too ashamed to join them, he went to wash the blood from his hands and then found a waiting room.

❑ ❑ ❑

A nurse asked Matt some questions, which he struggled to answer. After looking at the wounds, she added fresh gauze to the worst ones and then jotted something on Matt's chart before saying, "The doctor will be with you shortly."

The twenty-minute wait seemed like an eternity, but Matt was starting to think more clearly by the time the doctor arrived.

He looked at Matt's chart and then at Matt. "What happened to you?"

"I ran into a nightmare."

"Sorry? This looks worse than falling and bumping your head." Beyond the gashes, signs of bruising were already coloring Matt's face.

"I didn't say it was *my* nightmare."

"You took quite the pounding. Do you want to press charges? We deal with domestic violence all the time."

"No thanks. Please just stitch me up so I can get out of here."

"Take it easy, young man. You won't be going anywhere for at least two hours. Concussion protocol. We also need to make sure there's no bleeding behind this eye."

It took the doctor a while to sew up the worst cuts. When he finished, he said, "There. I think you should only have minimal scarring once the stitches are removed." Then he turned to Anna and the nurse. "Make sure Matt doesn't fall asleep for at least an hour. In the meantime, I will order a CT Scan. From the looks of it, I'm pretty sure that eye will need further attention."

The nurse put ice packs around Matt's swollen face and asked, "Are you comfortable? Do you need another pillow?"

"How about something for the pain?"

"I could give you something mild, but it probably won't help much. Anything stronger will make you sleep. Can you stick it out for a bit longer?" Matt nodded once. He stared at the ceiling with his good eye. "Okay, good. I'll be back to check on you in a bit. I'm not sure how long you'll have to wait for the Scan, but I'll give you something for the pain as soon as you're done. Here's your call button. I'm close if you need anything."

Anna stepped beside Matt's bed and pushed some stray hairs off his forehead. "Do you know what caused the nightmare?"

He started to shake his head, but quickly realized that wasn't a good idea. "No. Parker's my best friend, but I've never seen him act this way before. I can't imagine what triggered such violence."

"How long have you known him?"

"About three years, but we've never traveled together so I don't know if this is a regular occurrence."

"Let's hope not." Anna stayed with him for a while and talked about other things to help keep him awake. When two nurses finally came to wheel Matt away, she patted his arm and said, "I'm going to check on Parker. I'll be back."

Matt reached for Anna's hand. "Thanks. I don't know what we would've done without you. So much for trusting we'd be safe renters."

"Don't you worry about me, I'm fine. Right now, we need to focus on you getting better." She squeezed his hand and left the room.

❏ ❏ ❏

A waiting room was adjacent to the ER. That's where she found Parker with his head in his hands. "Hey, are you okay?"

Deep in thought, he hadn't heard Anna approach and her voice startled him. "Oh, uh, yeah. Well, not exactly." He sat back and briskly rubbed his hands over his knees before clenching them together. "How's Matt?"

"The doctor stitched him up and they just now took him for a CT Scan. Even if the eye's okay, he can't leave for a few hours. That means we'll be here for a while. Want a cup of coffee?"

"No thanks. I should take you home so you can get some sleep." He got to his feet.

Anna took a seat. "I'm not leaving. Matt is more important than sleep and besides, I have some personal time I can use. I'll call my boss in the morning."

"I can't let you do that." Parker remained standing and held out his hand.

Instead of taking it, she patted the chair next to her. "Come sit. I *want* to stay and you're not going to dissuade me."

He shoved his hands into his pockets and walked to a window. Anna stayed in her seat. When several minutes had passed and he didn't come back, she joined him. Gently touching his arm, she asked, "Hey, what's going on?"

He slowly tipped his head toward Anna, trying to figure out what to say. As soon as their eyes met, his courage faltered. He couldn't trust this new acquaintance to understand. It was easier to look out the window. To keep her at arm's length, rather than share the pain from his own past.

It was almost as if Anna could read his mind. "Parker, I'm here for you, you know? It's no different than you being there for me this morning when I told you my story. It only seems fair you share yours." Anna gave a reassuring smile—not the condemning look he expected.

"I haven't had night terrors in years." He shifted his stance and peered into Anna's eyes. "Your story woke memories of a past that I've tried to forget."

"How so?"

"My dad took off when I was ten. My mom had boyfriends from time to time, but none lasted very long. Finally, the summer before my junior year of high school, she met Mike. He had a good-paying job and treated her well. My mom worked, but we were living paycheck to paycheck, so when he asked us to move in with him, she jumped at the offer. The thought of living in a nice house instead of a small apartment sounded good to both of us. At first, things seemed to be fine, but as time went by, I started noticing bruises on my mom."

He stopped to rub his chin, realizing he had stepped across some invisible line of vulnerability, but Anna needed to know so she would understand the reason for the night terror. "When I would ask her about the bruises, she'd always say she fell or made some other excuse. I was busy doing teenage stuff, so I didn't give it much thought. Then, one night in the spring of my senior year, I came home about 11:00 to find Mike choking my mom. Thankfully I came in when I did. I yelled at him and tried to pull him away from her, but then he turned on me. In one fell swoop, he threw me to the floor and started beating the crap out of me."

"Oh no," Anna gasped.

"Well anyway, when you told us about Quinn hitting you, the memory of my past came rushing in. After that loser hurt me, my mom stayed with him, if you can believe such a thing. He never apologized to me and acted like nothing ever happened. At the time I didn't understand why she put up with him. Now I realize, she did it for me. For us. But was having nice things worth the trade-off?" Parker abruptly left the window and took a seat.

Anna joined him. "But what happened after that?"

He blew out a heavy breath. "While I was still recovering, I begged my mom to move out. I told her I'd get a job after school to help with the bills, but she wouldn't leave Mike." The more Parker talked, the louder he got. Wary eyes darted his way. He noticed and lowered his voice before continuing. "I couldn't bear to watch the abuse any longer. A friend offered me a place to stay and I moved out."

"But what made you attack Matt?"

"I was stuck in a graphic dream. When Matt grabbed my shoulder, I must have thought he was Mike and I was defending my mom. He wasn't going to win this time. I'm older now and stronger . . . I can protect my mom. I can protect myself . . ." Parker spoke as if he was reliving the scene, desperate to control the situation. Sweat began to bead on his brow. His eyes became dark and threatening as his hands again curled into fists.

Anna grabbed his arm and whispered loudly, "Parker, stop!"

The woman who sat closest to them gathered up her things and moved. This got Parker's attention.

For a moment he stopped speaking and scanned the waiting room. With most of the tension now abated, he unclenched his fists and buried his face in his hands. "And look what I've done; my best friend is in the hospital because of me."

"I'm sorry you and your mom had to live through that." Anna started to rub his back. "Are you and Mike on good terms now?"

Parker's head shot up. "Of course not."

Anna flinched, pulled her hand back, and fell silent.

He sat back and studied the concern in her eyes. "Sorry to take my frustrations out on you, Anna. To be honest, I haven't spoken to Mike since that night."

With eyes locked, she quietly asked, "Is your mom still with him?"

Parker shrugged. "How am I supposed to know?"

Anna frowned. "You mean to tell me that you don't talk to your mom, either?"

"I haven't talked to her since graduation. She came wearing heavy makeup to hide the bruises. Mike was with her. He strutted like a peacock and had his arm around her waist. It broke my heart to see my mom like that, but I knew I couldn't change her. What angered me the most was the fact that she chose that rich scumbag over me."

"Unfortunately, in her own struggle to survive, she lost sight of what was important," Anna said. "I'm guessing she regrets that now."

"Yeah, well, that's ancient history—abandoned by my father, overlooked by my mother. And here you are, a loving and kindhearted woman who cares more about me, practically a stranger, than either of my parents do."

"But it's not ancient history. You wouldn't have had such a strong desire to protect your mom, even in a dream, if you didn't still care about her."

"More like revenge. I actually thought I was hitting Mike and, as you noticed, I wouldn't have stopped if you hadn't intervened. I haven't seen my mom in nine years. I had no idea, until tonight, that much hatred still raged within me."

"Here's the thing, Parker. Hatred and bitterness are like cancers. They eat away at us, even when we can't see them on the surface. It sounds like forgiveness and reconciliation would help heal your heart."

Chapter 11

MATT'S REACTION

The hour was late when a nurse entered the waiting room where friends and relatives congregated in clusters hoping for news of their loved ones. "Excuse me, Anna? We've decided to admit Matt because he does have a concussion and hyphema. That's a bleeding in the eye caused by blunt force trauma. He will need to see an ophthalmologist in the morning. Our main concern right now is the vomiting; we must keep that in check, or it could cause more damage to his eye."

Anna frowned at the news. "Will he lose sight in that eye?"

"He could sustain some loss of vision, but if he strictly follows the doctor's orders, the eye should recover completely. To be clear, the healing process is slow and tedious. If not taken seriously, lasting damage can result."

"Can we go see him now? What's his room number?" Anna started for the door without waiting for an answer.

"Hold up." The nurse ran after her. "We prefer for you to wait. He's been given pain medicine and a sedative to help him sleep. He won't even know you're there. Give me your number and we'll call you if necessary."

"Okay."

"Do you have a ride?"

"Yes, my friend over there will take me home," she said, pointing to Parker. Anna wrote down her number and thanked the nurse again.

Parker started for the door when he heard Anna's answer. *My friend?* He wondered if that's what you say to a stranger when there's no time for the truth. *Why is she so generous? I certainly don't deserve it.*

They rode home in silence and when they reached the house, Parker immediately went to pack his things. Anna made a cup of tea and was sitting at the kitchen island when he came back. He couldn't leave without passing her, so he said, "I'll stop at the hospital in the morning. Please, don't worry yourself about us any longer."

"Parker, you don't have to leave. All is forgiven and with tourism in full swing, you won't find an empty room at this hour."

"Thanks, but I can't stay. We'll stop back to get Matt's things before we leave town. He'll want to thank you personally." Too ashamed to stay a moment longer, Parker hurried out the door and was gone before Anna could convince him otherwise.

Not knowing where to go, he drove around for a while and ended up at the mission. The lamplight, still on inside, cast a warm glow through the window and onto the sidewalk. He pulled over and mindlessly stared at the building. Unwittingly, his thoughts went back to Mike. In anger, he clenched the steering wheel. Then, without warning, Matt's bloodied face came into view. Parker shuddered and closed his eyes, hoping to erase the memory that was all too real and fresh.

That didn't help, so he briskly rubbed his face. Nothing seemed to ease his pain. Desperate for peace, he fixed his eyes on the mural of the children. Suddenly they began to move, to play. He could hear the sounds of their laughter. *No, this can't be happening. It's one thing to have the images change on my phone or computer, but this?*

He lowered his window, put an elbow on the door and leaned out of the Jeep to watch. The scene on the mission window changed to a playground. Children were everywhere. Some parents pushed swings, others followed their children from one apparatus to the next, and a few sat on benches chatting while their children played together. It wasn't long before everyone disappeared from the scene, except for a woman who could pass for a younger version of Anna. She was chasing a toddler who looked to be no more than two years of age. At one point, they stopped running and turned to face Parker. Seconds later, the vision ended, and the original mural appeared unchanged.

Wow, that was weird. Parker didn't understand how Anna could be so happy and loving after all she'd lost. How could she talk about forgiveness when she had every right to harbor hatred and self-pity? He put up the window and let his head fall back on his seat. *All we've done is stir up painful memories and then scare her half to death in her own home. It's not right.*

❑ ❑ ❑

Parker woke to the sound of pouring rain. It was morning. The mission door was open, and people were hurrying to get inside. His eyes moved to the mural and he wondered whether the animation actually happened. More than likely, it was a figment of his imagination brought on by Anna's story.

On a whim, Parker ran across the street and through the open door. Once inside, he grabbed his phone, accessed the cloud, and brought up one of the photos of the red-headed girl standing in front of that mission. He asked several people, but no one recognized her.

With slumped shoulders and a heavy heart, he walked into the rain and down the street. He didn't care that he was getting soaked; the rain brought him comfort. For a while, he thought of nothing.

Eventually, his mindlessness slipped back into reality, and whether he wanted to or not, he knew he needed to go to the hospital to check on Matt. The rain had let up, so he pulled out his phone to see what time it was. *Oh man, how'd it get so late?* Turning, he jogged back to his Jeep.

Using his phone's camera, Parker took a picture of the mural of the children before he drove away to find a diner. More than wanting food, he needed to wash up and get changed into dry clothes, which he quickly did while they made his breakfast.

On his way back to the table, he got a text from Anna. `'I'm at the hospital. Matt's awake, coherent, and asking about you. Room 461'`

Seriously? Parker couldn't believe that Anna used personal time so she could go to the hospital. Instead of taking his seat, he went to the counter and got the waitress's attention, "Excuse me, ma'am, but could I please get my order to go?"

"Sure, no problem." She disappeared into the kitchen and returned a moment later with the food and his coffee.

"Thanks."

❏ ❏ ❏

His nerves, usually of steel, faltered as he followed the orange signs to the trauma unit. It was going to be hard enough to face Matt, but he didn't see why Anna had to be there, too.

When Anna saw Parker, she greeted him with a warm smile and a reassuring nod. Then she promptly left the room without saying a word. *Huh, I didn't see that coming.*

Matt's bed was raised about halfway. His head was propped between two pillows and someone had brushed his wavy brown hair straight back to keep it off his forehead. The patch that covered his left eye concealed his stitches. His whole face was black and blue and swollen, along with smaller lacerations and a split lip.

It took all Parker's strength not to grimace or look away when he first saw him. He had predetermined not to make excuses or blame the night terror. Matt didn't look at him as he approached the bed. "Hey, um, how are you doing?" he asked and then added, "I'm so sorry."

"Me, too," Matt said. He slowly turned his head just enough to see Parker. "This changes everything."

Parker locked eyes with Matt, refusing to drop his gaze, but he didn't answer.

"I didn't sign up for this," Matt continued.

"Neither did I. You certainly didn't deserve this and unfortunately I can't take it back." He paused to reflect on the severity of Matt's wounds. "If you don't want to help me find the girl, I understand."

"Well good, because I'm not willing to risk my life on a hope that we can make sense of these pictures. You'll have to go it alone from here."

Parker knew Matt well enough to know this would be his reply and yet, the thought of doing it alone didn't seem right either. "How about we not worry about our mission right now and focus on getting you better. Then we can talk about it in a few days, okay?"

"Today, two weeks . . . it doesn't matter. My answer will be the same. I'm out!"

Matt was more adamant than Parker expected, but then after seeing his face, he had no recourse. Instead of pressing the issue, he pulled up a chair and sat there in silence for a while. Matt closed his good eye.

Parker didn't know what to do. If Matt was going to ignore him, he didn't feel like sitting there and yet he felt it would be wrong to leave.

Another ten minutes passed and still Matt hadn't opened his eye or bothered to speak.

With a sigh, Parker stood. "Well, I hope someday you can forgive me, and we can at least be friends again. See you around."

Matt opened his eye. "Parker, hold up. You're forgiven. Anna explained the reason for your night terror and just because I want out doesn't mean we're not still friends." Matt tried to smile, but the movement caused him to wince instead. "I'm simply not up for the challenge, especially after Haley, so don't take any of this personally."

"Thanks. That means a lot to me." Parker squeezed his arm. "I'll come back later, okay."

"Sounds good. Hopefully, by then, I'll be feeling a little better."

"I hope so, too. See ya."

Anna met Parker in the hall. His tall, strong frame looked frail and beaten down. "Hey, do you want to get a cup of coffee?"

"Sure." He didn't make eye contact and they walked to the hospital café in silence. They ordered and Parker paid while Anna found a free table by the window. Once they were situated, he asked, "Do you know if they've given Matt a time frame for his release?"

"Yes. The doctor said he could go home tomorrow. They want to keep him one more night for observation. But they also told him no traveling for at least a week, maybe two, depending on how quickly the bleeding behind his eye clears up."

Parker groaned. "That long, huh?"

"No worries. I told Matt he could stay with me as long as necessary."

"I don't get you. Why do you feel it's your responsibility to help us?"

"I'm happy to help and, more importantly, Matt doesn't want to keep you from your obligations. So, you see, it's a win-win."

"But Matt's stuck here because of me. I can't just leave him."

"He said he'd call his parents this afternoon to let them know what happened. They'll come to get him when he's able to go home."

"Great. Matt's parents used to like me and treated me like a son. Even when Matt was preoccupied with Haley, I'd occasionally go over and watch a game with Mr. Howard. Not having a family of my own, that meant a lot to me. Once they know what happened, they'll hate me."

"No one hates you. The same great guy I met two days ago is the same great guy sitting here. You're way too hard on yourself."

"I hate myself, so why shouldn't they? A 'great guy' wouldn't have done this."

"The issue is deeper than this one event, Parker. Because you can't forgive Mike and your mother, you don't believe anyone should forgive you. I hope you can find a way to at least restore your relationship with your mom. It would do you both some good."

When Parker didn't answer, Anna changed the subject. "Are you done with your business here in Virginia Beach? You said last night that you were leaving this morning to follow some leads."

"I don't think I'll be following any more leads. Especially when this is the result."

"What about the information you have concerning the girl in Memphis? Are you giving up on her because of one nightmare?"

"It wasn't just a nightmare. I was out of control! I almost killed my best friend and that freaks me out." Parker dropped his gaze and started fidgeting with his keys. "And anyway, I don't know who this girl is or if she even needs my help. Missing or not, no girl is worth what happened to Matt."

"What happened to Matt has nothing to do with this girl." Anna reached out to take Parker's hand and looked him straight in the eyes. "Maybe it's none of my business, but I know firsthand what her parents are going through and I wouldn't wish that heartache on anyone. Not to mention the horror or pain the girl might be suffering. Remember how you and Matt played a part in rescuing those two girls last week before they were hurt? I wish someone would've done that for us. I hope you'll reconsider."

Anna's bright eyes and sincere words pierced Parker's heart. She released his hand and sipped her latte. He shifted in his seat, knowing she was right, but not convinced he should go it alone. Finally, he asked, "What is it that makes you so passionate and caring? I've never met anyone like you."

"Do you have time for a story?"

"Sure."

"When I moved to Virginia Beach, I thought it would be a fresh start. But changing locations didn't remove the guilt that tormented me. Losing Nora was my fault and I couldn't forgive myself. You wouldn't have liked me then." She hesitated with an ever so slight shake of the head before continuing. "In time, I became good enough friends with a co-worker that I shared my story with her. When I told her, she began to weep. I felt she understood my pain. She didn't offer me condolences or cheap platitudes. Instead, she invited me to church and said Jesus could help me handle my loss and bring healing to my heart."

"So, did you go?"

Anna's hazel eyes sparkled as the light from the window hit her face. "No. I didn't see how I could trust in a God who allowed my baby to be taken from me and my marriage to be destroyed. I was bitter and angry!"

"But how are you such a loving and caring person then?" Confusion emanated from Parker's eyes.

Anna laughed. "I'm getting to that, now hush. I was broken and alone and I hated the person I had become. Grief and self-pity consumed me. Months passed. I started losing more weight and missing work. Then that same coworker asked me to go with her on a women's retreat. Her church had a list of reliable babysitters, so I wouldn't have to worry about Owen. The next day I told her I would go, but that my parents would come to watch Owen.

"While I was there, the guest speaker told her story of loss. How she had to watch her son struggle and eventually die of leukemia at the age of eight. I couldn't believe my ears. This vibrant woman wasn't mad at God. Instead she turned to Him for strength. I wanted that strength." Tears welled in Anna's eyes. "On that day I understood what it meant to be saved and Jesus came into my heart." With an endearing smile, she again took Parker's hand and said, "He is why I have such peace! Yes, the loss of my child and husband still hurts, but not nearly as much as it did before."

"That's quite the story, Anna. Maybe someday it'll make sense to me, too."

"Oh, I hope so. I'll be praying for you."

"Thanks." Parker squeezed her hand and rose to leave. "What time will you be back at the house? I forgot to get my laptop from your office."

"Let me say goodbye to Matt and I'll come now. I should get some sleep." Anna yawned as they parted ways.

Parker didn't have to wait long at the house before Anna arrived. He got his computer but didn't stay to visit and Anna didn't seem to mind.

Overtaken by fatigue and confusion, Parker didn't know what to do. Should he go back to Philadelphia and give Matt some time to heal and an opportunity to change his mind? Or should he stay in Virginia Beach and visit him? He knew it would drive Matt crazy having to sit with nothing to do. Parker only drove a few blocks before pulling over. He needed to gather his thoughts and make a plan.

"Hey, mystery guy—now what am I to do? Matt quit and you're conveniently silent." Frustration flooded over him and he hit the steering wheel. "How am I supposed to do this without Matt?"

He let his head fall back against the seat. "I should've known it was too good to be true. If you had any real insight, you would've known better than to choose me. How is it that you knew about Matt's breakup and those abducted girls, but didn't know about my night terrors or temper? You pretend to care about people and want us to help rescue them, yet you don't care about me. It's not fair." *This is stupid; I'm talking out loud to a phantom.*

Parker crawled into the back seat and fell asleep.

Chapter 12

PLEASE COME

It was late afternoon when Parker woke. He stopped to get coffee and then found a hotel near the hospital. Once settled in, he looked at the pictures of the ships. He was pleased with several and emailed his favorites to Anna.

Leaning back in his chair, he held the mug of coffee to his chin with both hands and started tapping his index fingers together. What should he do? Go to Memphis or stay? As he stared at his computer screen, his eyes landed on the file folder labeled, 'Redheaded Girl.' He set down the mug and opened the photos from the mission and the art gallery. Seeing the girl's face again gave him pause. *If the people at the mission never saw this girl before, then why use a mission? Unless our mystery guy thought a mission would help get our attention.*

Then he brought up Matt's photos. In the school portrait, the girl looked healthy and happy. Parker rubbed the back of his neck. *This is going to be harder than I thought. Does the girl need help or not?*

There was one photo left. The school. With the tap of his finger, the picture popped open. So did his eyes. "Whoa." Scrawled across the front of the building, in stark black letters, were the words: **PLEASE COME!**

Seized by a bout of nausea, Parker ran into the bathroom. When the moment passed, he placed his hands on the sink and stared slack-jawed into the mirror. *This is so creepy, yet, maybe my guy hasn't given up on me or the need to find this girl after all.* He hurried back to the desk, emailed the picture to himself, and immediately left for the hospital.

❏ ❏ ❏

Matt appeared to be sleeping when Parker walked in, so he quietly took a seat in the empty chair next to the bed.

Only a few seconds passed before Matt said, "Hey."

"Hey. How's it going?"

"With all the drugs, I feel too loopy to know, but at least I'm not throwing up."

"Well, that's good."

"Did you hear? They're going to release me in the morning."

"Yeah, Anna told me earlier. That's great. She also mentioned that you could stay with her."

"It seems like my best option, especially since I can't travel yet. Have you decided what you're going to do?"

"Yes." He got to his feet and handed Matt his phone. "Look at your photo of the school."

Matt read the words aloud, "Please come." He thrust the phone back. "Are you trying to make me feel bad?"

"Of course not! I didn't know what to do—stay here or head home. Confused and discouraged, I took another look at our photos. These words are blatantly obvious. I'd have to be heartless not to go. I came to let you know I'm leaving for Memphis after we get you to Anna's house in the morning."

"This is why he chose you; you're strong. I'm not sure why he wanted me to help." Matt looked toward the ceiling, presumably hoping that Parker wouldn't notice the tear that had pooled in his eye.

Parker did notice but didn't mention it. He knew if things were different, Matt would come. Since the images of the redheaded girl appeared, Matt had taken a keen interest in seeing where this story would lead. *This is a shame on so many levels.* "Don't be so hard on yourself. If I landed in the hospital, I wouldn't be going either."

Matt turned his head as far as the pillows would allow and closed his eye. This caused the tear to spill over and roll down his cheek.

"Hey, you'll be the first to know once I have any news, okay?"

"Yeah, okay, sure." A sigh escaped his lips as he rubbed the tear away. "If you don't mind, I'd like to be alone."

Parker winced, but he knew another apology wouldn't help. "Right. Um, hope you can get some sleep." With that, he hung his head and walked away.

❏ ❏ ❏

The next morning Parker arrived on time to help an orderly steady Matt into a wheelchair, while the nurse gave Anna a list of instructions. "Doctor Charvat needs to see Matt in his office tomorrow. Here's his appointment card. In the meantime, he must sit and sleep with his head elevated. A recliner with extra pillows to immobilize his head would be ideal. If you have any questions, you can call the number on this card 24 hours a day."

Once they had Matt situated at Anna's house, Parker said, "I'll stay until tomorrow and take Matt to the doctor."

"There's no need, I can take him. Don't you need to get going?"

"I do. So, if you're sure you don't mind, here's a check to cover Matt's rent and any other expenses, like rides to the doctor." He winked.

Anna did a double take when she saw the amount. "I can't take this. You already gave me your credit card info; I was only going to charge you for the two nights you already stayed."

"Now that you mention it, put the next two weeks for Matt's room on my card. The check can be to thank you for helping us out of a tough spot. We can't pay you enough for all you've done."

"Yeah," Matt said. "Please accept it without an argument. That way I won't feel like a burden and you won't need to worry about getting other tenants right now."

"Exactly, and if Matt needs to stay longer than anticipated, add those nights to my card."

"No arguments then; you're both very kind." Anna smiled and turned to face Parker. "So what have you decided to do?"

"Well, with your prodding and some new information I received last night, I've decided to follow our leads on the girl. I'm not thrilled to go it alone, but it's the right thing to do."

"I'm so glad to hear it."

Parker looked at Matt, who had already closed his good eye, and said, "Hey, feel better, man. And keep me posted on your recovery. I'll let you know when I stop for the night."

Matt didn't bother to open his eye, but he did give him a thumbs up.

Anna walked out with Parker. When they reached his Jeep, she said, "If you don't mind, I'd like to be kept in the loop."

"I'm sure once I have information worth sharing, Matt will be glad to fill you in." He leaned down and kissed her on the cheek. "Thanks again for everything."

❏ ❏ ❏

It was early afternoon by the time Parker left for Memphis. He reached Knoxville before calling it quits. As soon as he was settled into his hotel room, he texted Matt. `Only six hours to Memphis. I'll touch base with you tomorrow.` He didn't expect a reply, so he set his alarm and fell asleep almost immediately.

❏ ❏ ❏

Before getting out of bed the next morning, Parker checked his phone with the hopes of finding a new text or voicemail from his mystery guy. Nothing. *Huh, if I were the one giving information, I'd offer more details. Oh well.*

He was on the road by daybreak and reached Redford High before noon. The sign out front and the building looked exactly like his picture, which brought him some small comfort, even though it didn't make it any easier to go inside. He pulled into an empty spot across the street from the school and sat there for a few minutes before driving away to find a hotel. He also went for a short run—partly procrastinating and partly preparing for his encounter with the girl. The lack of information made him nervous, not to mention that he was usually the one behind a camera, *not* the one making inquiries.

After showering, he took the time to trim his beard, something he hadn't done since leaving Philly. When finished, he put on dark blue khakis, a light blue polo shirt, and loafers. With one final look in the mirror, he smiled at his appearance and reassured himself. *You've got this.*

It was a little after 1:00 by the time Parker reached the school. He hoped new information about the redheaded girl was only a question away. Raising to his full height, he approached the welcome desk and confidently asked, "Can I please speak with an administrator?"

The young woman looked up from her keyboard and gave him a onceover. "Do you have an appointment, sir?"

"No ma'am, but it won't take long. I just have a few questions about a student I'm trying to find."

"Let me see if anyone is available to speak with you." Parker anxiously drummed his fingers on the satchel that was slung over his shoulder while she made a call and explained the reason for his visit. When she hung up, she said, "Our Principal is free and said he could try to help. Would you please take a seat?" She gestured toward a small room off the lobby. "He'll be with you in a few minutes."

A few minutes turned into fifteen. Finally, a distinguished looking man in his mid to late fifties walked in. "Sorry to make you wait. My name is Mr. Edwards; I'm the principal here at Redford High, and you are?"

"Parker Jackson, sir. I've been hired to find this girl." He handed him his phone with the photo already open. "Can you tell me if she's a student here or if she has already graduated?"

Mr. Edwards peered at the picture with narrowed eyes. A scowl abruptly darkened his features and his tone became harsh. "Is this some kind of sick joke?"

The pointed question caused Parker to flinch. Because he came into this blind, he had no idea what to expect, but this response caught him off guard. *Could Mr. Edwards suspect me or my employer of foul play?* With little time to contemplate the severity of the situation, he quickly regained his composure and said, "No joke, sir. I don't understand. A client hired me to find this girl and the only information I have is this picture and the name of this high school."

Mr. Edwards crossed his arms. "And who hired you? Her father?" His brow creased into an ominous line. He looked both skeptical and concerned about to whom he should give information.

Parker fought to maintain eye contact. *Interesting, there seems to be a problem with her father.* His mind frantically searched for the right answer, not wanting the conversation to end before it got started. "I'm working with Matt Howard, a reporter in Philadelphia. We're looking into a few cold cases. I know nothing about this girl or her father. Can you please help me?"

The sincerity in Parker's tone must have caused Mr. Edwards to soften because he said, "Well, I guess at this point it probably doesn't matter what I tell you; the school's been cleared of any wrongdoing."

"Wrongdoing?"

"The girl's name is Melissa Stanton; she went missing a few years back. One of her teachers, Mrs. Weber, might be able to provide you with some information. I'll forewarn you, though: Melissa's never been found and is presumed dead. Come with me."

Mr. Edwards stopped at the welcome desk and asked the woman to call Mrs. Weber and have her come to the conference room as soon as her class was over. Then he had Parker follow him to a room adjacent to the administrative offices.

"It will be easier to talk in here." He glanced at his watch. "You won't have to wait long. Her class ends in a few minutes. Good luck with your search." As he left the room, he muttered, "Though I doubt any good will come of it."

"What's that?" Parker called after him.

Mr. Edwards stepped back into the doorway. "There was a lot of unsavory gossip at the time of Melissa's disappearance."

"Care to enlighten me?"

"Not really." Darkness again shadowed his face. "It's not the kind of thing people want to talk about. Most are happy to sweep it under the rug and forget it ever happened."

"Maybe so, but if it helps me find the truth, any information you have would be helpful," Parker countered.

"There's the bell. Mrs. Weber will join you shortly. She knew the girl personally. Now, if you will excuse me, I have other business to attend to."

Parker took a seat. *This doesn't sound very promising. But then again, why would I have to come to Memphis if it's already too late?* That thought gave him hope as he pulled a pen and notepad from his satchel. While he waited, he jotted down a few key points from the conversation.

It wasn't long before a tall, stocky woman with umber skin and short, black hair entered the room. She looked to be about forty years old with kind eyes and a broad smile. "Hello. Parker, is it?"

He had already jumped to his feet. "Yes, ma'am." He took her extended hand. "Thanks for meeting with me."

"I'm happy to help. My name's Aleta." They both took a seat before she continued. "I understand you have some questions about a former student of mine?"

Parker slid his phone across the table with the picture opened. "I'm trying to find this girl. Mr. Edwards seems to think there's no hope, but I'm not willing to give up on my search quite yet. What can you tell me about her?"

Moisture filled Aleta's eyes; her smile disappeared. She gazed thoughtfully at the picture for a moment, subconsciously whispering, "Melissa, oh my dear Melissa, what's become of you?"

Parker gave her time to regain her composure and then leaned forward with his elbows on the table. "I know none of the details. Can you please tell me what happened?"

She looked at Parker and then back at the picture before answering. "To be clear, I can't help you find her. I haven't seen or heard from Melissa since the day she left." Pain emanated from her eyes as she slid the phone back to Parker. "Mr. Edwards told me I was at liberty to answer your questions, but I don't have a lot of time because I need to prep for my next class."

"Well, in that case, it might be easier if you just tell me what you know. Does that work?" Parker wasn't sure a smile was the right expression, but it was all he knew to do.

She nodded. "Hmm, where to begin? I suppose at the beginning. I met Melissa in her freshman year of high school. She was competitive, outgoing, and smart. She loved sports and played on a few of the school teams. I believe the picture you have is from her sophomore year. At that point, she seemed to love life—carefree and happy, but by the beginning of her junior year, things deteriorated rather quickly. She smiled less, her grades began to fall and . . ."

❏ ❏ ❏

The gym overflowed with screaming fans; less than a minute remained in the game that would decide the winner of the Girls' Sectional Basketball Championship. Finally, the buzzer sounded, and the Redford Lady Badgers had hung on to win 68-64. Fans flooded the court and the team piled on top of each other. The trophy presentation would soon follow.

"Coach Weber?"

"Oh, hi Melissa; come in and have a seat. I was reminiscing about last year's championship game as we get ready for this season. Wasn't that awesome?" Melissa nodded as she entered the office but didn't sit or answer. "We should be even better this year, maybe winning States."

"Yeah, about that." Instead of looking up, Melissa fidgeted with a strap on her backpack. "I came to tell you that I'm not playing."

"Seriously? But why not? I thought you loved playing basketball."

"I do, but some things have changed and that's all I can tell you at this point." Tears filled Melissa's eyes.

"Oh my . . . What's going on?"

"I'm not at liberty to talk about it and if you truly care about me and not just my athletic ability, please don't ask again and whatever you do, don't contact my parents."

❏ ❏ ❏

"Mrs. Weber?" Parker finally ventured.

"Oh right, sorry. And please, call me Aleta. Now, where was I?"

Chapter 13

UNSAVORY GOSSIP

"Melissa's grades began to fall . . ." Parker reminded her as he jotted down the word, 'Troubled.'

"Yes. Couple that with the fact that she didn't play basketball that year, which as the team's coach, threw me for a loop. We got along great, but I couldn't convince her to play. All she told me was that she 'didn't have permission' and abruptly left my office. Within a week, we heard her mom had cancer, so everyone assumed that Melissa was needed at home after school. Sometime later, maybe the beginning of March, I asked her how things were going. She said her mom's cancer seemed to be under control and the doctors thought she'd recover. To my surprise, she showed *no* emotion.

"Too often Melissa's eyes were bloodshot and swollen. She would always say everything was fine and blamed it on allergies. Other teachers started asking questions. There was a consensus that something was wrong." She shook her head. "Yet, none of us tried to find out what. Then one day in April, Melissa was gone. Mr. Stanton had called the school and said his daughter had the flu. We expected her to be out a few days, maybe a week, but before she came back, the police showed up. They peppered everyone who had contact with her with a barrage of questions, but sadly, no one knew the answers. Nor did we understand the severity of the situation. She never returned."

Parker waited for Aleta to continue, but she seemed to disappear back into that *troubled* place. So far, the only information he gained was that a few years ago Melissa had been acting strangely and then ran away. No one knows where she is or if she's even alive.

"If you don't mind me asking, Mr. Edwards mentioned some 'unsavory gossip.' Do you know anything about those rumors?"

Aleta's broad smile had disappeared when she started telling Melissa's story, but now she shifted in her seat and looked downright distraught.

"Are you able to tell me what happened?" Parker wanted her to continue, but he didn't expect what came next.

"Oh for the shame of it!" Aleta slammed her hand on the table. "We all knew something was wrong; so why didn't we try harder to find the truth? Why didn't we help her?" Tears scurried down her cheeks, looking for a place to hide. Through her sobs, she cried out, "Why? Why do we always wait until it's too late? Why?"

Aleta abruptly stood. "Excuse me. I need to go." She wiped her cheeks and quickly headed for the door.

"Wait." Parker shot to his feet and stepped in front of her. "I didn't mean to upset you, but there's obviously something that you're not telling me. What is it?"

She pulled a tissue from her purse and blew her nose. "I think you'd be better off hearing the rest of the story from her friend, Susie. A few years after Melissa's disappearance, she came to me with news that she felt ashamed that she had kept a secret. Apparently, Melissa talked to her the night she ran away. She's the only person I know that could offer you any kind of helpful information. Are you free tonight?"

"Yes. Where do you want to meet and when?"

"Here, give me your cell number." She handed him a piece of paper. "I'll text Susie to see if she's free—say 7:00. If she can make it and is willing to talk to a stranger about this, I'll give you a call."

Parker scribbled down his number and handed the paper back. "Thank you. I look forward to meeting Susie."

"Until later, then," Aleta said.

Parker stepped away from the door. "Later."

She gave him a small smile and left the room.

His thoughts lingered on the prospect of meeting Susie. A shiver shot down his spine. Despite the fact that he needed to hear her story, he wasn't sure the truth was something he was ready for. The bell rang, pulling his attention back to the empty conference room. It was time for him to leave.

On the way out he passed a trophy case and stopped to take a look. One of the trophies was for the Girls Basketball Sectional Championship Mrs. Weber had told him about. Melissa was in the team picture. Her red hair was pulled back into a ponytail and she was grinning from ear to ear, right along with the rest of her teammates.

Mrs. Weber is right . . . Melissa, what has become of you?

Parker took a seat on a bench in front of the school and wrote down Aleta's story. Before he finished, a text came telling him to head into Memphis. A street address and building number were the only other information given.

Nice, I didn't want to sit and do nothing for the rest of the afternoon. His camera bag was already in the Jeep, so he left immediately.

Parker found the place near the border of East Memphis in an area where individual two and three-story buildings lined both sides of the street. The buildings were older, but in good condition with storefronts and office entrances painted and maintained. Most had flower pots and awnings to spruce up their properties. Above the doors or on the windows were the names of each business. At first glance, the building in question looked like all the rest. A brand-new, silver Porsche parked in front of the building distracted him. *Wow, that's a sweet looking ride.*

Parker quickly found a place to park on the opposite side of the street and grabbed his camera. He snapped a few pictures of the car, before getting out of his Jeep.

Then turning his attention back to the building, he realized this business didn't have a name. The gold-leaf street number was carved into a small, dark green sign mounted beside the glass door. Nothing about the property seemed eventful except for the number of security cameras strategically placed around the building.

Hmm, I wonder what goes on here that they're so paranoid.

Though it was ever so slight, Parker did notice that someone inside had moved the curtain from the only window on the front. A few seconds later, a young man came out. He wore a dark gray suit with a red tie and looked to be in his early thirties. As he approached Parker, he straightened his glasses and said, "Excuse me, sir. Why are you taking pictures of our building?"

"I'm a photographer and take pictures of all kinds of things. Is there a problem?"

"Yes. We have clients coming in a few minutes and I don't need you scaring them off."

Parker shrugged. "They're just pictures. I don't see a reason to be so uptight about it."

"You can leave now, or I'll call the police."

The man's threat caused Parker to raise his hands in surrender. He walked to the next storefront, took a few photos, crossed the street, took a few more of a different building, and then returned to his Jeep. The man had disappeared, but Parker noticed he was being watched from just inside the door. *This is too weird.*

His original plan was to go back to the hotel. More than likely, the photos he already took would show him what he needed to know. While waiting at a red light, he decided to loop around and park on a side street about two blocks from his original location. From there, he walked to the corner and slipped onto an empty bench. Just as he was switching out the standard lens for a zoom lens, an older man came from the same building. Parker quickly snapped a picture before the man got into the Porsche and sped away.

He didn't have much time to ponder whether that guy was relevant or not because just then a blue Subaru Forester parked in front of the building. A young couple got out and went into the office. He took a picture of them, and then one of their vehicle. Close to a half hour passed before they came back out carrying a toddler. *Huh. This must be an adoption agency.*

He snapped another picture of them and then started back to his Jeep. The whole concept of taking photos when and where he was told was certainly interesting, but it was also confusing. *What does this building have to do with Melissa?* Lost in thought, the ringing of his cell startled him.

It was Aleta. "Hi Parker, good news. Susie agreed to meet with you. We can be at Randy's Pub by 7:00."

"That's great. I'll see you then."

❏ ❏ ❏

Randy's Pub was just down the street from Parker's hotel, so he walked. He sat at a table by the front window and ordered a burger with fries. While waiting for his food, he sent Matt this text: 'How are you doing?'

'Feeling a little better today.'

'That's good.' Parker hesitated before sending the text and added, 'Do your parents hate me?'

'Of course not, but they did mention counseling. How are you making out? Any news?'

'Yes. Meeting people shortly. I'll call later.'

❏ ❏ ❏

Aleta and Susie arrived promptly at 7:00. Parker stood to greet them and asked if he could get them anything. They both took him up on his offer and got drinks. "Nice to meet you, Susie. Thanks for coming."

"Well, I hope I didn't make a huge mistake, but Mrs. Weber seems to trust you. To be honest, I think it's weird that you're bringing this up after all these years, especially if you don't have any new information to share with us." Susie was a pretty woman, but the crease between her brows and her piercing blue eyes were intimidating, even for Parker. "I haven't heard from Melissa and all I have are the horrifying memories from the last time I saw her. What information could I possibly give you that could help now?"

"Well, uh, actually, I have some pictures to show you," Parker said. He was thankful he thought to add the other images of Melissa to his phone before coming to the Pub. "I was hoping you could clear up some confusion. I don't know if it's the same girl in all three pictures." He handed his phone to Susie. "As you can see, the first one is a girl who looks to be eight or nine. The second is the portrait I showed Mrs. Weber and she confirmed it was Melissa. In the third one, she's a bit older and could pass for the same girl, but she looks in rough shape. Can you tell if the first and third photos are of Melissa?"

"This one with her mom is definitely Melissa. I could recognize that smile and long red ponytail from a mile away. Plus, I was there. Her family took me with them on vacation that summer to Virginia Beach. We had a blast! Oh, how I wish things had never changed." Susie sighed and scrolled to the picture of the mission. Stretching the image so just the girl's face showed, she excitedly asked, "Is Melissa alive?" Her eyes sparkled with anticipation. "Is it her?" She turned and offered the phone to Aleta. "Could it possibly be her?"

"I think it is, but this picture doesn't give us much hope. Look at her."

"Except that she's alive. I assumed she was dead, especially since no one's heard from her since she left town." She lowered her voice. "I was with her the night she ran away. To be honest, I figured she'd get scared and come back, but then again, I wouldn't have come back, so I guess I'm not surprised."

Susie took the phone back from Aleta and stared at the picture of her frightened friend. "Where did you get these?"

"I don't know."

She met Parker's gaze. "How do you not know?"

"These photos and the name of Redford High here in Tennessee are all the information I have. My client sent me the pictures and asked me to find out what I could. I hoped you'd be willing to fill in some of the blanks for me. What can you tell me about Melissa?"

"Are you sure you want to know?" Her cheeks flushed. "I try not to think about it because it makes me so angry."

"I need answers, so please." Parker wished Matt was with him; he was better with people and could've wooed the story out of her.

Susie rubbed her chin as sharp lines again creased her brow. Abruptly, she raised a hand to flag down the bartender. "I'd like a shot of whiskey, please." As soon as he brought it, she threw it down in one gulp and winced. "Ahem. Before the start of our junior year of high school, Melissa changed. She became closed-off and distant. She stopped inviting me to her house and seldom came to our parties. I'm sure Mrs. Weber already told you she didn't play basketball that year."

Parker nodded but didn't interrupt.

"Well, we all thought it was because of her mom's cancer, but even when her mom started getting better, Melissa seemed to get worse. We were best friends from kindergarten, so I tried to get her to open up, but all she would say is, 'I can't talk about it.' One time she got so angry, she whispered, 'Stop! If I tell you, he'll kill me.' Her glare warned me not to say another word. Then unexpectedly, she pushed away from the table and ran out of the cafeteria. I was too frightened to tell anyone and never asked her about it again.

"Then one day in April, she broke the silence. Her parents were out of town celebrating their anniversary and she was home alone. She called to see if I could come over. She needed to talk. The tremble in her voice worried me so I went as quickly as I could. When I arrived, the Melissa I knew was gone. Her eyes were bloodshot and swollen. Her long, red hair was chopped short and dyed raven black. As soon as I saw her, I freaked out. Let me tell you her story."

Chapter 14

QUIET DISAPPEARANCE

"I'm leaving this horrid place! Don't try to contact me. No texts. No calls. And absolutely no going to the police! You can't tell anyone, not even Coach Weber." She grabbed Susie's arms and forcefully shook them. "Promise me you won't tell anyone."

"Whoa, what's gotten into you?"

Melissa looked like a scared cat with her black hair and green eyes adding to the intensity of the moment. Her voice began to falter. "Promise me . . . promise."

"Okay, I promise, but why? What's going on?"

Melissa let go and buried her face in her hands. Through muffled sobs, she said, "I can't take the abuse any longer." Then fighting to regain control, she clenched her fists and looked at Susie. "I asked you to come so I could let you know that it wasn't my choice to block you out. I've basically been under house arrest."

Susie's eyes turned to a sea of glass. "Abuse?"

"My life has been a living hell since last August. Mom went to Book Club, like she always did on Wednesday mornings. Then my dad came home. I didn't think anything of it until he came into my room and started kissing me and touching me inappropriately. I pushed him and tried to get away, but I wasn't strong enough . . ."

"Oh my god," Susie gasped. "I can't believe he would do that to you!" Seeing the anguish on Melissa's face, she quickly realized there were no words, so she reached out to hold her friend. They both crumpled to the floor and cried for a long time.

Eventually, Melissa dried her eyes and leaned against the wall. "You need to hear the rest of my story, so you understand why leaving is my only option. He told me if I said anything to anyone, he'd kill me. The next time she went to Book Club, I made sure I wasn't home. Later that evening he said if that happened again, I would pay. I quickly learned that if I didn't do as he demanded, he would hurt me in places no one else could see."

Susie wanted to scream but bit her lip instead.

Consumed with grief, Melissa continued, "When school started, my mom volunteered twice a week at an after-school program, and he demanded I be home. I begged him to stop. He was my father for god's sake. He laughed at me! He said there wasn't any harm in having sex with me because I wasn't his daughter."

"You're adopted?"

"That's what he said. I didn't know it either."

"What a monster! I would've left a long time ago if I knew that."

"I wanted to, but I was scared and didn't know where to go that he couldn't find me. Then my mom got cancer and even though she isn't my real mom, I love her. She was so sick that I didn't dare tell her. I didn't dare tell anyone."

"What a wretched pervert!" Susie's anger could no longer be contained. "And here we all thought he was such a great guy and an upstanding lawyer."

Melissa shuddered. "But about the adoption. He showed me the paperwork, standing over me with his smug smile while I read it. Before I could even get my head around the idea, he said they didn't see the need to tell me sooner because my teenage mom never wanted to see me again.

"His betrayal and total disrespect for me as a person left me feeling like the scum of the earth. It was like I became his plaything. He even had the audacity to say that I'd grown into an endowed young woman and that he figured he'd enjoy the fringe benefits of rescuing me from the poor and worthless life I would have had.

"On another day he said, 'Why don't you lighten up and enjoy the ride?' I spit in his face and told him he was a monster; that I would never enjoy the ride!" Melissa hugged her arms across her knees and started rocking back and forth. "The sexual abuse is destroying me. Mentally, emotionally, and physically. I've got to leave before I go crazy or give in to the urge to commit suicide."

Susie tried to focus on the options and said, "I can go to the police with you. There must be something they can do. I'll ask my parents, I'm sure you could come live with us. Let's go to the station right now."

Melissa lost it and started screaming, "Don't you understand? You said it yourself; my dad's a successful lawyer. He's gotten many a criminal off on a technicality. He would convince the judge or jury that what I said was a lie and then things would be ten times worse for me. This is just a game to him, and I can't take it any longer!

"There were times when I wished I was strong enough or brave enough to kill him, but I'm not a murderer. I'm the victim! My *only* hope of safety and sanity is to disappear. This is why you can't tell anyone. If he finds me, I'm dead."

❑ ❑ ❑

Pain filled Susie's eyes as she looked at Parker. "This picture of Melissa makes me feel so helpless." She flagged the bartender for another shot before continuing, "How can we protect innocent girls from such abuse? Here's a beautiful and talented young woman living on the streets all because of the selfish desires of a strong, influential man. If he was a plain old Joe, she might have had her day in court."

Downing the shot—hoping to wash the memories away—Susie concluded her story. "As I mentioned, Melissa cut her hair and dyed it black. She did it at a dumpy gas station south of the city so no chemicals, pieces of cut hair, or any signs of *change* to her appearance were left at the house. It looked odd with her fair skin and freckles, but she didn't care. She couldn't risk being recognized on security cameras. It seemed like she thought of everything, even wearing a new St. Louis Cardinals baseball cap and big gaudy sunglasses. That morning she emptied her savings account and only took with her what she could fit into a new duffel bag. Nothing on her person had ever been seen by either parent.

"I walked her to her mom's car, and we said our goodbyes. She hugged me and wouldn't let go. Through her sobs, she said,

'I'm scared, Susie, I'm so scared.' We both cried some more and then as if bitten by reality, she pulled away, jumped in the car, and drove off.

"It was three days before her parents returned home and discovered that Melissa was gone. The police found her mom's car on a side street in St. Louis where there were no surveillance cameras. Inside the car they found the note explaining why she ran away, along with her phone and a sealed bag containing DNA evidence of the abuse. She hoped these items would verify her story. Without her phone to track her, and not knowing what she looked like, the trail went cold. No one has seen or heard from Melissa since.

"What adds to our grief is the fact that Mr. Stanton was never found guilty. He was able to get the DNA proof dismissed from the case because, without Melissa, there was no evidence it was hers or that any abuse had taken place. I can't prove it either, but I can personally attest to the fact that Melissa—a smart, outgoing, and precious girl—mentally and emotionally died that winter, even though the official report only says that she disappeared on the 12th of April."

"One last question, if you don't mind," Parker said. "Do the Stanton's still live in the area?"

"Mrs. Stanton must have believed the note and put it together with Melissa's change in behavior because she filed for a divorce even before the police stopped their search. She moved to New Orleans to be close to her sister's family. I think she hoped Melissa would go there; she loved her aunt and uncle and got along well with her cousins. To my knowledge that never happened, but then, they might have kept it a secret for safety reasons."

"And Mr. Stanton?"

"Though never convicted, the evidence Melissa left was enough to ruin his reputation. After the divorce, he closed his law practice, sold his house, and moved away. It makes me feel better knowing he's not here."

"Wow. When I came to Memphis, I had no idea what I would find. I hope you'll be able to sleep tonight." He thought of his own night terror after hearing Anna's story. "I know this was difficult, but thank you for sharing Melissa's account of what happened. This information is helpful. I trust new leads will surface and, who knows, we might find a silver lining."

"You have more hope than I do, but now it's my turn to ask a question. I find it odd, that after all these years someone would hire you to find Melissa. Who is it and what's their connection to her?"

"That *is* the million-dollar question because I honestly don't know. I'm a photographer and these images, along with some others, magically appeared on the pictures I took. I know that sounds crazy and you probably figure I'm making it up, but something similar to this happened recently in Philadelphia which ended with rescuing two abducted girls. When this new information appeared, I trusted there must be a purpose and drove straight here from Virginia Beach as soon as I could." Parker's eyes brightened. "If you think about it, it's pretty cool that the picture I took at the art gallery a few days ago, is the same gallery you attest to being at with Melissa when you were kids. That's why I believe there's still hope."

"Yes, this *is* irrational, not to mention impossible. To my knowledge, that picture's never been on social media and some of the elements in the background are too modern to be the actual picture taken back then. I don't know how you did it, so I must be the one who's going crazy because strangely enough, I believe you. It's comforting to know someone cares and is looking for Melissa." Susie stood, but before leaving she handed Parker a business card. "Here's my number." She met his gaze with a hopeful smile. "If you ever find her, please let me know."

"I will. Thanks again for meeting with me on such short notice."

"No problem."

Aleta rose to join Susie. "I need to get home, too. Good luck with your search. And please, let us know either way."

Then for the first time since they met earlier that day, her broad smile returned. "I feel optimistic. When you find Melissa, let her know she's been missed and if she ever gets to the place where she feels it's safe to contact us, we'd love to hear from her."

As soon as the ladies left the Pub, a well-dressed man, who looked to be in his fifties, took a seat across from Parker. "Excuse me, but I couldn't help but overhear part of your conversation."

Parker's eyes widened. "Do you have information about Melissa?"

"I don't know where she is, if that's what you mean. But you need to know the truth."

"The truth?"

"I mean, you can't believe everything you hear. Melissa Stanton was an ungrateful spoiled brat. Her parents rescued her from an unhealthy situation and raised her like their own. When she got older, she became rebellious. If she didn't get her way, she'd throw a fit and cause them all kinds of grief. Then one day she took off, leaving unbelievable lies in her place. The Stanton's were good people—well-liked and respected in the community. Mrs. Stanton was involved in programs to help kids and Mr. Stanton took on several pro bono cases to defend innocent people when they couldn't afford a good lawyer. After Melissa left, the rumors ruined their lives."

Now Parker didn't know what to believe. His eyes narrowed as he leaned forward. "If the rumors weren't true, how did they hurt the Stanton's?"

"As soon as people heard about the sexual accusations, Mr. Stanton never had a chance. He was convicted in the court of public opinion, even though he was never found guilty."

❑ ❑ ❑

As Parker sat on his bed, writing Susie's story, a twinge of pain shot through his chest. *Why am I taking this so personally?* He let his head fall back against the headboard. Since taking off after high school, he'd become successful and self-sufficient. He didn't give much time to thought or concern for others, and forgetting his past seemed to make that easier. But now he felt his heart breaking for a person he'd never met. And to add to his confusion, the man defending Mr. Stanton sounded quite convincing. Eventually, his meditation turned to Matt and the pain he had caused him.

A battle raged within Parker. His self-made walls of defense were coming down, things were changing, and he couldn't run. But then, for the first time in a long time, he didn't want to.

A text from Matt interrupted his introspection. 'I've been waiting for an update. When can you call?'

Parker tossed his notebook on the bed and made the call. "Hi, Matt. How are you doing."

"I'm okay, but what were you able to find out about Melissa?"

"It's not good. I wish you were here, so you could've heard it firsthand."

"Me too, but that's not exactly my fault."

Matt's tone wasn't as harsh as his words, but it still felt like getting hit with a bucket of cold water. "Um, I thought you wanted me to call?"

"I did. It just stinks being stuck here; that's all."

"I'm sure, but maybe you'll change your mind and want to join me after you hear my story . . . and you're feeling better, of course."

"Oh yeah? Well then, fire away, mate."

Matt's reply made Parker smile. "Wow, what's with the mood swings? Are you high on pain meds or something?"

"That could be it." Matt stifled a laugh. "But seriously, the lack of movement is getting on my nerves. I have to limit screen time and my good eye tires quickly when I try to read—so please, distract me for a while."

"I can do that." Parker took his time and explained the entire day's events. "Oh, and I've written down the important things. I'm trying to help with your part of the parchment until you come back."

"You still expect me to join you?"

"Why not? I haven't found Melissa yet and there's no way I can write this story by myself."

"Except the more we learn, the more I'm not sure I want to write about it." Matt sighed. "I thought Anna's story was heart wrenching enough. Now this girl's plight sounds even worse. I wish our guy would stop leading us down rabbit trails and let us find her."

"But they're not rabbit trails. Think about it. The sheer fact that I met Susie is fascinating, especially after she told me she was with Melissa at that art gallery in Virginia Beach. This means our photos are of actual events and prove we're being led in the right direction."

"Yes, that was pretty cool, and she happened to be the last person to talk to Melissa before she disappeared. I do have a question though. What do you make of the man at the pub?"

"I'm sure his *assertions* about Stanton are true. But like Mike, closet abusers don't usually go around bragging about their exploits. I believe Susie. You should've seen the pain emanating from her eyes and heard the inflection in her voice . . . it was so much more than memories of a long-forgotten friend."

"And like you said, Susie was with her when they came to Virginia Beach. I agree that it was her story that you needed to hear."

"It also adds purpose to the photos we took in Virginia, even though it did seem out of the way."

"But don't forget, we've met Anna. She treats me like family, not the inconvenient house guest that I am."

"I still can't get over how she dropped everything for us. Has she had any more relapses about Nora?"

"Not at all. And she was excited to hear that you were meeting with people tonight. Except now, I'm not looking forward to telling her what you learned."

Parker slipped off the bed and started pacing. "I'm not sure why you're surprised. Don't you remember our pictures of her at the mission? She was a mess."

Matt moaned, but Parker continued unabated. "It's obviously a reality that no one wants to hear, and no matter whose story is right, both Susie and Stanton's friend confirmed she's missing. If Anna asks, give it to her straight. I think she'll be glad to hear we're moving forward, even though the news sucks."

"That's for sure. I also appreciate that you thought to take notes for me. I don't want to fall too far behind before I can join you and do it myself,"

"Seriously?" Parker stopped in his tracks.

"Yeah, I'd already been thinking about it before you called."

"That's fantastic!"

"Well, let's not get the cart in front of the horse. I still have some healing to do and when I can't see out of my left eye and I have a splitting headache, I second guess myself—" Matt's voice trailed off, but Parker didn't interrupt the silence. When Matt did finally speak again, he asked, "Have you received any more messages?"

"Now that you mention it, I took some pictures earlier today, but haven't had a chance to look at them yet. I'll let you know if anything shows up."

Chapter 15

LEARNING TO TRUST

Parker woke to sunlight streaming into his hotel room. He lay there for a while, contemplating what to do next. It was then he remembered fatigue had overtaken him the night before and he hadn't bothered to look at the photos.

Scrambling out of bed, he grabbed his camera's SD card and laptop and hurried to the small desk.

The first few pictures were of the Porsche. Then there were the photos of the buildings and finally the ones he took of the Forester and the young couple with the child. No extra images had shown up in any of his pictures. Looking more closely, in hopes of finding something, he noticed the Forester had a Texas license plate. He scrolled back to the Porsche, enlarged the photo, and saw the car was from Missouri. *Huh.*

He drummed his fingers on the desk and wished Matt was there to help. "Hey, mystery guy, you haven't given me a new lead, or if you did, I'm not seeing it."

Once the photos were saved, he went to take a shower. No new info had come by the time he was packed and ready to leave. *Maybe he's waiting until Matt's better.* That thought was enough to give Parker a plan. He would head back to Virginia Beach and hang with Matt until they got more info.

The only stop he made before leaving Memphis was at a Dunkin drive-through. As he reached the outskirts of Nashville, he saw a sign for a rest area and decided to take a break. To his great pleasure, he had a new text.

`Take pictures of the Ryman Auditorium.`

"Sweet." With the directions at his fingertips, he reached the building in less than twenty minutes. In his haste to get there, he hadn't taken the time to stretch out his legs, so he decided to park a few blocks further away and do just that. When he arrived, several people were lingering out front. Some were in clusters chatting, while others were taking pictures or on their way inside for a tour of the historic building. With camera in hand, he started his own photo shoot.

An elderly couple with Irish accents noticed him and asked if he would take their picture. Happy to oblige, Parker slipped his camera behind his shoulder as the man handed him theirs. When he gave the camera back, the gentleman offered him a business card. "Thank you, young man. If you ever visit Ireland, be sure to look us up. We own a Bed & Breakfast on Liffey Lake, southwest of Dublin." Tipping his beret and smiling, he took his wife's hand and headed toward the entrance.

Parker quickly grabbed his camera and snapped a few shots of the couple as they walked away. *Cute.* After checking his camera display screen and seeing he had several good pictures, he started back to the Jeep. Then he realized he should probably look at the photos before leaving town. He passed a café and figured that'd be as good a place as any to look at the pictures.

His first photo changed to the engraved look, like their previous destinations. It was an open-wheeled race car. *Well, my guy is making this easy for me. I should at least end up in the right state.* Parker smirked at the thought as he got out his phone. The image was on the state coin of Indiana. Of all the photos he took, only one more had extra details. In the windows of the auditorium was a reflection of a two-story brick building. Above the door, there was a sign that read, 'Hope Mission House.'

After lunch, Parker found a bench away from the hubbub of people and called Matt. "Hey, can you look something up for me?"

"Sure. Does this mean you have new images?"

"Yeah, I'm in Nashville, but before leaving town I need to know where to go. I have two clues; the first is the state coin of Indiana. The second is a place called Hope Mission House. Can you see if they have a website and get me an address?"

"I'll look. Text me the picture so I can make sure it's the right place."

"Sending now. I'm going to hang here until I hear from you."

"Okay. It shouldn't take long."

The call ended and Parker lay on the bench, grateful for the cool breeze and a chance to close his eyes for a few minutes.

A half hour passed before Matt called. "I found it. It's located in the heart of Indianapolis. Their website says the mission is set up to give homeless men a place to stay while they help them overcome addictions. They currently house twenty men."

"Interesting."

"It sure is. I didn't call back right away because I started reading about their mission. It sounds like a great place. The website has several testimonies from men who've gotten back on their feet because of the mission. They even help them find jobs and work toward restoration with their families. The director says it's through the power of God that these men are made whole and are able to function in society again."

"Like I said, interesting." Parker sat up and ran his free hand through his hair. "I mean that's great and all, but what does this have to do with us? I assumed we were still looking for Melissa."

"Well, if nothing else, it appears our guy has a soft spot for missions. I'm sure there's a reason," Matt said. "So far, what didn't make sense at the time, like staying at Anna's house, ended up being important. If she wasn't willing to let me stay while I heal, you wouldn't be out there gathering information. This is clearly your next step and I think you should go. Indianapolis isn't that far from Nashville."

"Okay, text me the address. I'll drive as far as Louisville tonight. There's no need to get to the mission before morning."

"Sounds good. And Parker?"

"Yeah?"

"Thanks."

"For what?"

"For asking me to help when you could've just looked yourself."

"We're friends, right? Now get better so you can help firsthand."

"It's a deal."

Parker heard the smile in Matt's voice, which made him smile, too.

"Hey Matt," he hesitated, "you *do* know that I am sorry, right?"

"Yeah, yeah, I know, and you don't have to keep apologizing! Every great story needs conflict. I believe this is going to turn out to be a great story."

"Ha, you've been talking to Anna, haven't you?"

"Yes. She's quite the optimist."

□ □ □

Before Parker went to sleep that night, he found the Hope Mission House website and read as much as he could about the place and the people who ran it. He wanted to see if he could figure out why he needed to go there. *Matt's right, this is quite the place, but I still have no idea what I'm supposed to ask them.*

□ □ □

By the time Parker arrived the next morning, several men were standing on the sidewalk in front of Hope Mission House. Some were bent over, trying to catch their breath, while others had their hands on their hips or were wiping sweat from their faces.

Parker jumped out of his Jeep and joined them. "Hey guys, it looks like I'm late. I love to run."

"Are you crazy, man? This sucks," one of the men wheezed.

"At the beginning, when you can't breathe and everything hurts, yeah, it's no fun. But once you build up your endurance, I bet you'll look forward to this part of your day."

"See, guys, I told you so," the group leader said with a grin. "Hi, I'm Brandon."

"Parker." He reached to shake his hand.

"Did you stop just to give my guys a pep talk or did you want to see our mission?"

"Actually, I was hoping to speak with the director."

"Sure, he's inside. Hey, guys, start doing your stretches, I'll be right back."

Parker followed Brandon. They entered a decent-sized common area with tables set up in clusters. To his right was a group of men doing a Bible study. Beyond them at a small table sat a man and a woman and across from them an older gentleman, who appeared to be counseling them.

Brandon pointed to a bald, clean-shaven, middle-aged man with black-rimmed glasses. A few guys were talking with him to the left side of the room. "Hey John, you got a minute? Parker, here, wants to talk to you."

John excused himself from the group and came to say hello. "Good morning and welcome to Hope Mission House."

"Hi. Is this a good time to talk? I'd like to ask you a few questions."

John looked at his watch. "Now works. Can I get you something to drink? Coffee, soda, water?"

"Coffee would be great, thanks."

After getting their coffee, John led him to an office in the back. Photos of men, some with their families, covered the walls. Parker took a minute to look at them.

"Wow, are these pictures of the people you've helped?"

"Some of them." John pointed to an empty chair as he took his seat behind the desk. "We opened this mission about twelve years ago and I'm happy to say there are too many success stories for these walls to hold them all. Occasionally, I switch them out for new ones."

"It's impressive."

"Yes, but it's not always easy. Most of the guys we help are pretty messed up. When I get discouraged because one of them drops out or returns to his destructive behaviors, I come in here to remind myself that what we do here is worth it."

Parker scanned the room again. "If these photos don't motivate you, I don't know what could."

"Thanks. Now, what can I help you with?"

"I have a question about a girl, which I know sounds foolish because this is a mission for guys, but my information led me to you." Parker reached across the desk to hand John his phone. The same distressed photo that he had shown Susie was already open. "Have you ever seen this girl before?"

John looked thoughtfully at the girl. It appeared that he was trying to connect the picture with a memory. "I see lots of new faces every week and most of them I couldn't pick out of a crowd. Jordan was different. It took me a minute to recognize her because her hair was dyed an unnatural black. These eyes are the same though, and the fear that is emanating from them is hard to forget. Yes, this girl came to our mission."

After the disturbing story in Memphis, Parker hadn't realized he forgot to breathe. He gasped for air and choked out, "Jordan?"

"I know that's not her real name. With the way time flies, I don't remember exactly how long it's been . . . but it was years ago. Anyway, she was almost out of money with no place to stay. She told us that she was afraid to get a job because she didn't dare use her real name and social security number for fear of being found." He slid the phone back.

"You were able to help her, right?" Parker put pressure on his knees to keep them from bouncing. "Where does she live?"

"Slow down and I'll tell you what I can recall."

Parker frowned.

John rested his arms on the desk and clasped his hands around his coffee cup. "We discovered that Jordan had run away from home months earlier. I had a woman from the kitchen and a few other staff members join me. We tried to encourage her to go home and work things out, but she burst into tears and told us her heart wrenching story. We offered to go to the police with her and that's when she really flipped out. I specifically remember how the pain and fear that was in her eyes abruptly turned to anger. She started screaming, 'I'm not going back into that hell-hole to get more proof! I don't care if you don't believe me. I'll never go back! Never! I'd rather die!' She grabbed her bag and ran for the door.

"A few of the men standing at the entrance heard the disturbance and stopped her. I quickly joined them and told Jordan she could stay with my family until we had time to figure something out. I called my wife and asked her to come to the mission. In the meantime, our cook brought out a plate of food and that was enough to make her stay. She wolfed it down like she hadn't eaten in days.

"While she ate, one of my staff found her picture in the missing person's database. Because the authorities were still looking for her, we'd be guilty of obstructing the search if we concealed her. We had no way of knowing if they were close, and at the time, I didn't know what we could legally do, because she wasn't yet seventeen. That sounds silly now in retrospect, but we couldn't risk damaging the integrity of all the great work we do here.

"Anyway, we thought we had gained her trust, so we offered to contact Child Protective Services. The situation was more dire than I expected."

Parker furrowed his brow but didn't interrupt.

"I remember it as if it were yesterday. She said her adoptive father was a respected lawyer with too much power and too many connections in high places. He had the means to find her and if he did, he'd force her to come home. She again burst into tears and begged us to help her without letting anyone know. Even now, her story haunts me."

"What do you mean, *still haunts you*? Weren't you able to help her?" A pang of anxiety shot through Parker's chest as he shifted uneasily.

John straightened his glasses and looked thoughtfully at him. "I'm sorry I can't tell you what you want to hear."

Sadness extinguished the light that had been in Parker's eyes at the realization that something went awry. "Well, it sounds like you tried. What happened?"

"The one thing we knew to do was to keep her talking. I thought things were going well. She started to relax and seemed less frightened. I let her know my wife would be there any minute. Then she asked to use the bathroom. She must have slipped out the window because, like a vapor, she was gone. Several of our staff and even a few residents helped look for her, but we couldn't find her."

"But why'd she run?" Parker knew his disappointment was obvious, but he didn't care. He didn't understand how Melissa could be so close to getting help and in a moment vanish without a trace.

John ran his hand over his chin a few times before answering. "To be honest, I don't know. We had never encountered a situation like that before. Hope Mission House is a place to help homeless and drug-addicted men, not runaway teenage girls. I suppose it could be possible that she thought one of my staff had called the police and she needed to run before it was too late."

The room fell silent. The only noise to be heard was the low hum of voices in the common room. Parker put his head in his hands and stared at the floor. He knew he shouldn't fault John or the mission; they did what they could with the information they had. Without looking up, he muttered, "I don't get it."

John walked to the front of his desk and leaned against it. "Parker, are you okay?"

He sat back and stared at John with pensive eyes. "No." He shook his head. "No, I'm not okay. Melissa's story makes me sick and now I've hit another dead end."

"Who gave you the lead that you should come here?"

"The man who hired me to find Melissa."

"Are you sure it wasn't her father?"

"I just came from Memphis, where I heard the first part of her story from a close friend of hers. The woman confirmed that Melissa was abused. So yes, I'm confident my leads aren't coming from him."

"What are you going to do now?"

"I have no idea, but I appreciate you taking the time to tell me what you could." Parker got to his feet. "Thank you."

"I wouldn't lose heart," John said, reaching to shake his hand. "I've seen plenty of hopeless situations turn around for good, so why not Melissa's?"

"Let's hope so."

"When you find her, please be sure to let me know."

"I will."

As Parker walked away, he opened his phone to the picture of Melissa. *If you'd only stayed a bit longer, I know these kind people would've figured out a way to help you.*

Chapter 16

DIVINE INTERVENTION

Parker called Matt and was surprised when he didn't answer. *Huh, now what am I supposed to do?*

He could head for Virginia Beach as planned, but his gut told him to wait. As a matter of habit, he checked his phone for a text, even though he knew it hadn't vibrated. The lack of communication from the man who set these events in motion would not have bothered him so much if he felt at liberty to go and do what he wanted. Yet being his own man and doing his own thing seemed petty and small since hearing Melissa's story. All he wanted was to find her. He shoved the phone back into his pocket, but instead of driving away, he got out of the Jeep and took a walk around the block.

When he returned, John was talking with a few men on the sidewalk. "Hey Parker, I didn't know you were still here. Is there a problem?"

"No, I just needed to stretch my legs. Do you mind if I use the bathroom?"

"Not at all. Someone inside can show you where it is."

When Parker saw the window that Melissa had used for her escape, he was surprised to see how small it was. He shook his head, unable to imagine living in constant terror of being found. He'd left home because of Mike's abuse, but he never feared that he would come after him. For all Parker knew, Mike was happy to have him gone.

Parker walked to the window. Though he was tall enough to see out, the bottom half was frosted so he couldn't tell what was on the other side. On a whim, he opened the window and stuck his head out. The drop to the alley was ten, maybe twelve feet; not only making Melissa's flight from the mission difficult, but quite dangerous.

He suppressed the urge to climb out of the window, doubting at this point he would find anything of value.

As he started to pull his head back into the room, he saw a piece of fabric caught in the gap between two bricks on the outside sill. With some effort, he pulled it free. It looked to be a weathered piece of clothing. *Huh, she obviously got caught as she climbed out. I wonder if she got hurt.* He put the cloth into his pocket and left the bathroom.

Matt still hadn't returned his call by the time he got back to his Jeep, so he used his phone to see what was in the area. A park was close, and it was a beautiful autumn day. That would be as good a place to wait as any.

With his camera bag slung over his shoulder, he started walking through the park. It wasn't long before he spotted a pond with some ducks swimming at the far end. An elderly couple was throwing bread to the ducks from their bench. Parker took a seat opposite and watched for a while. They seemed oblivious to everything else around them, so he snapped a few pictures before writing down John's story.

Matt finally called. "Hey, sorry I missed you, I was busy."

"Busy doing what?" Parker asked. "I thought you were confined to a recliner."

"Well, that's changed. I had an appointment with the ophthalmologist earlier. When he took off the patch, he marveled at the improvement. After an in-depth look, he said it was a miracle and he'd never seen an eye injured this badly heal so quickly. He made me promise that I wouldn't overdo it but also said I was free to go about my normal activities."

"That's fantastic!" Parker pumped his fist and didn't try to hide the excitement in his voice. "This means you can join me, right?"

"If you still need me, then yes. The doctor did tell me that if my eye starts to feel strained, I need to be sure to rest it, and if any blood returns, to call his office immediately."

"I'm not an expert on miracles, but I'm guessing that won't happen. This is great news."

"It sure is. Anna said it's an answer to prayer and I agree. Then get this, I wasn't home more than five minutes before I got a call from our guy."

"Oh yeah, what'd he say?"

"He said now that I can resume my normal activities, there's no danger in taking a walk. He told me to get my camera and he gave me directions to where he wanted me to take pictures. Then he said, 'You know the drill,' and he hung up." For the first time, Parker could hear Matt's enthusiasm wane. "I'm resigned to not having his name, but I still don't understand why he has to be so abrupt."

"You should be glad you get a voice. All I get lately, if anything, are texts." Parker felt a bit jealous even though he knew he shouldn't be.

"Don't get me wrong, I'm grateful for his voice. His methods just throw me off, that's all. I was also thrilled to get an assignment, because even though I said I wanted back in, I struggled with the idea and didn't get much sleep last night. It appears our guy thought I needed a little push."

"That works for me," Parker said with a laugh.

"I knew you'd be thrilled. But now back to the photo shoot. I couldn't believe how good it felt to be moving again. My eye is fine, and I don't have a headache for the first time in days."

"Sweet. Have you had a chance to look at the photos yet?"

"No. I'm just walking back to Anna's place now."

"Oh, okay. Well, I've hit a dead end, so I don't know what to do next."

"Does that mean the people at the mission didn't know Melissa?"

"They had met her, which means we followed our lead correctly."

"Hey, I just got to the house. How about you tell me about Melissa while I get out my laptop and load the pictures? I'll email them to you. That way we can both look and be sure we come to the same conclusion. Deal?"

"Deal." Parker wasn't done with his story by the time he got Matt's photos, but it seemed more important to catch him up than worry about where to go next.

When he finished, Matt said, "I can't believe she ran. To be so scared that she didn't trust anyone, not even at a mission." He sighed loud enough for Parker to hear him. "I'm sure it never even crossed her mind that she'd end up homeless."

"Unfortunately, I don't think she had a plan beyond leaving," Parker said.

"You'd think someone would've been able to help her."

"Yeah, but she was so afraid of her *dad* finding her that she didn't trust anyone. John still regrets that Melissa took off before they had time to find the right resources to help her."

"That's a tough one because the internet is full of sites that explain where abused runaways can go, not only to get help but also to be protected."

"True, but Melissa didn't have her phone or access to the internet."

"Lots of places have free Wi-Fi and public computers," Matt countered.

"From what I could tell, she was so paranoid of lurking eyes that she avoided public places."

"I certainly can't relate."

"Neither can I. But to stay on point, why did I need to come to this mission? It's not like we're any closer to finding her." Parker found himself getting upset, so he got to his feet and started walking back to his Jeep.

"Maybe our guy gave you this extra connection to validate Susie's story. And if you think about it . . . it gave me time to get better and over my pity party."

"No one thought you were having a pity party, but I do like the sounds of having you back in the search." Matt's reasoning filled Parker with fresh hope. Even though he wasn't as adventurous or as daring, he approached things from a different vantage point which Parker found helpful. "Let's see what shows up in the pictures, so that we know where to meet up."

Before Matt could look at the photos, he was interrupted by a text from his mom.

'How are you doing today? Unfortunately, we can't come to Virginia Beach until Tuesday. Your dad got called away on business.'

Instead of texting back, he called. "Hi, mom. Guess what?"

"By your tone, I'd say you have good news."

"Ha, you know me too well. I got great news from the ophthalmologist. He gave me a clean bill of health. I'm free to travel."

"So soon?"

"He said it was a miracle."

"Well, praise the Lord! That's wonderful. This means that you can take the train home tomorrow, right?"

"No. I'm going to rejoin Parker. We have new leads and he needs my help."

"Excuse me? I thought you were done with this whole adventure thing. I know it kept your mind off Haley, but do you trust Parker?"

"Mom, do you even hear yourself? In one breath you're praising the Lord for my eye, but then in the next, you don't believe that I'll be okay. Parker had a nightmare; he didn't become a pathological abuser. Yes, I trust him. Besides, this has become so much more than getting my mind off Haley. We're connecting with people and seeing how their lives have been impacted by our search for the missing girl. I need to go."

"Well, okay then. On a different note, have you talked to Haley yet?"

"I've tried. She won't answer her phone. I even left a voicemail."

"It's such a shame. I don't understand why she's being so unreasonable."

"I do. She knows she made a stupid decision and doesn't want to own it," Matt said. A few choice words darted through his thoughts, but he did well to keep them to himself.

"Tell you what, I'll get ahold of Haley to confirm she sent wedding cancellation notices, and if she hasn't, I'll take care of making sure our side of the family knows."

"Don't be surprised if she doesn't answer."

"This has to be done and soon. If she won't answer, I know where she lives."

"Be nice now," Matt said, half joking.

"She doesn't deserve nice, but for your sake, I'll be the epitome of grace."

"Thanks, Mom. I know her actions are reprehensible, and you probably think I should hate her, but I don't."

"I don't hate her either, but that doesn't keep my heart from hurting for you."

"I know and I appreciate your love and support. Please keep me posted on the wedding front. Haley booked the reception so that's on her, even though I'm sure we've lost our deposit. I already called the pastor to cancel the church. Let me know if there's anything else I still need to take care of."

"I will. Bye."

Matt leaned back in his chair. Fresh thoughts of Haley angered him and he wished he could hate her. It would make things so much easier. To deflect from the pain, he turned his focus to the new pictures.

Just then, Anna walked in with the mail. "Hey, Matt, who did you give my address to?"

Confusion scurried across his brow. "I didn't give it to anyone. Why?"

"Because there's a letter here with your name on it." She handed him the business-sized envelope.

Matt didn't recognize the handwriting. "Huh, that's interesting. Let's see what's inside."

Anna watched as he pulled the contents from the envelope. "What is it?"

"Here, take a look. It's a flight itinerary and a note that says a ticket has been purchased in my name."

Anna took the papers and read the note. "Why Indianapolis?"

"Because that's where Parker is, but neither of us ordered the ticket. The flight leaves tonight at 7:00."

"Let me guess, your mystery man!" Anna grinned.

"It would appear so. Who else knew my eye was better or where Parker is?" Matt was thrilled because he had figured the first flight he could get would be for some time tomorrow. "Oh, and my dad got called away on business, so my parents aren't coming either." On this point alone, Matt was disappointed.

"Well, I'm sorry I won't get to meet them, but this is too perfect to be a coincidence. I think it's great that you get to join Parker and be a part of the search. Now you'll have a firsthand account to draw from when you write your novel."

"I'm surprised you believe in our mystery guy and the impossible way we get our information . . . especially being a Christian and all. This doesn't seem like something you'd believe in."

Anna smiled at the remark. "I'm glad you mentioned it. Let me give you an example of why I believe this *is* God's intervention: I love the ocean and the sound of the waves, but I also respect its power and the reliability of the tide. So if God can supernaturally part the Red Sea while millions of Israelites pass safely through on dry land, and then destroy the Egyptian army with the same water, or if He can allow Peter to walk on water—both of which are naturally impossible—why can't God *still* supersede His own creative order to accomplish His will today? I believe He can do anything He wants, even if it is unconventional."

"Interesting perspective. I was raised in a Christian home but never considered it to be God's intervention. It's certainly the most plausible explanation at this point."

"I haven't told you this, but you and Parker are the first people I ever had stay at my house."

Matt's eyes widened.

"Owen suggested I do it to help with the bills, but I was a bit apprehensive, so I had you meet me at Casey's Café. I'm guessing it wasn't by *chance* that you found me. I think this is all very fascinating and I'm honored to have a small part in your journey."

"No wonder you're such a great hostess. I'm glad we saw the ad." Matt thought of how ungrateful he was only a few days earlier when he didn't want to stay at her house.

"Me too. I'll give you a ride to the airport."

"Are you sure? I don't mind using Uber."

"With you leaving, this will be our last opportunity to chat."

"Great, then I'll have time to give you Parker's latest update."

"Sounds good. I have a few things to get done before we leave. We'll talk on the way." Anna left for the kitchen.

Matt ran upstairs. Lost in the moment and giddy with excitement, he forgot to look at the photos. *Parker will be stoked to find out that I can come tonight, and I get to help find Melissa.*

A call interrupted his musings. "Hey, what did you think of the new images?"

"I, uh, didn't look yet. But before you get upset, I'm packing so I can catch a flight to Indianapolis tonight."

"How'd you manage that?"

"Mixed in with Anna's mail was a letter addressed to me, which included a one-way ticket. I arrive at 11:20. And before that my mom called, saying she and my dad would have to postpone their trip to Virginia Beach. Now they don't have to come at all. How sweet is that?"

"More like unbelievable, but then with the other things you told me earlier, this wouldn't even be a stretch . . . though it all seems too good to be true."

Matt laughed. "It's improbable for sure, but you know as well as I do that there's no sense in trying to figure it out. It's happening and I'll see you later tonight."

"And here I thought I had news."

"What news?" Matt asked.

"The pictures we took with the film are now on my cloud. We have the ones that changed to parchments and the ones with the names on them from Chestnut Street."

"That's cool. Now I can get the one I like printed and framed after all."

"Hey Matt, are you ready?" Anna called from the bottom of the stairs. "We need to leave soon."

Matt pulled the phone away from his mouth before saying, "Okay. I'll be right there." Then he said to Parker, "I've got to get going. We'll have to finish this conversation in person."

"Works for me. I'll make hotel reservations and meet you at the airport."

Chapter 17

HOLMES AND WATSON

Parker enthusiastically reached out to shake Matt's hand. "Holmes and Watson together again. Good to see you, man."

"Good to be here, Sherlock." Matt's grin matched his excitement. "And speaking of great but unorthodox detectives, I looked at the photos on the plane. It appears our next destination is St. Louis."

"Yeah, that's what I thought too, but I'm not sure why. From what we've learned about Melissa, I don't think she'd go back to St. Louis."

Matt shouldered his bag. "Maybe there's something else we need to learn before we find her."

"That sounds more like it. I never told you about the other pictures I took when I was in Memphis." As they made their way out of the airport, Parker told him the story about the building with too many security cameras. He concluded with telling about the Porsche. "I took a few pictures of the car because I thought it was sweet, not because I thought it had anything to do with why I was there. But then, when no extra images showed up in the photos, I looked closer and noticed the Missouri license plate. Not that Missouri means St. Louis, or that the driver has anything to do with anything except for the fact that he came from that building.

"Then, as you already know, I was directed to take new photos in Nashville, which brought me to Indianapolis. Geographically, it would have made more sense to go to St. Louis first."

"Sure, but the information you received to go to Memphis, and now Indianapolis, has been in chronological order. You say you hit a dead end, but it seems like we're only given what information we need at the time and not a step further. The more we learn, the more I'm convinced that our guy has this story all mapped out for us. I say it's worth seeing where this road leads."

When they reached the exit, a blast of heavy air met them, adding to the weightiness of their discussion.

As they walked to the Jeep, Parker asked, "Why do you think this guy chose us? I mean think about it—how does he know that we won't get tired of all this back and forth and give up?"

"To be clear, in the beginning it bothered me that he knew so much about us, yet in all that knowing, he must've figured we have what it takes to see this through and find the girl."

"Yeah, except our first mission only took a day so it seemed exciting—"

"You don't find this exciting?"

Parker mindlessly swung his key chain around his index finger. "I suppose so, it's just that we have no idea how long or drawn out this assignment will be."

"Well, you were told it was a cold case. Those aren't usually solved overnight, or the case wouldn't have gone cold." Matt gestured quotes. "And anyway, I don't see why it matters how long it takes. You got paid a hefty amount in advance. That doesn't usually happen, does it?"

"No, but then I don't expect my clients to pay first."

"Exactly. I'd say this proves our guy trusts us to finish the job. Now we have a girl to find and I have a story to write. Our road trip continues in the morning."

"Oh, so now you're Sherlock?"

"When you stop your grumbling, I'll gladly give you back your hat."

❏ ❏ ❏

They got on the road early and reached the outskirts of St. Louis by 9:30. While still on the east side of the Mississippi, Parker got a text.

'Take highway across the river. Use second exit, head south until you reach a small business district. Photograph number 437.'

Doing as directed, they drove through a residential area before reaching a part of the city where commerce wasn't thriving, but businesses lined both sides of the street. Number 437 looked similar to the brick, two-story office in Memphis. It was well-kept with large flowerpots on both sides of the door, but again no signage to indicate what was inside. Parker's curiosity piqued when he saw all the security cameras for a place of no recognizable significance. Even though this was disconcerting, he didn't mention it to Matt.

They were there for less than three minutes when a new text came.

'LEAVE, NOW!'

"Hey, let's go!" Parker ran to his Jeep.

Matt stumbled in his haste to follow. "Whoa, what's going on."

"Just get in!"

The moment the doors were closed, Parker sped away, making sure to keep an eye on his rearview mirror. "Here, look at this." With a shaky hand, he tossed his phone to Matt.

"'Leave, now!' What's this about?"

"I don't know, but I didn't want to wait around to find out."

"Good point, especially after that guy in Memphis threatened to call the police. Should we find a place to stay so we can look at the photos? There were a few decent looking hotels back—"

"No!" Parker cut him off. "I'd rather get further away from here. That place gave me the creeps, or maybe it's the text, but either way, those hotels are too close to that building." He drove several blocks, turning at most of the intersections. Once he was confident no one was trailing them, he asked, "Can you use your phone's location services to see where we are in relation to number 437? With all the turns I just made, it's hard to tell if we've put a decent distance between us and them."

"Sure, but who's them?"

"I have no idea."

"We don't actually have a reason to be afraid, do we?"

"I probably overreacted." He smacked Matt's arm with the back of his hand, trying to squelch the lingering anxiety. "Let's just forget about it."

Matt got out his phone. "Hey, hold up a minute, now I have a new text. It says, 'Continue south, take third left and then second right, take photos of the abandoned building near river.'"

They drove a mile or two before they spotted a deserted factory. Parker wasn't sure if they were in the right place, but the building had artistic potential, so he pulled into the driveway. They split up and started taking pictures.

Matt only got a few before his phone rang. "Hey, Parker, it's my boss. I've got to take this."

"Okay, I'm going to look around." He walked out back and was pleased with the way the light hit the building. After taking a few more digital pictures, he got out his film camera and started focusing on the details. *I wonder if this was meant to be a perk to help settle my nerves after our last photo shoot.*

When Parker got back, Matt was still on the phone, so he leaned against his Jeep and started looking through his camera's viewfinder. *Sweet, some of these will be good enough to sell.*

"Sorry about that," Matt said, as he hung up.

Parker shrugged. "Not like it's a problem, but I thought you used vacation?"

"I did."

"Then why'd he call?"

"He wanted to run an idea by me. You'll never guess what he asked."

"You're right; I have no clue, and what's with that ridiculous grin?"

"He thought we should write a story about the abandoned building on Chestnut Street. What are the odds?"

"You said it's been empty like forever. So what's the urgency that it couldn't wait until you got back?"

"Apparently some businessmen want to buy it. My boss thought it would be advantageous for us to do a background story for the paper. That our readers would be excited to find out why the building sat empty all these years with no attempt to sell. I can start doing the research in my spare time."

"But do they want to sell or are the businessmen pushing because it's prime real estate?"

"I'm not sure, but that's part of the intrigue; apparently the taxes are paid in full. Because they aren't in arrears, the city can't make them sell. Hopefully, the offer is good enough that they'll want to let it go."

"Do you know who owns it?" Parker asked as he put his cameras away.

"My boss didn't say. I told him I'd see what I could find out and he said he'd email me what information he had to help get me started. But don't you find the timing curious?"

"What's the big deal? It's just a building and it would be good for the historic district to have it functional again."

"I know, but I've lived in Philadelphia my whole life and I never gave that building any thought until we photographed it a few weeks ago. Don't you remember telling me I should find out what happened there?"

"Yeah I remember." Parker smiled a little. "But right now we need to focus on why we're in St. Louis. I say we find a place to stay so we can look at our pictures."

They jumped into the Jeep and Parker continued south.

Matt punched motels into his phone. "Hey, turn right at the next light. There's a motel off the beaten path about three miles from here. And yes, it's in the opposite direction of number 437."

"Anything away from 437 works for me."

The motel was old and dreary, but it suited their purpose. The first thing Matt did was to open the blinds. "There, nothing like a little sunshine to cheer things up."

"And make it easier to see." Parker checked to make sure the desk lamp was plugged in. "The bulb must be blown." Not wanting to waste any more time on the light, he set up his laptop and loaded the pictures from his camera. While he waited, he looked over his shoulder toward Matt, who had flung himself on the bed closest to the door. "How about finding a diner or somewhere we could get a decent cup of coffee? I need caffeine!"

"Ah, me too." A moment later he had a list of local places opened on his phone. "We have a few options within a ten-minute walk from here. Are you coming?"

"I'd rather stay if you don't mind." Parker had already turned back to the photos.

Matt rolled off the bed. "No problem. I'll get us something to eat while I'm out. What sounds good?"

"Surprise me." He didn't even look back as his focus was already on the first picture.

Matt put his camera in his satchel and headed toward the door. "Well . . . if you change your mind, text."

Parker mindlessly said, "Uh-huh." But then he must have heard Matt's heavy sigh because he looked up. "Sorry I'm preoccupied. That 'leave now' text is still bothering me. I want to find out why we're here."

"Well then, Sherlock, you've regained your hat." Matt grinned.

"Come, Watson, the games are afoot. Now off with you!"

They both laughed before Matt stepped out of the dark, musty room into bright sunlight. A deli was only three blocks from the motel, so he walked. There was no need to hurry; Parker and the clues would be there when he got back.

Though it was only 11:00, Matt's stomach growled. They had left Indianapolis early that morning and hadn't taken the time to eat. When he reached the deli, a group of people were already in line waiting to order, so he grabbed a newspaper before walking to the end of the line.

With only two people still in front of him, Matt felt his phone vibrate. He assumed Parker had changed his mind and wanted something specific for lunch. *Oh.* The text was from a blocked number.

Chapter 18

AN UNWELCOMED VISITOR

Parker felt a bit tight after their morning drive . . . and the stressful 'leave now' text. Pushing away from the desk he stood to do some stretches. *I should've gone with Matt.* A few minutes later, he sat back at the desk and refocused on the task at hand. Three of the five pictures he took showed people standing in front of the office. The first was a young couple who looked to be in their mid-twenties. The second, a couple who looked a bit older, maybe in their early thirties; and the last, two older gentlemen dressed in sharp, black suits.

One by one, he enlarged the photos to get a better look at the people's faces. It was then that he realized the guy in his early thirties was the same man he'd talked to outside the office in Memphis. "Huh, that's interesting."

Puzzled by this discovery, Parker cropped each of the images so that only their faces showed, saved them under new file names, and then went back to the originals to see if there was anything else of importance. In the last picture, one of the older gentlemen was handing a large, manila envelope to the other. Parker zoomed in to see if there was any writing on it. Just as he leaned in to get a better look, the motel door opened. Not bothering to turn, he said, "That was fast."

The voice that answered *wasn't* Matt's. Parker quickly spun on his chair to see a man in the doorway. "Sorry man, but you

155

have the wrong—" was all he said before jumping to his feet. The man had a gun and it was pointed straight at him.

"Don't take another step." He came further into the room and elbowed the door shut behind him.

Parker recognized him from the pictures he'd just saved. The man looked to be in his mid-twenties, clean shaven with a black crew-cut and wearing the same outfit of dark jeans and a light green polo. Nothing about his appearance suggested he was a criminal, let alone a hit man.

Parker swallowed hard as he scanned the room for a way out.

"Do you seriously think you can get past me? You're trapped and I need answers."

"But I'm not even from around here. You must be mistaking me for someone else."

"No mistake. Why are you taking pictures of our properties?" The man's voice sounded more worried than harsh.

Parker raised his hands slightly. "Um, can you clarify? I don't know what buildings you're talking about?" He kept his tone casual, in hopes that it would lighten the mood.

Even though the gun shook in the man's hand, he took a step closer. "Who hired you and what do you know?"

This caused Parker to step back, but the desk stopped him from going further. "I'm a freelance photographer. I have a large fan base and most of my stuff is sold at galleries or online."

The man came closer and struck him in the face. "Don't mess with me, Parker Jackson. You must have a reason or connections, especially when you photographed our buildings in two different cities."

Blood gushed from Parker's nose and into his beard. He quickly looked up and put pressure on it to see if he could stop the bleeding. "What's your problem?" He wiped his upper lip with the back of his hand. His fear now turned to anger. "Such a mess, and for what?"

Their eyes locked. The man's expression grew colder by the second. "I've had about enough of your playing dumb." He cocked the gun. "Who hired you?"

Parker finally dropped his gaze and when he did, blood dripped onto his light gray, Henley shirt. With no way out, and the man now visibly upset, he was at a loss. Looking up, he said, "How are your threats going to help when I have no idea what you want me to say?"

"Shut up!" the man barked. "Did you think we wouldn't notice you? We let your intrusion go as a legitimate *chance* a few days ago in Memphis, but now you're here in St. Louis. That's no coincidence. You must know something."

Parker's mind raced back to Memphis. *So there is a connection between the buildings, but that doesn't help me now.* He decided not to answer.

The man seemed to be gaining confidence. His hand now steady, his voice brash. "If you're foolish enough to remain silent, I can permanently help you with that."

"If you kill me, you learn nothing. Besides, I have connections you apparently don't know about." Parker was surprised by the lack of fear in his answer, especially in light of the threat just made against him.

"Do you mean your dimwitted friend who just left?" The man laughed a dry, mocking laugh. "This isn't a game to us. If you care about your life or the life of your friend, I suggest you start talking."

"I seriously have no idea what you want from me. As you can see by my license plate, which is probably how you found me, I'm from Pennsylvania. I travel around the country and take photographs. When I get home, I use the best ones and sell them online or at galleries. Do you want to see my business card?"

"Wow, you're unbelievable. No matter; your cover is blown, and we don't plan on letting you go until we find out what we need to know." A wry smile crept into the corners of his lips as he pushed Parker from the desk. The photo of the older men in front of the office was on the computer screen. "Hey, how did you get that picture?" Panic enveloped his voice.

A moment later a young woman burst into the room. She wore too much makeup, her hair was pulled into a ponytail, and she sported skinny jeans with a tight top. "Ryan, what's the hold up? We need to get going."

"But we can't leave without finding out what this guy knows. Look!" He pointed to the computer screen. "I didn't know the boss ever made transactions in plain sight."

"Oh man, this is worse than we thought." The woman hurried to the desk. "That picture could ruin us if it gets into the wrong hands."

"What are you saying, Allison?"

"It's obvious that this guy knows too much. We need to bring him with us, like now. I'll bag up his computer. You keep an eye on him while he gets the rest of his camera equipment."

The urgency in her voice caused Parker to tense. A groan escaped his lips.

With a mixture of anger in his eyes and fear in his voice, Ryan snapped, "You heard the lady."

Parker shot a look at the men on his screen before Allison closed the laptop. *What's in this photo that has these people so worked up?*

As nonchalantly as he could, he wiped more blood from his nose and smeared it onto the desk as he passed. *It's probably too late for that to help, but what else can I do. Without a miracle, I'm toast.*

Before leaving the room, Allison took another quick look around. Seeing nothing of interest, she grabbed his keys off the dresser. "I'll drive while you keep an eye on the photographer here. Vincent can wait for his friend and bring him to us."

Ryan shoved the gun into Parker's back. "Now, we're going to walk out of here like nothing's wrong. If you try to make a run for it or do something stupid, don't think I won't use this. Got it?"

Parker, still shaking from the chill that ran down his spine, stiffly nodded.

"Good. Let's go."

He only had a moment to scan the street for Matt before Ryan shoved him into the back of his Jeep. What started as a hopeful mix-up, turned quickly into fear and now culminated in full-blown terror. He had no idea where they were going or what they would do to him. What troubled him even more was the fact that he had no answers.

"Hey, Allie, do you have something we can use for a blindfold?"

"Probably." She took the next right and drove a few blocks before stopping. Then she looked through her handbag and pulled out a scarf. "Here, this should work." She tossed it to Ryan. Then in one quick motion, she pointed a taser at Parker. "Don't get any ideas."

Ryan pulled the scarf tighter than necessary and said, "You better get your story straight before you talk to the boss."

Allison pulled out again.

By now Parker's nerves were frayed. He tried to convince himself to relax, but his heart seemed to pound louder and louder.

Twenty minutes must have passed before they came to a stop. Parker instinctively raised his hand to remove the blindfold.

"Hey!" Ryan grabbed his arm and pulled it down.

"Do you want me to give him a jolt from my taser?" Allison asked.

"No, we're good. Just get the door."

Allison jumped from the Jeep and a moment later Parker heard a loud metallic groan. When she got back in, they inched forward, only to stop again a few seconds later. The groan again ensued, ending with a bang and the rattling of a chain.

Even though Parker still wore the blindfold, he saw, as well as felt, the darkness. Ryan pulled him from the Jeep and pushed him forward. They led him over a smooth concrete floor before heading up a flight of steel-grated stairs. At the top, they turned left and walked down a long, sporadically lit hallway.

Then, without warning, Ryan shoved Parker so hard that he lost his balance and fell headlong onto a dusty linoleum floor.

Allison flipped on the light. "You can remove the blindfold now." She and Ryan watched as Parker tore off the scarf and scrambled to his feet. "What's the password to your cloud account?"

Parker reluctantly gave it to her.

"The boss will be calling soon, so you better be ready to tell us how you got that picture and what you needed it for." She stepped back.

Parker swung his hands upward. "But I don't know—"

Ryan rolled his eyes and slammed the door in his face.

Parker waited for them to walk away before quietly trying the knob. The door was locked. He found himself in a room with one working fluorescent light, peeling paint and boarded-over windows. Several of the ceiling tiles were missing, which exposed the steel I-beams. The place also smelled of rust and grease, but seemed too big to be a garage, so he assumed they had brought him to an abandoned factory.

After a quick scan of the room, he turned his focus to finding a way out. To his great disappointment, the plywood that covered the windows could not be loosened. The only other possibility was the rafters, but they were too high. He was trapped.

Like a caged animal, Parker paced back and forth for several minutes before taking a seat opposite the door. He let his head fall back against the wall. *What have I gotten myself into? These people are obviously afraid of something.*

He had no idea how much time had passed when the door abruptly flung open. Ryan didn't come in. Instead he stood in the doorway and waved the gun toward Parker. "Get up. Allison needs you in the next room." He stepped back into the hall and waited for him to pass.

Though Parker had no choice but to comply, he moved slowly, hoping he could think of an answer that would satisfy them.

He was surprised to find the room he entered to be fully furnished and even though the windows were still boarded over, it was much brighter, and the ceiling tiles were all intact. At the far end of the room, a living area was set up with lamps, end tables, an area rug, and a couch. They even had a TV mounted to one wall with a DVD player on top of a small refrigerator. Closer to the door was a desk that looked like a piece of original office furniture with another lamp on it.

This must be a permanent hideout, but for what?

Allison sat at the desk with Parker's laptop open. Pictures of the buildings in question filled the screen. She spun her chair toward him and crossed her arms. "Where's the picture we saw at the motel?"

Parker stifled a relieved sigh when he looked at the images and saw no people in any of them. This gave him hope. "I don't know what you thought you saw earlier, but you have them open on the screen. That's why I couldn't figure out why you were so upset."

Ryan leveled a blow to the side of Parker's head.

Parker turned to retaliate, but Ryan put the gun in his face. "Nice. I haven't done anything wrong, yet because you have a gun you think it's okay to keep hitting me. Well, news flash, buddy, that's not going to make pictures that don't exist magically appear."

He cocked the gun and yelled, "Where's the damn picture?"

Parker didn't back down. "I don't know what picture you're talking about. All my photos are right there." He pointed. "Maybe you've made a mistake."

"There's no mistake," Allison said. "We saw the photo."

"And who shut my computer? It's not like I had a chance to delete the photo you're talking about, even if it was *really* there." He gestured quotes.

Ryan leveled another blow to the back of Parker's head, this time with the butt of the gun. Parker stumbled forward and fell to his knees with a groan.

Everything within him wanted to retaliate, but instead he blurted out, "I don't have what you're looking for. If you let me leave now, I won't go to the police and I'll forget that I ever met you."

"Yeah right." Ryan knelt in front of Parker and put the gun in his face. "That's not going to happen."

"Ryan, stop. Maybe in my haste to leave the motel, I accidently deleted it. I'll look."

"Check his email, too. We need to know who else has it."

"Oh, right." Allison turned back to the computer and started a fresh search. "Nothing! I don't get it."

It was then that her phone rang. She quickly scooped it off the desk. "Hello . . . We have him with us now . . . Okay, just a sec." She put the phone on speaker. "We have a problem, boss. I found the pictures of our buildings, but I can't find the one with you and Stanton in it."

Parker's heart skipped a beat at the mention of that name, and though the probability of this guy being Melissa's dad was low, he didn't want to take a chance. Quickly he lowered his face and started rubbing the back of his head. No one seemed to notice his cover.

A low gravelly voice pierced the silence. "Mr. Jackson, if you value your life, I suggest you start talking. Who are you working for?"

"Like I already told Ryan, I'm a freelance photographer." Parker looked his way. "May I?" Ryan nodded and Parker got to his feet. "I do all kinds of commission jobs."

"I didn't ask for your life history. Who hired you to photograph our buildings?"

"I don't know, sir."

"Yeah, right!" Allison sneered. "Then how do you get paid?"

"The first photos I took for this guy I sold at my art gallery in Philadelphia and that was my payment. I don't know his name or why he wanted pictures of these buildings. How about you delete the photos you're concerned about and then let me go."

"That's not going to happen, Mr. Jackson. We never leave loose ends. Now, you either tell us who you're working for or we'll start adding some serious pain."

"What? Am I supposed to make something up in hopes that you'll let me go?" He took a step back, making sure he was out of Ryan's reach. "I've never met the guy and have no idea who he is. He never mentioned your name or the purpose for the pictures."

"Ryan, take him back to the other room so we can talk."

"Yes, sir."

Allison clicked the phone off speaker and put it to her ear.

"You heard the man. Let's go." Parker obeyed. Once he was back in the first room, Ryan added, "We don't have time to waste on a scumbag like you and our patience is running out. You better have answers when I come back."

Again, the door was locked behind him and Parker was left alone to contemplate his fate. This time he pulled on the plywood with frantic desperation, even using his feet as leverage. Without a pry bar, it was hopeless.

Maybe I could spring myself off the wall to reach the rafters. He looked for the closest opening in the ceiling from the wall to an exposed I-beam. Without another thought, he ran and jumped, pushing himself upward off the wall. His hands reached the beam, but he couldn't hang on and dropped to the floor.

He quickly tried again. This time he was able to hang on, but before he could swing himself up, Ryan ran into the room and pulled him down. Parker fell hard, which knocked the wind out of him.

"Where do you think you're going?"

As he gasped for air, Parker got to his knees, and when he didn't see a gun, he charged his head straight into Ryan's gut. In a rage, he threw him to the floor. "I told you, I don't know anything." Then he hit Ryan as hard as he could and ran down the hallway.

Allison must have heard the ruckus because she sprinted out of the next room in time to hit Parker in the back with her taser. He dropped to the floor. "Enough already! This is ridiculous. Since you won't cooperate, I guess we'll have to restrain you."

Ryan came sheepishly into the hall and dragged Parker back into the room while Allison went to get some rope. She tied his hands together and threw the rope over a rafter in the middle. Together, she and Ryan pulled Parker's arms up until his toes barely touched the floor.

"There, some time stretched out like that should make you talk," Allison said. "If not, we'll raise it."

She left the room, but Ryan stayed. He glared at Parker for a minute before saying, "I don't know why the boss won't let me kill you. You're not worth the trouble."

A moment later, Allison came back with her phone on FaceTime and held it where the boss could see Parker, but Parker could not see him.

"Nice little escapade, Mr. Jackson," he said. "I'm impressed by your tenacity, but I'm also getting tired of your foolishness."

Parker had barely recovered from the fall and his encounter with the taser but remained resolute. "Why should I cooperate? It seems like if you're going to this length to get information, you probably have no scruples about killing me. I'd say we're at an impasse."

"Still feisty, I see. That's not very wise in your current position. As you've heard my employees say: I'm the boss. You won't get my name or see my face, but you will answer my questions if you know what's good for you. Now, last chance, are you ready to tell me who you're working for?"

"Well that's going to be a bit of a problem," Parker scoffed, "because I have a nameless, faceless boss, too."

"Oh, so now you're trying to be funny. Well, let's see if this is funny. Ryan, let him have it."

Ryan showed no mercy as he used Parker's defenseless and already hurting body as a punching bag. He even hit him in the face a few times. Parker momentarily blacked out and his head fell forward.

"Ryan, that's enough. You've had your revenge. We don't want to kill him; we want him to talk."

"Yes, sir."

"Leave him to hang there. Eventually, the strain will take its toll on his body and he'll be begging for you to come back and take him down. Don't do it until he gives you his boss's name."

The haze cleared from Parker's mind, but he didn't lift his head so they didn't know he could hear them. Just then, he heard the door in the boss's office open.

A new voice said, "Hello, Davis."

"Stanton."

"We have a problem."

Allison quickly ended the call and left the room.

Ryan turned off the light and followed her. With Parker tied up, he didn't bother to shut the door.

A relieved sigh escaped as Parker struggled to catch his breath. *How am I supposed to appease them? I have no idea who I'm working for or why I took pictures of their buildings.* Sharp pain shot through his ribcage with each breath and his head hurt even worse. In desperation, he frantically pulled at the rope, but with his feet barely touching the floor, he had no leverage to free himself. In the darkness his thoughts turned to Stanton. *I wonder if this guy is Melissa's dad, and if he is, what does he have to do with Davis and what has them so worried?*

Chapter 19

UNLIKELY HELP

Matt found an empty table outside to wait for his order. He took a seat and read the text.

`'Stay at the Deli until I call.'`

That's odd. Maybe Parker couldn't figure out the latest pictures and I'll need to take more. When his phone rang, he was ready to answer. "Hello."

"Listen carefully; Parker's in trouble. Some bad people have taken him. Do not, I repeat, do not go back to the motel. The perpetrators left a man to apprehend you."

"Wait, Parker's been abducted?" Matt asked. "Please tell me you're kidding."

"This is no laughing matter. Now focus. You must do exactly as I say. After you get your food, walk west; a few blocks from here is a busy park. It will be a perfect place to disappear because the man at the motel will grow restless and come looking for you. He has your picture but doesn't know where you went. When you reach the park, sit on the bench nearest the fountain. Start reading your newspaper and wait for further instructions. If you get a call from Parker—do not answer." The call ended.

Matt's eyes darted around the crowd of people who were mingling outside the deli, but no one looked suspicious. That didn't stop the pounding in his chest or keep sweat from beading on his forehead.

"Here's your order, sir." The voice of the teenage girl caused Matt to jump. "Oh, I'm so sorry; I didn't mean to startle you." Then she noticed his countenance. "Is everything alright? You don't look so good."

It took Matt a moment to regain his composure. "Oh, uh, yeah, I'm fine. I just got some bad news."

She set his food on the table and said, "That stinks." Not knowing what else to do, she went back inside.

Matt quickly scanned the street. None of the bystanders looked suspicious, which helped to bolster his courage. Throwing his satchel over his shoulder, he scooped up the coffees, grabbed the bag of food, and hurried toward the park. Even though it made his flight more obvious, he couldn't keep from glancing back. So far, he was safe, but what about Parker? His mind raced to the worst possible conclusions.

Eight minutes later, sweaty and out of breath, he entered a large park. The fountain was nowhere in sight. His heart sank. After another quick look around, he got out his phone and brought up a map of the park. *There you are.* He followed the winding, paved path and reached the fountain without anyone in pursuit. Relief washed over him, but then evaporated as quickly as it came.

Matt's phone vibrated. `Stay calm. Help is on the way.'

This text didn't do much to bring him comfort. How would he know if the person meeting him was the guy on his way to help or the perp?

To shroud his stress, he opened the newspaper and pretended to read.

Several people passed the fountain before a tall, lanky guy with straight, blond hair that hit his shoulders came and sat on the bench. He wore sunglasses, holey jeans and a white T-shirt under an unbuttoned plaid flannel.

He handed Matt a St. Louis Cardinals baseball cap and a pair of clip-on sunglasses. "Here, put these on and let's eat. It seems a little weird that you're sitting here with food, but not touching it."

"Are you our mystery guy?" Matt tried to sound composed, yet the quiver in his voice betrayed him.

The man laughed. "No, I'm not your 'mystery guy' as you call him. He did send me, though. I started helping him about a year ago and occasionally he sends me on missions. He provides me with the info I need to help people who find themselves in situations that are outside their control, much like your involvement in rescuing the two girls back in Philadelphia."

This helped steady Matt's nerves; he didn't see how Parker's captors would know anything about that.

The man removed his sunglasses long enough to introduce himself. "My name's Joel—Joel Thomas. I received information two days ago telling me to meet you here at 11:45. Your friend Parker needs rescuing. You won't be able to save him alone, so I've been sent to help."

Joel opened the bag. "I'm guessing the turkey wrap is yours?"

Matt nodded.

Joel handed it to him and then got out Parker's roast beef sub and started eating.

Lunch was the last thing on Matt's mind; he needed answers. "Wait, so you're telling me there are more of us?" He seemed surprised.

This time Joel held back a laugh, but not his smile. "It would appear so."

Matt watched water splash into the pool below the fountain for a minute before turning to face Joel. "I guess that makes sense. I mean, I know there's nothing special about Parker and me. The thing is; I keep thinking we'll wake up and discover this was all a crazy dream. But now with Parker's life in danger and you sitting here, it's all too real. How do you receive your information?"

Joel finished chewing a bite of the sub and then said, "Eat and I'll explain. My messages show up on my computer. One night I was working on an app for a client of mine when, out of nowhere, a random code appeared. I thought I was hacked, so I cut the Wi-Fi and ran a quick security scan. When it ended without an issue, I restarted my computer. Before I even turned the Wi-Fi back on, the code still streamed across my screen. I was at a loss. I'm a computer programmer and know how to read code, but this was something I'd never seen before."

"Huh. We can certainly relate to that. I'd call our first few encounters perplexing." Matt's slight grin quickly turned into a bigger grimace. His thoughts went to Parker and he hoped Joel's story wouldn't take much longer.

Joel didn't seem to notice Matt's impatience. "Ha, perplexed. That's such a good word and an accurate description for sure! Well anyway, I hadn't seen code like that before, so I did a web search but couldn't find anything similar. It was quite late, and I was ready to call it quits for the night when my phone rang. Some guy asked me what I thought about the future of our industry. He went on to explain the purpose of the code and how to interpret it. Since I'm a computer geek, my first thought was that it would be an interesting challenge and I agreed to help the man.

"I followed his instructions and as soon as I had the last snippet of code aligned, it vanished, and a floor plan appeared with video links to a crime. It was then that I realized these encryptions contained information that could be used to help people out of difficult situations. Sometimes messages show up on my phone, like this one." He reached over and handed it to Matt. "It looks like a floor plan, probably of the building where Parker is being held.

"When the messages first started coming, it took me a while to figure them out and a few times I was wrong. That didn't make it impossible to complete my missions, but it did make it harder. That's why I'm not in a hurry right now. We can't afford to make a mistake this time. So we're going to finish our lunch and not panic. Good choice, by the way." Joel held up his sub and took another bite. "When we finish eating, we'll load this image onto my computer and determine the safest route to rescue Parker without getting caught ourselves."

They ate in silence. Joel crossed his legs and looked like he didn't have a care in the world. Matt, on the other hand, grew more anxious by the second and rapidly tapped his foot. He wasn't happy with Joel's cavalier approach and finally asked, "So riddle me this Batman, if you knew Parker was going to be in trouble before it happened, why didn't you come sooner . . . before it was too late?"

Joel gave Matt a sidelong look. "Because it's *not* too late," he said confidently. "This is all part of the process. Yes, it's hard. Yes, bad people who want answers are interrogating Parker. He's taken some blows, but he's strong and not giving in. The piece you're missing is the fact that there's more to this than rescuing or helping others."

"What do you mean?" Matt asked.

"Have you ever known someone who went through a difficult time and came out of it stronger?"

Matt's first thought went to Anna. She'd suffered more heartache than anyone he'd ever known; yet her care for others, despite her own pain, was exactly what Joel was talking about. He nodded.

"Have you thought about how the events of the last two weeks are changing you?"

"I guess not."

"Sometimes we have to stop and look inward before we can continue to move forward. Both you and Parker are at that point. This will not destroy you, but it will make you stronger. You will also gain important information that will help you finish the mission. People's lives depend upon our success and not just Parker's. I'm here to help you through this next phase," Joel concluded and finished his sub.

After a bit, Matt said, "I don't see how we can rescue Parker. It's not like we're Navy Seals or ex-Marines." He was too overwhelmed to be hopeful, and too numb to be scared. They had to do something and do it soon. "What good are your floor plans if we don't know where the building is?"

"Have a little faith, man. We'll figure it out. And don't forget, we have the element of surprise on our side. Now let's go; we have work to do."

Matt's phone rang. It was Parker.

❑ ❑ ❑

Parker struggled to breathe. The pain in his extremities grew. In that state of hopelessness, he heard the faint, inconsolable cry of a small child. Shock mingled with confusion as the crying got louder. A woman, whose voice he didn't recognize, was now yelling at it. *Why is there a baby here? What are they going to do with it? Hey, mystery guy, what's going on? I followed your directions and it got me here, strung up with no way out and no hope of helping that poor child.*

Sweat dripped down his face and arms. Exhaustion seeped through every muscle and into his thoughts. Parker knew there was no way to free himself. Each breath came harder than the last. *It's hopeless, and I'm a dead man.*

Thinking of the terrified child lessened the pain coursing through his body, but it also broke his heart. In desperation, he whispered a prayer. "Dear God, please help us both."

About a half hour later Allison flipped on the light and entered the room. Without speaking, she held her phone in front of Parker, who was wet with sweat, his breaths now short and choppy.

"Hello again," the boss said. "How are you feeling?"

Parker heard another man snicker before he answered, "I suppose if I could see your face, you'd be grinning. I'll play along; I'm doing great." He forced a smile through clenched teeth even though every muscle burned, and his head pounded.

"Nothing about your presence is funny, Mr. Jackson. However, we've made some progress toward discovering at least part of the purpose of your surveillance. Is that him?" The boss asked the man who had laughed.

"Yes, that's him. A friend of mine sent me his picture this morning. He said he was at Randy's Pub a few nights ago asking questions about Melissa Stanton."

"If you're Melissa's dad, do you dare show your face?" Parker goaded.

The boss cleared his voice. "See, I told you this guy is gutsy. He should be begging for his life, instead, he wants to see you."

"Allison, let him see me."

"Yes, sir." She hit the icon to switch the camera toward her and then turned the phone toward Parker.

"There, are you happy?" Stanton said with an arrogant smirk. "I'm not afraid of you. Even if we didn't have you in our custody, you have nothing on me. So yes, I'm Melissa's dad."

Parker looked at him for a minute. His mind raced, trying to find the right question in his current predicament.

"What, cat got your tongue?"

"You must be afraid that I know something, or you wouldn't have sent Ryan and Allison to find me."

"No, that just happened to be a lucky coincidence. What's the expression, 'kill two birds with one stone?' Except at the moment we only have one bird," Stanton quipped. "That is until you tell me where Melissa is. I miss my pretty little bird."

Parker shuddered at the implication and spat at the phone.

"Hey!" Allison pulled her phone back to wipe it off and accidentally hung it up. "What'd you do that for?"

"Your friend, Stanton, is a rapist," Parker said. "Abusing his adopted daughter was a favorite pastime of his until she couldn't take it anymore and ran away."

"So that's what this is all about? I thought it had to do with the children."

"What children?"

The look on her face revealed that she had said too much.

This was the first time Parker saw a chink in Allison's tough façade. "See, I know nothing. Can't you please let me go? You could tell your boss, and that pervert, Stanton, that I escaped."

"Oh right. What do you think would happen to me if I let you get away? Besides, I've never even met Stanton."

"You should be thankful for that; as pretty as you are, I'm sure he'd find a way to have you."

Allison's sneer returned. "Stop trying to change the subject. I'm not going to turn on my people."

"Now you're twisting my words," Parker said, trying to smile through clenched teeth. "I'm giving you some friendly advice. Keep your distance from Stanton."

"I know how to watch my back. It's you I know nothing about."

"Listen, this isn't my fight. I just want to get out of here and go home."

"You should've thought of that before you started spying on our facilities. We even caught you taking pictures of this place. That's when we realized we needed to find you. You obviously know more than you're letting on."

"Wait, are we at the abandoned factory by the river that I took pictures of earlier today?"

Allison glared. "See, you know too much."

"Actually, I don't. I just thought this building would look cool in black and white." Parker gasped for air. As he pushed up with his toes, he pulled on her emotions. "Why do you hate me?"

"I don't hate you." Allison looked away. "I just don't want to spend the rest of my life in prison."

"So what do you do with the children?" Anna's story flashed through his mind. "Sell them?"

Allison's head flung up. Fear shot from her eyes like fireworks.

Parker saw he hit a nerve, so he continued, "You keep saying you need answers, so I guessed. Apparently, I'm right."

Without warning, Allison pulled a gun on him. Parker winced, not realizing she had one. The tremble in her hand forced him to say no more. He didn't need her to hastily pull the trigger.

Ryan started upon entering the room. "Whoa, Allie, what's going on? And why do you have my gun?"

"He knows about the children."

"Only because you told me," Parker blurted out, now hoping to turn his captors against each other.

"Wait, you told him?" Ryan threw his hands onto his hips. "But why?"

"I thought he already knew, but even if he didn't, he knows now." The gun shook in Allison's hand as she kept it in Parker's face.

Ryan gently put his hand on hers and said, "Allie, put the gun down. Let's see what the boss wants us to do."

Parker knew time was running out. He had to give them something. "Listen, guys, I'm a photographer and I've been hired to find Stanton's missing daughter, Melissa. My friend just came along for the ride. When we followed the leads, we had no idea they would lead us to the dad or discover that he's doing something illegal."

"See? He knows too much. Stanton will want us to kill him." Allison rubbed her forehead.

"If he's after Stanton, why should we have this guy's blood on our hands?" Ryan asked.

"I agree. We don't have time to get all of our stuff out, but we could wipe the place down before we disappear."

"What should we do with Parker?"

"Leave him! If Stanton wants to come back and kill him, that's on him. You know as well as I do, we're expendable."

"Excuse me." Parker interrupted them. "If you're expendable, why not let me go? You know Stanton won't come back and I'll die of dehydration. Then if he gets caught, he'll pin my death on you."

The ringing of Allison's phone caused her to jump. "It's the boss."

"Put it on speaker," Ryan said. "He'll know what to do."

"Have you been able to get our captive to talk?"

"Yes, Parker knows about Stanton's shady past," Allison said. "I think he should take care of this problem seeing it's his fault we're in this mess."

"What's with the attitude?" the boss asked.

"I'm scared. You know Stanton has the power to bury us. It might be time for us to part ways."

"Are you crazy? This is a lucrative business and I've always been more than generous with both of you."

"And we're grateful for that, but if Parker gets killed, his boss will just send someone else."

"So you still don't know who he works for?"

"No. He figures he's a dead man, even if he talks, but he's willing to give his life to protect his interest. Something Stanton won't do for us. It's one thing to avoid getting caught when we take the children, but murder was never part of the deal."

"You're right and I'm sorry. Extenuating circumstances have forced our hand and we must make an exception this time. I don't like it either, but because he can identify you, it's for your own protection. Ryan, I need you to dump Parker and his Jeep into the Mississippi."

Allison pulled the trigger.

Chapter 20

THE STAIRWELL

Parker's smiling face filled Matt's lock screen.

"You gonna answer that or what?" Joel asked.

"I was told not to." He hit the button to end the call.

"Sorry, man."

"Yeah, me too." Matt waved his phone at Joel. "What if the people who took Parker decided to dump him along the side of the road or maybe he escaped and is trying to reach me? I should call him back."

"No, don't." Joel put out a hand to stop him. "You were warned for a reason. You can't feel bad about not answering." He got to his feet. "Come on, let's go find him."

They walked in the opposite direction from where Matt entered the park. Joel's car wasn't far from the entrance. He drove until they found a large plaza where he was able to park in between two bigger vehicles. "There, this should conceal us while we look at our info." Opening the floor plan on his laptop, Joel began to study it.

"You said you have a building's floor plan. Does it have an address with it?" Matt asked.

"Wow. You have no patience."

"Patience?" Matt whipped off his glasses and barked, "Parker could die, and you think it's okay to lecture me about having patience?"

"Whoa, dude. If you can't trust me, trust what you know. Like your ticket to Indianapolis or the fact that I met you exactly when I was told to. I'm here to help, man, so let me help. We'll figure this out."

Matt felt awkward around Joel and stressed about Parker. To keep himself from saying something he'd regret, he put his glasses back on and looked at the newspaper he bought. At first, he didn't notice the color, but when he did, he grabbed a pen and a small notepad from his satchel.

"Find something?" Joel asked with an air of 'I told you so.'

Matt rolled his eyes. Joel was a bit too smug for his liking. *Focus, it doesn't matter if I like this guy, I need his help.* "Yeah, see here? Random words in this article are now in red. It looks like an address."

"That's fantastic. While you figure out the location, I'll try to find a way to access the building."

It didn't take Matt long to pull the info together. He opened his phone and brought up a satellite view of the building. "I found it, and get this, Parker and I took pictures of this place this morning. I bet that's how they spotted us and were able to track us to the motel."

"Cool. Well, not cool that they tracked you and took Parker, but cool that you're at least somewhat familiar with the area. Do you happen to have your SD card with you?"

"I do." Matt fished his camera from his satchel, ejected the card and handed it to Joel. "I only took about three before my boss called, but I'm sure if we need more information it will be in these pictures."

"Great! Now you sound like you believe."

Maybe Joel isn't so much conceited as he is confident. He's been doing this longer than we have.

"Um, you have six pictures here and two different buildings."

Matt looked and then started shaking his head. "Do you see how crazy our clues are? I only took pictures of this building." He pointed to the bigger one. Then he looked again at the satellite image. "There it is! The other building is across the street." He held his phone out for Joel to see.

"Ah, now my floor plans make sense. I have two, but they didn't look like the same building. See this stick figure? That shows us where Parker is currently located. He's in a room on the back side of the second floor in the bigger building. We'll have to keep an eye on it to make sure they don't move him. The front entrance is too far from Parker; we'd get caught before we could help. The door on the back could work as a point of entry, but according to your picture, it's chained shut and all the windows are boarded over. We'll have to dig a little deeper to find a place of entry." Joel still seemed unfazed by the obstacles in front of them.

Even though Matt didn't expect a favorable reply, he still asked, "Is there anything interesting in the building across the street? I don't see why you'd need that building's floor plan if there wasn't a purpose for it."

"Hey, now you're thinking." Joel reopened both diagrams and placed them side by side. Matt leaned over to watch. Suddenly a line of code appeared, connecting the two buildings.

"So I'm guessing those numbers mean something to you?" Matt asked.

Joel nodded with a huge grin. "They sure do! It's our way in."

"Really? What is it?"

"It's binary for the word tunnel! The floor plan of the office has the stairs to the basement marked. Now that I know what I'm looking for, I see a stairwell that we can access once we reach the factory. That will be our way in. The perps will never see us coming. Ready?"

"Yes," Matt said confidently. He knew when they got there his nerves might falter, but for now, rescuing Parker was the only thing on his mind. "There's a parking lot behind the office. Hopefully, we can access the building without too much trouble."

Joel drove past the factory on the four-lane. He wanted to get a feel for how big the place was and the distance between the two buildings. Then he looped around the block and pulled behind the office as planned. Grass grew through the pavement and weeds surrounded the building, yet most of the windows in this one-story structure were still intact.

Joel grabbed two small flashlights out of his glove box and handed one to Matt. "Here, we're going to need these."

The building was locked. Too desperate to care, Matt found a pipe, busted the glass and reached through to turn the lock. Thankfully, no alarms went off.

"Whoa, power to ya, dude. Way to break and enter." Joel smirked as he passed him. "Now, let's see what we see. There will be a hallway to our left and the third door should be the stairway to the basement."

The floor creaked with every step, magnified by the silence. Sun streamed into the open space to their right, where cubicles formed what must have been a large office. "This place doesn't look that run-down. It might even have been rented more recently than the closing of the factory," Matt said, more as an observation than an important discovery. Talking aloud seemed to help calm his nerves.

The hallway wasn't far from where they entered, but the further they walked, the darker it got, adding to the eeriness of the situation. When they reached the right door, Joel pushed it open. A cold, damp draft and total darkness met them. They turned on their flashlights and made their way down the concrete stairs. Rats scurried into the shadows as they reached the floor.

"Now where?"

"The floor plan shows a passage on the back wall. I'm guessing this is how the managers used to access the factory without having to cross the highway. Look for a door."

Scrap metal, wire, and old furniture cluttered the space, making it difficult to maneuver. "Should we move some of this stuff, so it doesn't slow us down on the way back?" Matt asked.

"No time. We've got to find the door, or it won't matter." Several minutes passed and neither of them had found the passage. "Check the side walls. It has to be here somewhere." For the first time, Joel sounded concerned. From what Matt could tell, he had no plan B. To make matters worse, time was ticking and neither of them had any idea about Parker's current condition.

Matt searched the wall opposite of Joel. He pushed a table out far enough to shine his flashlight behind a pile of scrap steel where he spotted a door. "Here it is. Quick, help me move this stuff." They hurried without worrying about the noise they made because they were too far away from the other building for it to matter.

Once they pushed the door open, Joel said, "Sweet, this is it. Let me show you the plan to make sure we're both on the same page." He held out the phone for Matt to see. "Parker's icon hasn't moved, so that's good. This passage brings us to the back corner of the other building. The five offices located over there are all on the second floor and along the back wall. See how there's a narrow hallway in front of the offices?"

"Yeah, I see it. How don't they know about this stairway?"

"They probably couldn't get the door open and didn't worry about what was on the other side. Anyhow, when we reach the second floor, Parker will be in the second room. His captors most likely will be in one of the rooms down the hall, closer to the main staircase that they use to access this area. Let's hope our timing is good and that Parker is alone."

Matt whispered a prayer.

Though the passage was clear of debris, the light from their small flashlights got swallowed up by the sheer volume of cobwebs. It was obvious that no one had walked through there in years.

"Hold up," Joel said. He stepped back into the basement and grabbed a few old broom handles. He handed one to Matt. "I admit, I'm not a fan of spiders."

Ha, I guess he's not so bad after all. "Good call."

"Thanks." Joel took the lead.

Several minutes passed before they reached the other end of the tunnel. "Before we open this door, should we turn off our flashlights until we see what's on the other side?" Matt asked.

"Yeah, there's no sense in drawing unnecessary attention."

Once both their lights were off, Joel turned the handle. The door opened without difficulty or much noise. All they found was more darkness, so they flipped their lights back on. To the left and the right were concrete walls. Straight ahead of them, but further than expected, were the stairs.

They quietly made their way to a landing and then turned to go up to the first floor. Once on that level, they saw a solid metal door with rusty hinges and a big lock and chain.

Great, Matt thought, *that doesn't look very promising.*

The further they got from the tunnel, the hotter the stairwell became. More than once, Matt had to wipe sweat from his brow to keep it from running into his eyes. He wondered if Joel could hear the pounding of his heart.

Neither dared speak as they made their way to the next landing. Then the darkness that had followed them gave way to a faint glimmer of light.

They quickly turned off their flashlights.

"Whew. Thank God for that small window," Joel whispered. "I wouldn't want to enter the hall blind."

Matt nodded, thankful for the poor lighting so that Joel couldn't see the fear in his eyes.

When they reached the door, it had both a deadbolt and a combination lock. Joel cautiously looked through the window. He could see the full length of the hallway and counted five doors. "It looks just like the floorplan. And if I remember correctly, there were three random numbers below the binary code." He quickly pulled his phone from his pocket. "Here, hold this where I can see it."

Matt took the phone and held it by the lock, which also gave Joel a little extra light. He was surprised to see Joel's hands shake as he quietly turned the dial. When he pulled on it, the lock didn't release. Joel blew out a short breath, wiped his hands on his shirt and tried again. It still didn't open.

Joel slumped to the floor. "Maybe this isn't the combination."

Bam!

"Whoa." Matt instinctively ducked and then pressed his body against the wall. "We're too late." When he heard no more shots, he slipped onto the top step and buried his face in his hands.

"We don't know that for sure."

Matt was too distraught to answer. *No, Parker can't be dead. Please God, don't let Parker be dead.*

Joel slowly stood and peeked through the window. "Hey, a man and a woman just left the room Parker's supposed to be in."

Matt moaned.

"Quick, hold the phone close, they just went into the next room." Joel spun the dial a few times before starting. He leaned close and carefully turned the dial to the first number and then back the other way. He took a deep breath before moving to the final number. This time it opened. Joel pumped his fist. "I'd say the lock not opening the first two times was a blessing in disguise."

Matt didn't share in Joel's enthusiasm. "Don't you think we should go to the police?" He shuddered at the thought of what lay beyond the door.

"There's no time. They might've just inflicted a flesh wound to get him to talk. And anyway, it's not over till it's over and if it's not over, we still need to rescue Parker."

"How are we going to do that? They have guns."

Joel didn't bother to answer. He removed the lock and set it beside the door. He stole another look before sliding the deadbolt. "The hall's empty. Let's go."

Opening the door as quietly as possible, they quickly crept down the hall and into the fated room unnoticed.

Parker gasped.

"You're alive!" Matt's courage redoubled. "Are you shot?"

"No. I'll explain later," Parker murmured. "The hook that holds the rope is behind me."

Joel went to pull the slip knot, while Matt wrapped his arms around Parker's waste to keep him from collapsing to the floor. His legs buckled and he still went to his knees. With teeth clenched, he fought to stifle a cry. Pain shot through his ribcage; short breaths were all he could manage.

"You're hurt," Matt said as he removed the rope from his wrist and Joel came to help him up.

"Just give me a second." Parker sat back on his heels and flexed his fingers.

"We don't have time to wait," Joel whispered.

"He's right." Matt helped swing Parker's arm over his shoulder. Joel got on the other side and together they got him to his feet. "We saw two people go into a room down the hall. If they heard you fall, they could be here at any moment."

Joel let go to peek out the door. "No one's coming, let's go."

Matt helped Parker down the hall and into the stairwell.

Joel closed the door behind them, slid the deadbolt, and secured the lock. "That should keep them at bay . . . at least for a bit." Without waiting, he took off down the stairs.

Parker stumbled on the first steps, his legs still rubber. Thankfully, he caught the railing. "Steady now," Matt said, giving him a hand.

"Quiet back there!" Joel snapped.

"How about you give us a hand then," Matt barked back. "Parker needs help."

Joel came back and together they slowly made it down the dark stairwell. By the time they reached the bottom, they heard the echo of a heavy banging from above. Matt flinched. "They're onto us."

"Not necessarily," Parker said. "They probably just discovered I'm gone, and that door would be the first place to check."

They hurried as fast as they could into the tunnel and Joel quickly shut the door. "I hope your right, but there's nothing here to use as a barricade, so I say we run!" He turned on his flashlight and took off.

Matt got his light out, too, but stayed to help Parker.

"Go. I can make it." With fresh adrenaline coursing through his body, he followed close behind Matt. They reached the office basement with no one in pursuit and slammed the door behind them.

"Help me shove this table back in front of the door and let's get out of here," Matt huffed.

Parker made his way up the stairs while they moved the table. Moments later they were hard on his heels, all running for the back door. Joel passed Parker and looked out to make sure the coast was clear. Then he motioned for them to follow him. They rushed out and climbed into his orange Fiesta.

Joel quickly spun the car around, throwing loose gravel in all directions.

"Slow down and think!" Parker yelled. "If you peel out of here, it will draw unwanted attention and those people mean business." He lay down in the back seat.

Matt followed Parker's lead and ducked below the dash.

In typical Joel fashion, he took the time to put on his sunglasses and then pulled out at a reasonable speed. But as soon as he was on the four-lane, he gunned it, leaving the factory, and hopefully the perps, behind him. Ahead of them were signs for the Interstate, so he headed toward it and within minutes they had disappeared into heavy traffic.

Parker, exhausted and still shaken by the day's events, didn't bother to sit up. "Matt, how did you not get caught? They left a man at the motel to apprehend you."

"Our guy sent me a text when I was still at the deli. While I waited for my order, he called to let me know what happened and directed me to a park. Joel, here, met me at the designated location and we worked together to find you." Matt looked back at Parker with a huge grin. "I can't tell you how relieved I am that you're alive."

"That makes two of us." Parker winced as he mustered just enough strength to sit up. "And Joel, it's nice to meet you. I can't believe you guys risked your lives to save me. Thanks."

Joel smiled into his rearview mirror and said, "No problem, man. Now, how about we stop and get you something to eat? Then you can tell us what happened."

Dried blood matted sections of Parker's beard and his shirt was stained, too. Purple bruising surrounded his left eye, and his cheeks were still red and swollen from Ryan's revenge. "Okay, but can you go to a place that has a drive-thru? I hurt everywhere and don't want to be seen in public."

"You got it."

After a short silence, Parker said, "I certainly didn't expect this kind of rescue, Matt. I thought maybe if you were safe and figured out where I was, you'd send the police."

"To be honest, I didn't think about going to the police until after we heard the gunshot. By then, there wasn't time—" Matt's voice trailed off as he pondered the reality of his own actions. A smile crept into the corners of his lips.

Joel kept an eye on his rearview mirror. When he didn't see anyone following him, he took the next exit and followed signs to a fast-food place. As soon as he had the order, he drove down a side street.

Parker took the bag Matt handed him but didn't open it. He let out a heavy sigh as a tear rolled down his cheek.

"Hey, what's going on?" Matt had never seen Parker cry.

Chapter 21

IT'S TIME

Parker cleared his throat. "These people traffic children."

"Seriously?" Matt winced. "That makes me sick."

"Me too." Another tear slid down Parker's cheek. "I even heard a child crying."

"What?" Joel hit the brakes hard enough to throw them all forward.

"Whoa, what the—" Parker grabbed the back of the seat with one hand and his ribs with the other. "Ugh! Man, that hurt."

Joel whipped the car into an empty spot along the street and swung his head around. "Sorry, dude, but we gotta go back and save the kid. That's what we do."

Parker blew out a quick, painful breath. "Ahem. We could, but remember, they have guns and we don't. Also, if we save the child, the top guys will simply relocate and keep selling children. They're the ones who need to be put behind bars. The people who kidnapped me are just puppets."

"Yeah, well, they're still guilty of deplorable crimes." Matt's words dripped with disdain. "Stealing the children and destroying innocent families is indefensible."

"I never said they shouldn't pay for their offenses, but that's the point; they will take the fall while the big fish go free. The gunshot you heard was to get the boss off their backs. I should be dead."

Joel shuddered. "And we're glad you're not. So, what are you thinking?'

"Take the whole outfit down at once."

Matt flipped his hands upward. "How do you expect us to do that?"

"I don't. It's time to go to the police. I'm hoping they'll catch these people during the adoption."

"Did you hear them say where?"

"Yeah, the office we took pictures of this morning. But that might have changed now that you guys rescued me."

"If the boss thinks you're dead, I doubt your captors would admit you escaped," Joel said. "Not yet anyway."

"I hope you're right." Matt reached for a pen and paper. "When?"

"Three o'clock."

Matt looked at his watch. "We need to go now. Joel, how about you head back toward the city while I find a police station near number 437."

"You got it." Joel checked his mirrors and then started back toward the city. "Do you think the police will believe you?"

"I would hope so." Parker stretched his hands over the front seat so Joel could see the rope burns. "These, along with my bruised face and bloody shirt should be enough to get their attention. We also have an address for the office and the abandoned factory."

"Well, there's only one way to find out." Matt punched the address into his app and then held his phone toward Joel. "Here you go. I found a police station within four blocks of number 437."

"Oh, and get this," Parker said, "Stanton, yes, Melissa's 'dad', is helping them. He was one of the older men in the picture that had them so worried."

"But how do you know that?"

187

"The older men never came to the factory. Davis, the guy they called boss, played it safe and wouldn't show himself. Stanton, on the other hand, wanted to see me. A friend of his had sent him my picture from the pub in Memphis. They called Allison on FaceTime. When Stanton realized I was the same guy, he admitted he was Melissa's dad. The tone in his voice was incredibly arrogant so I goaded him to show himself. He took the bait. But then, he probably figured I was a dead man so it wouldn't matter."

Matt rubbed his chin. "Wow, I figured there was more for us to learn in St. Louis, but never in a million years would I have thought we'd catch Stanton doing something illegal."

"Right, and if he gets convicted for the child trafficking, Melissa won't have to stay in hiding."

"That'd be wonderful!"

"And there's one more thing you should know. These people own the building I photographed in Memphis, too."

❑ ❑ ❑

By the time Parker finished his story, Joel had already pulled into a visitor parking spot at the police station. He and Matt followed him inside. They were met by two, armed security officers who asked the purpose for their visit. After a short explanation, they stepped through the metal detector and were escorted to a room that served a dual purpose on the second floor. There was a conference table with chairs to the right of the door and a desk with a computer and three different monitors against the wall to the left.

It wasn't long before two officers entered the room. The older gentleman sported a dress coat and looked a bit younger than his white hair implied. He wore wire-rimmed glasses and had a protruding waistline. The other man was short and stocky with dark brown hair. Muscles bulged from under his tight dress shirt and he looked to be in his mid to late thirties.

"Hello, I'm Captain Smith. This is Lieutenant Reade," the older gentleman said as he reached to shake Parker's hand. "You say you were abducted?"

"Yes, sir. My captors thought I had information about their illegal activities, so they brought me at gunpoint to an abandoned factory."

"Well, did you?"

"Did I what?"

"Have information on their illegal activities?"

"No, I'm a professional photographer and happened to take pictures of two of their buildings. That's when they got worried."

"You didn't know the buildings were connected in any way?" the Captain asked with a wary eye.

"How would I? One of them is an abandoned factory."

"Okay, if you were taken at gunpoint, how did you escape?"

"Matt and Joel," he pointed with his thumb, "figured out where I was and rescued me."

The Captain turned toward them with furrowed brows. "That was a bold move, but not very wise. Why didn't you come to us first?"

"Our only thought was to free Parker," Matt said. "We knew we hadn't done anything wrong so we figured it couldn't be that serious."

"Yeah, and we didn't know they had weapons until after," Joel interjected. "Once we heard Parker's story and realized what these people were involved in, we came straight here."

"And what exactly is that?"

"They steal and sell children."

Captain Smith did a double-take at Parker's candid answer. "Can you prove this?"

Parker nodded. "I discovered they sell children when they were interrogating me. I even heard a child crying at the place I was being held. They weren't very careful about what they said because they had every intention of killing me. These guys came just in time."

"We'll get to your rescue and take everyone's statements in a minute, but right now I need the location of the place you were held so we can go save the child."

"We have that address, but they won't be there. The adoption is to take place at 3:00 this afternoon."

The Captain looked at the big clock above the door. "We don't have much time. Did you happen to get the address of the drop-off point?"

"I didn't hear them say an address, but they said they would proceed with the sale as if nothing had changed." Parker handed Captain Smith a piece of paper. "Here, the top address is for the office building I took pictures of this morning. I believe that's where you'll find them."

"And the other address is where they held the baby?"

"Yes, sir."

The Captain quickly glanced at the addresses before handing the paper to Lieutenant Reade. "We only have about forty minutes; bring up a satellite image of these buildings and send them to my computer."

While he did that, Smith asked Parker a few more questions. "Reade, it sounds like we better get a search warrant first."

"Yes, sir. I'll start that now and get it sent to Judge Miner's office ASAP. The info you requested has already been emailed."

"Thanks. I'll call the judge to explain the urgency for the warrant. Gentlemen, excuse me. I've got work to do."

As soon as the Captain was gone, Parker asked Reade, "When you're finished with that, can you find my Jeep? It has an electronic tracking system."

"I can. This won't take much longer."

While they waited, Parker gingerly took a seat and rested his arms on the table.

When Reade finished, he faxed the warrant, and then spun his chair toward Parker. "What's your license plate number and the tracking code?"

Parker wanted to come watch, but he couldn't muster the strength to move, so he wrote the info down and gave the paper to Matt. He brought it to Reade and Joel followed.

A few minutes later, Reade pointed to a red dot on his screen. "There it is. Here, I'll put it on the big screen, so Parker can see it from over there." With the click of a button, they all watched the red dot move while Reade pinpointed the location. "It's not far from the factory."

"I don't get it," Joel said. "Shouldn't that dot be on a road? All I see is a few buildings and the river."

"The Jeep isn't on a road," Reade said. For a moment the dot stopped. Then it moved rapidly toward the Mississippi. Less than thirty seconds later, the signal was lost.

Parker's face flushed. "Oh man, they really did it. They really dumped my Jeep." He flopped back in the chair and immediately grimaced. Caught up with losing his vehicle, he had momentarily forgotten about the beating he took earlier. "Oh well. At least this proves my story is true."

"Yes, and we also know where to find your Jeep," Reade said. "It's become a valuable piece of evidence for our case."

"And even better, you weren't in it." Matt grinned at Parker.

"Yeah, thanks to you and Joel."

❑ ❑ ❑

It wasn't long before the Captain returned with another officer at his side. "I put my best undercover agents on this case. They're staking out number 437 even as we speak."

"That was fast, what about the warrant?" Joel asked.

"The Judge signed it and faxed it back shortly after Reade sent it."

"Sweet."

Matt walked to the table. "Now what?"

"Now we wait." The Captain looked at his watch. "In the meantime, Parker, go with Officer Rodrigues here." He pointed with his thumb. "He will take pictures of your face and wrists and get your official statement. He has the right to determine if you should be taken to the hospital for further examination."

"Wait, Parker," Matt said. "What's the password to your cloud account? Shouldn't we show them the pictures from Memphis?"

"What does Memphis have to do with anything?" Smith asked.

Parker looked from Matt to the Captain. "I took pictures there a few days ago." He wrote down the username and password and gave it to Reade. "My captors told me that I took pictures of their building in Memphis, too. Look for a file called Memphis."

Reade opened the file. "There are several pictures here. What am I looking for?"

Parker slowly got to his feet and came to look. "Open the ones with vehicles in them. Notice how both have out of state license plates; one from Missouri, the other from Texas. If you enlarge the plates, you should be able to read the numbers."

Reade got the number from the Porsche first and ran the plate in the Missouri DMV database. "The vehicle is registered to a William Davis who lives here in St Louis."

"Makes sense," Parker said. "The guy, my captors called *the boss*, is named Davis. Now, if you go to the next picture, you'll see a young couple walking from the same office with a toddler. Unless this is a legitimate adoption agency, I believe you'll find another stolen child."

Reade punched in the plate number and brought up the name and address of the couple from Texas.

The Captain looked at the pictures for a moment and then turned to Parker. "It's hard to believe that you have this much information, especially when you told me you weren't even investigating this group."

"I'd say it's a lucky break. We were following leads to find Stanton's missing daughter."

"Who's Stanton?"

"One of the other top guys. We had no idea that either of these buildings had anything to do with Mr. Stanton or the trafficking of children," Parker said.

"If we can take down this ring, it will be *more* than a lucky break." The Captain looked hopeful. "Do you have an address for the office in Memphis?"

Parker reached for his phone and sighed. "I don't remember, and I can't look. Are there any street signs in the photo? The building was in East Memphis."

Reade stretched the image. "I don't see any signs, but the building next door has a name on it. I'll look for their website and get the address that way."

"Once you have the location, see if the same Davis owns either of these office buildings. Even if he doesn't, bring him in for questioning." Captain Smith abruptly left the room.

"Hey, where'd he go?" Joel asked.

"To contact the FBI. Memphis is out of our jurisdiction. Parker, go with Officer Rodrigues." After they were gone, Reade handed Matt and Joel some paperwork. "We need to get an official statement from each of you, as well. The form has several questions. Answer the ones that are applicable and then give a detailed description of how you rescued Parker. When you're done, I'll take you to the lounge."

The room fell silent as the men filled out their reports. When they finished, Reade had them sign the affidavits and then he put them in the appropriate file. "There, now that we have that done, follow me."

The officer's lounge was only two doors down. Reade didn't bother to enter, but he did let them know they could help themselves to the coffee or, if they preferred, water and sodas were in the fridge.

"Thanks Lieutenant." Worry suddenly creased Matt's brow. "But can I ask you a question before you go?"

"Sure."

"What are the chances that the top guys get convicted?"

"If we catch them in the act of selling a child this afternoon that will be huge."

"But I doubt Stanton or Davis will even be at the office, especially since they don't know who Parker's working for."

With shoulders squared, Reade placed his hands on his hips. "Yeah, about that, who *are* you working for?"

"We don't know. We've never met the man and he paid us through the sale of Parker's photography."

"Huh, well that's a first. Do you know why the girl went missing?"

"Yes. Sexual abuse."

Reade cringed. "Her father?"

"That's what we were told by the people who knew her personally. None of them have seen or even heard from Melissa in years."

"I should let the Captain know this Stanton guy is guilty of more than trafficking children."

"I hope you can convict him."

"It's too soon to say, especially since we don't know how much evidence we'll be able to gather. But because Parker was abducted and he talked to Stanton and Davis, we should be able to link them to the kidnapping charges as well."

"Yeah, but then it will be Parker's word against theirs. Stanton is a lawyer, and apparently pretty good at manipulating the law in his favor. Melissa ran away because she knew she couldn't beat him in court."

Reade bit his lip. "This story just keeps getting worse, but at the moment, I can't give you any assurances and I have work to do." With that, he nodded and hurried down the hall.

Joel grabbed a soda and took a drink before getting comfortable on the sofa. "I think it's cool that this mission has become about so much more than *finding* Melissa. It's clear she doesn't want to be found; so technically you're not doing her any favors unless Stanton is put away for good."

"Ah, right, where he can't ever hurt her again."

"Exactly." Joel grinned as he got out his phone and started surfing the web.

Matt brightened at the thought and went to get himself a cup of coffee.

A moment later, Reade popped his head through the door. "I thought you should know that Parker was taken to the hospital."

"I'm not surprised," Matt said. "He took quite the beating. Thanks for telling us."

"No problem." And just that quickly, Reade was gone again.

Matt took a seat at the table and began to contemplate the day's events, both amazed and grateful that things turned out the way they did. He smiled at the realization that he had actually helped *save* Parker's life. *If only Haley could see me now.* At that thought, a stab of pain shot through him and sadness started to invade his mood. To keep dejection at bay and force his thoughts elsewhere, he got out his phone and began a search for articles about the building on Chestnut street.

No one spoke for a long time. Finally, Joel broke the silence. "Man, all this waiting is hard."

"It sure is." Matt got to his feet and went to look out the door. When no one was in sight, he started pacing the room. Occasionally, an officer or two would come in, but none offered any information, nor did they stay long.

❏ ❏ ❏

It was over two hours before Parker returned. "Any word yet from Captain Smith?"

"Not yet, but how are you doing?" Matt asked.

"Better. They took x-rays and found I have a few cracked ribs, which they wrapped, and then they hooked me up to an IV. I knew I was weak, but I didn't realize I was that dehydrated."

"Makes sense," Joel said. "You didn't touch your lunch or drink before we came here, and Matt mentioned that you didn't have breakfast either."

When the conversation ended, Matt got out his journal and started writing down the day's events.

Joel got out his phone and went back to surfing the web.

As for Parker, the pain meds had started working, so he lay on the couch and quickly fell asleep.

So much time had passed that Matt finished his story and was again pacing the room. "Joel, do you think our information was wrong?"

"Why do you ask?"

It seems like if they were able to catch these guys, we would've heard something by now, that's all."

"With the way you get your information, it's not likely. And anyway, it's such a big case, I'm sure they're just being extra thorough."

A few minutes later, Lieutenant Reade popped his head into the room. "We have news. Captain Smith will be with you shortly."

Matt walked over to Parker and gently touched his shoulder. "Hey, the Captain is coming."

Chapter 22

THE STING

"Ow!" Parker yelped. His whole body screamed at him when he sat up too quickly.

"Settle now, there's no hurry," Matt said. "Captain Smith isn't here yet."

Parker didn't move again until the door opened and, only then, did he straighten himself but a little.

"Well men, everything went down just as we hoped it would. My people have also confiscated a treasure-trove of evidence."

"That's fantastic!" Matt pumped his fist. "And were you able to rescue the child?"

"Yes. We allowed the perps to finish the transaction and let the couple drive away with the child before my people moved in. We had other officers ready to stop the family. They had no idea that this wasn't a legitimate adoption agency."

"I know it stinks for them, but the real parents will be ecstatic." Matt's smile was priceless. "Have you notified them yet?"

"Slow down with the questions, we're as excited as you are, but it's not that simple."

"What do you mean?"

"Unfortunately, it might take some time to locate them. The children are usually stolen from other states, so it makes them harder to find."

"Where's the child now?" Joel asked.

"We've taken him to the hospital to make sure he's not been hurt in any way. We have the suspects in a holding room, now let's hope they cooperate. The sooner we can return the child the better for everyone."

"You know, Captain," Parker said, "I'd love to be a fly on the wall when the real parents get their boy back."

"It will be a glorious day for them, for sure . . . and it's all because you were willing to come in. Most people in your situation would've been too afraid to get involved."

"It broke my heart to hear that frightened cry. There was no way I could worry about my own safety over the safety of the child."

"Well, this city owes you a debt of gratitude."

"What about the factory?" Matt asked.

"It was empty, but our timing was good—the first officers to arrive saw a vehicle leaving the crime scene, so they pursued. We have those two in custody. The rest of my officers searched the place to make sure no one else was there. Once we got the 'all-clear', I sent in the forensic team. They will be there for a while because apparently there's a lot of stuff to process."

"Yeah, I was surprised to see that at least one room was furnished. Were my camera equipment and laptop still there?" Parker asked.

"No. We found those in your Jeep. I doubt any of it can be salvaged and even if it can be, it will be kept here for evidence."

"Wow, when did you have time to get the Jeep?"

"I didn't. Reade is the one who sent a crew with a crane to pull your Jeep from the river." He turned to face Matt and Joel. "Reade also sent your accounts of Parker's rescue to the officers at the factory. They found the tunnel."

Joel grinned. "Pretty cool, huh?"

The Captain's smile vanished, and his tone became unexpectedly harsh. "To be clear, you and Matt are fortunate you weren't caught or killed. It would've been safer and wiser to come to us first."

"Yes, but if we did that, you wouldn't have caught these scumbags in action," Joel countered.

Before the Captain could reply, an officer knocked. "Excuse me, sir. We have the lineups ready."

"Great. Parker, come with me. You need to see if any of these people were your abductors."

Parker took his time getting to his feet. While he did that, Matt and Joel were told they could leave.

"I'll wait," Matt said. "I'm with Parker."

"I'd like to stay, too, if you don't mind," Joel added.

"Okay, you can stay here."

The Captain brought Parker to a long narrow room with one-way glass running the length of one wall. On the other side of the glass, six men were lined up and facing toward them.

"Do you recognize any of these men?" Captain Smith asked.

Parker pointed. "The third from the right is the man who took me at gunpoint. His name is Ryan. His partner is a woman named Allison." A few minutes later they brought in a row of six women. "Allison is second from the left." Parker turned to face the Captain. "Just so you know, even though Ryan gave me quite the beating and these two are obviously a part of a criminal enterprise, they didn't kill me when the boss told them to. Allison was on the phone with him when she pulled the trigger. Davis thinks I'm dead. I didn't make a peep and when the call ended, I asked her why she did that."

"What'd she say?"

"'I'm not going down for murder.' They were planning on leaving me there though, so it's a mercy that Matt and Joel found me."

"Well, as far as being in trouble with the law, stealing and selling children isn't much better. You, on the other hand, are a lucky man to have such good friends. Though I still don't understand why they didn't come to us first."

"At that point, I'd only been missing for a few hours and I'm a grown man. Would anyone here have actually dropped everything to come look for me?"

Smith bobbed his head thoughtfully. "You're probably right, especially seeing how Matt and Joel didn't realize how dangerous these people were. How'd they figure out your location, anyway? And, even more, how'd they know about the tunnel?"

Parker was thankful the Captain asked the second question, so he didn't bother to answer the first. "Joel's dad is a manager at a factory up north. His plant has a passageway under a highway, similar to what he hoped they'd find here. That info is probably in his report, but from what I know, they broke into the office building and looked for the tunnel. I'm sure if there wasn't one, they would've come to the police."

Smith shook his head. "Well, it's quite remarkable that so much good is coming out of this terrifying situation. We have another lineup ready. I don't know if you'll recognize this guy, but we might as well be thorough."

When they brought out six different men, Parker wasn't surprised that he had seen one of them before. "The man furthest to the right is the same guy I talked to in Memphis a few days ago. He told me to leave and threatened to call the police if I didn't."

"That's ironic." The Captain cracked a crooked smile. "I'll pass this information on to the FBI."

"What about Davis and Stanton? Have you caught either of them yet?"

"So far, Stanton has evaded us, but we have a BOLO out for his arrest. It's only a matter of time before he's apprehended. We have Davis in interrogation. I don't usually listen, but because I've been more involved in this case, I want to hear firsthand what he has to say. I'm going there now."

"Can I come?" Parker asked like a kid who just won a prize at the fair. "I'm the reason you caught him in the first place."

Captain Smith furrowed his brow. "You already know that you can't, so why'd you even ask?"

"Just a little excited, that's all. Sorry. It's clearly more important to convict this man than to watch him squirm now."

"Exactly. We will contact you with a court date as soon as we have one. You and your friends will need to testify."

"We look forward to that."

"Good to know. I'll have Reade escort you back. You are free to go."

❑ ❑ ❑

Matt and Joel jumped to their feet when Parker and Reade walked in. "Hey, guys, we get to leave."

"Sweet!" They said in unison and everyone laughed.

"Thanks again for coming in," Reade said. "I know it's been a long day for all of you, but I hope you realize it's been worth it."

"Totally," Joel said.

The Lieutenant shook each of their hands before crossing the room to get a cup of coffee.

As they got ready to leave, Matt smacked Joel on the shoulder. "Thanks for helping me rescue Parker."

"Yeah, though a simple 'thanks' doesn't seem like enough," Parker added.

"You guys don't owe me anything. I was happy to help."

"In a strange, reassuring kind of way, it's good to know that there are more of us out there. Maybe someday we'll be able to repay the favor."

"I hope not," Joel said with an expansive grin. "But seriously, it was fun working with you guys." He started for the door, but then turned back. "Hey, do you need a ride to the motel or something?"

"Oh right, I don't have a vehicle."

Lieutenant Reade hadn't left the room yet so Parker asked what they were supposed to do about transportation and if he thought it would be safe to go back to the motel.

"Sorry, with all that's going on, I forgot to tell you; we have your things here. The motel is a part of the crime scene. The Captain sent officers and a forensic team there earlier. Leaving a blood trail was brilliant."

Parker nodded with a half-smile. "Not like it was hard—I couldn't get my nose to stop bleeding. Oh, and what about replacing my Jeep?"

"After we retrieved it from the river, I had one of my people submit a criminal claim and damage report to your insurance company. You'll need to call them to work out the rest of the details. For now, we can help you get a rental." Just then the Lieutenant got a call. He held up a hand, motioning for the men to wait. "Okay, Captain . . . Yes, sir . . . I'll let them know."

"Know what?" Parker asked, as soon as Reade was off the phone.

"There's been a change of plans. I need you all to come with me." He led them back to the conference room. "The Captain is still listening to Davis's testimony. He should be here shortly."

Matt shoved his hands into his pockets. "Should we be worried?"

Reade shrugged. "I have no idea. Please, take a seat and we'll find out together."

Several minutes passed in silence before Captain Smith entered the room. He took a seat at the head of the table and let out a heavy sigh. "Sorry to keep you longer. Davis said a few things that made us believe it might not be safe for you to leave."

"So apparently he knows I'm not dead then?" Parker said.

"Right and he's not a happy camper. Stanton's still out there and at the moment we don't know how many other people are involved."

"Have you arrested a man named Vincent?"

"No, why?"

"They left him to wait for Matt, so that makes at least two of them."

The crease in the Captain's brow deepened. "Davis spewed a whole lot of anger. I'm sure if any of his cohorts find Parker, it will be kill-on-sight. We're not letting anyone in our custody go on bail."

All three men started speaking at once, but Captain Smith held up a hand to stop them.

"Reade, arrange for these men to stay at our safe house tonight."

"Yes, sir." With a nod, Reade left the room.

"Isn't this a bit of overkill?" Parker asked. "I mean, how would they even find me?"

"They found you once and it's a risk we're not willing to take."

"But they have no way to track me."

"Your phone wasn't in the Jeep, so they have all your contacts and know where you live."

"A safe house sounds good to me," Matt said. "At least for tonight."

"Parker, you'll need to warn your family. If they can't get to you, they could go after them to smoke you out."

Parker shrugged. "That won't be necessary. I haven't talked to my parents in years and I don't have a number or address for either of them on my phone. The only relative I have contact with is my uncle and his family, but they're currently stationed in Japan."

"How about you, Matt?"

"My parents live in Philadelphia and Parker has their numbers on his phone."

"Yeah, but not their last names or address." It had been a long day and Parker sounded more defensive than he meant.

"Well, that's good," Smith said. "Matt, you should still call your parents and tell them what's going on. If they get a call

203

from Parker's phone, or from a number they don't recognize, tell them not to answer. To be on the safe side, have them also turn off location services. We don't know how big this group is or how many connections they have, but we do know how serious they are about protecting their interests."

No one doubted the severity of the situation. Matt had already talked to his mom earlier in the day but was eager to give her an update, so he stepped into the hall.

The Lieutenant returned. "Excuse me, Captain. When you're through here, we're set to take these guys to the safe house."

"Okay, thanks." He turned to Parker and Joel. "We'll know more in the morning. Good night."

After Captain Smith left the room, Reade said, "We need to swing by evidence so we can get your things that were left at the motel. Parker, we'll have you put on a clean shirt and keep your bloody one here. Then I'll have my deputy take you to the safe house. Follow me."

"What about my vehicle?" Joel asked.

"For tonight, we'll keep it here."

Chapter 23

A LOUD CRASH

The men were exhausted after their long and stressful ordeal. A secure place to sleep was a welcomed relief.

The safe house had two bedrooms upstairs, reached by an open staircase. The smaller room held one twin bed. The other was larger with a full-sized bed on one wall and bunks on the other. They all decided to use the bigger room and encouraged Parker to take the bed. With his cracked ribs and a splitting headache, he didn't argue.

Once they were settled in, Matt said, "Hey, Parker, do you think Anna is in danger, or is there anyone else in your contacts that we should warn?"

"No. When Allison looked through my photos, none of them had extra images or clues. I'd wager that my contacts were either empty or altered somehow. I know I can't prove that, but I'm not concerned about your parents or Anna."

Matt grimaced as he pulled out his phone and opened it to recent calls. "Here, look. Earlier today someone called me from your phone. Our guy told me not to answer if I got a call from you."

"Oh, you better get ahold of Anna then. While you do that, I'm going to take a shower."

Matt nodded and took a seat on the couch.

"See you guys in the morning," Joel called from the stairs. He didn't wait for an answer but climbed onto the top bunk and fell asleep.

❑ ❑ ❑

About 2:00 in the morning, Parker woke to a loud crash. Bolting upright, he grabbed his ribs and stifled a cry. "Hey, guys, did you hear that?"

Matt didn't answer.

Joel propped onto his elbow. "Yeah, what was it?"

"I don't know, but wake Matt up and get dressed. I'm going to go look." Parker threw on some jeans and went downstairs. A nearby streetlight cast a dim glow into the space, giving him enough light to get around without knocking anything over. He didn't see or sense movement in the house, so he stood to the side of the front window and peered out. From there he could see the unmarked cruiser parked in between a few other cars further down the otherwise lifeless street. This was comforting, but he still went to the kitchen to look out the back door. All was quiet.

Fear, mixed with stress from his recent abduction, caused every muscle to tense in his already aching body. Slowly, he walked back upstairs and said, "Matt, can I use your phone?"

"Sure, it's on the nightstand."

Parker called the Deputy on duty. "Hey, uh, we just woke to a loud crash. Have you seen or heard anything?"

"I sure did. It was the funniest thing. A dog was chasing a cat and to escape, the cat ran between two garbage cans. The dog plowed so hard into those empty cans they went flying."

"Ha, that's good to know."

"You have nothing to worry about. Try to get some sleep."

When he hung up, Matt asked, "Is everything okay?"

"Yeah. Apparently, a couple animals were making all the racket." He handed Matt his phone. "Sorry to wake you."

"No worries. Better to be safe than—"

Just then, two blasts shattered the front windows and exploded inside the house. All three men went flying.

"Holy crap," Joel said as he scrambled to his feet and ran to the door. The hallway was a ball of flames and part of the floor was missing. "We're trapped!" Slamming the door, he ran to the window and forced it open. "The porch roof is close. We can make a jump for it. Hurry."

Parker helped Matt to his feet, and they made it to the window. Fire had already burned a hole in the wall and the room was filling with smoke.

"Go, go, go!" Joel cried. He seized a blanket and tried to beat back the smoke and flames while Matt and Parker climbed out.

"Forget about it, Joel," Parker shouted. "Let's go!" Smoke gushed through the window. "Quick, give me your hand." Joel popped his head out, choking and gasping for air. Flames licked at his heels. Parker grabbed him by the back of his shirt and pulled him out. Neither could sit and catch their breath because the roof was starting to burn. Clambering to the edge, all three jumped.

Parker let out a piercing scream as he rolled to his feet.

"You okay?" Matt yelled from the bush he landed in.

"Yeah, it's just my ribs reminding me they're cracked."

"Joel, how about you?"

"I twisted my ankle."

Parker ran to help him. "Here, put an arm around my shoulder." Together they hobbled as quickly as they could toward the back. Matt had freed himself and was just ahead of them.

As they rushed toward the fence the gas line exploded and the rest of the house blew up. The blast threw them all to the ground again and they were hit by flaming debris.

Joel let out a shriek and fell silent.

Parker lay motionless.

Matt rolled onto his back with a groan. "Hey, are you guys hurt?"

Neither answered.

Sirens blared and flashing lights filled the street, so Matt started yelling, "Help! Help! Somebody help us. Men down. Help!"

It didn't take long for a firefighter to come running into view with his headlamp on.

"We're back here."

When he saw them, he radioed for assistance. Then he knelt by Parker first and felt for a pulse. "Good, he's still breathing. I can't believe you guys had time to get out."

"But what about Joel? Is he alive?" Matt had gotten himself to a seated position.

Before the fireman had a chance to answer, three medics were at their sides.

□ □ □

Matt lay on his left side in a hospital bed in the ER. He had burns on his back and arms, along with a gash on his right calf. A piece of debris had torn through his jeans.

Two nurses came in with a cart full of supplies and started tending to his wounds.

Despite his own pain, he asked, "Where are Parker and Joel? Are they okay?"

"I don't know," the older nurse said. "We can check later, but right now we need to get these burns cleaned so they don't get infected."

The younger nurse cut the gauze from Matt's leg. "Ooh, that's nasty. A doctor will need to see this one." She added some fresh gauze and then hurried out.

A few minutes later, she returned with more supplies and a doctor.

"What about Parker and Joel?" Matt asked again.

"I heard they were both taken to surgery. We won't know more until they're out," the doctor said as he leaned in to get a better look at Matt's leg. "I'll give you some Novocain around this gash to help deaden the pain while I clean it."

"Okay, thanks." Matt squeezed a fistful of sheet and clenched his teeth. Though pain riddled his body, it was his frayed nerves that caused tears to spill out when he closed his eyes.

He had no idea how much time had passed from the time the doctor and nurses left him to when Lieutenant Reade popped his head through the curtain. "Can I come in?"

"Sure."

"I don't usually make hospital calls, but this is simply too bizarre. How are you doing?"

"How do you think I'm doing?" Matt snapped. "I'm freaked out and in a lot of pain. And so far, no one's told me anything about Parker and Joel."

"I just came from the nurses' station. They said Parker was fortunate that his ribs were wrapped. Apparently, it slowed the momentum of a sharp piece of shrapnel that just missed his lung. He needed that and some other pieces of debris surgically removed from his back, shoulders, and right arm."

"No burns?"

"Oh, he had burns, but I assumed that was to be expected." Reade pointed to the bandages on Matt.

"What about Joel?"

"They said he's still in surgery, so I don't know. And for what it's worth, I'm impressed that you were able to get out before the house blew to pieces. Most non-trained personnel would have panicked or froze."

Matt winced. "We have Joel to thank for that. He took charge and made sure we both got out before saving himself. I hope he's going to be okay."

"Me too." Reade sighed and then pulled up a chair.

"It seems like this nightmare is never going to end. Did you catch the monsters that did this?"

"The officers watching the house called for backup and pursued them. They blew out the back tires, and after a short standoff, they got the men to surrender."

"Are they connected to Stanton or Davis?"

"Maybe, I don't think they've had a chance to interrogate them yet. I offered to come straight here to check on you. The Captain doesn't know how the safe house was compromised. He sends his deepest regrets."

"Originally I thought the safe house was overkill," Matt said. "An unnecessary precaution, but now, it's clear that someone wants us dead."

"This has certainly become more serious than any of us expected."

"Have you found Stanton yet?"

"No, but we've cast a big net. He'll have to surface at some point."

"Let's hope that's soon." Matt eased onto his back and adjusted the cold pack that was on his forehead.

"Excuse me, Lieutenant." A nurse joined them. "We've already admitted Parker and want to keep Matt for the rest of the night too. The doctor feels this would be the safest place to keep them for now. Do you have an officer who can stand guard?"

"Yes, ma'am." Reade pointed to the man in the hall. "Conley will stay. He's already here and been instructed to allow *no* visitors."

"Thank you. We can also help with that." The nurse smiled as she left the room.

Reade turned back to Matt. "I'm going to leave, too. Try to get some rest."

They moved Matt to the other bed in Parker's room. The steady hum of monitors eventually lulled him to sleep.

Later that morning the doctor stopped by to check on them. After asking a few questions, he had the nurse explain how to tend their wounds. "Because you plan to leave the area, you'll need to have a medical professional check them to make sure you're not getting an infection within the next few days."

"We can do that, sir. Thank you," Parker said.

"What about Joel," Matt asked. "Can he come with us?"

"No. His injuries are no longer life-threatening, but he needs continued medical attention. We'll keep him here for at least two more days, maybe longer."

"Do you mind if we stop by his room to see him before we leave?" Parker asked.

"At the moment we have him sedated. He might be up for company tonight. I suggest that you call before coming. Now I have other patients to attend to." With a nod, the doctor left the room.

The officer on duty was instructed to bring Parker and Matt to the Precinct as soon as they were discharged. On their way, Parker leaned his head against the window and closed his eyes. Exhaustion, along with two life-threatening encounters in less than twenty-four hours, had taken its toll on him.

To take the focus off himself, he turned to Matt, who was fidgeting with the corner of his untucked shirt. "How are you holding up?"

He shrugged. "Alright, I guess. To be honest, I think I'm probably still in shock. It helps to keep my mind on the mission. If we haven't learned anything else, we certainly know why Melissa was so afraid of Stanton."

"Yeah, it will be interesting to see if he's the one who hired these heavy hitters."

"That or Davis got the word out to some of his men." Matt shuddered. "I wonder what else they're trying to hide that's worth killing for."

"My guess is revenge. With their records seized and being caught red-handed with a stolen child, they have no other recourse."

❑ ❑ ❑

Captain Smith and Lieutenant Reade were already in the conference room when they arrived.

"Gentlemen, please have a seat," the Captain said. "I'm sorry we didn't do a better job of protecting you."

Parker sat and rested his bandaged arms on the table. "Who would've known taking pictures could be such a dangerous thing?"

"They would've been better off by ignoring you, but it's too late for that now. We were able to press our bombing suspects and discovered that they were hired by an anonymous source that paid in cash."

"Probably Stanton," Matt muttered. He'd been leaning on his crutches.

"But how did these guys know about the safe house?" Parker asked.

"Two of the three men have criminal records and they all run with one of the more powerful gangs in the city. They wouldn't disclose how they knew about the safe house."

Without warning, Matt blurted out, "Is Stanton still out there?"

Reade got to his feet and motioned for Matt to sit. "We'll find him, I promise."

"For now, we have to piece together the safehouse crime scene and get your official testimonies," Smith said. "If the money trail leads back to Stanton, he will also be tried for attempted murder."

Reade turned on the recording device and said, "Tell us how you had time to escape."

"Because we happened to already be awake and dressed," Parker said.

"In the middle of the night?"

"Yes, sir. Not long before the blast, we heard a loud crash outside. I called the deputy on watch and he said the noise was caused by neighborhood animals. He was even joking about it.

"Thankfully we were in a bedroom on the back side of the house and, though it threw us all to the floor, Joel quickly got to his feet and shut the door. That didn't keep the flames at bay for long, but enough that we could climb out the window."

Smith jotted something on a notepad. "Huh, so basically it was bad timing by these guys; otherwise you would have all been asleep—"

"More like dead," Matt snapped. His hands visibly shook. "And I'm not leaving this building until I know Stanton and his cohorts have been apprehended."

"You've been through quite an ordeal and no one blames you for being upset," the Captain said, "but we need to finish getting your statements. When we're done, we'll find a quiet place for you to lie down. Sleep would do you both some good."

❑ ❑ ❑

Reade came into the lounge later that afternoon and found Parker and Matt sound asleep. He woke them and then gave them a few minutes to get their bearings before saying, "Stanton has been apprehended by the FBI. He was caught trying to board a plane in Memphis under an alias. It was the same alias that was on the paperwork we seized from the Memphis office before anyone had a chance to destroy it."

"That's a relief." Parker slowly got to his feet. "Man, I hurt everywhere."

"Ow." Matt struggled to sit up and had to use his hands to swing his leg off the couch. "Me too."

"Sorry I can't ease your pain, but I have some interesting news. Stanton withdrew the exact amount of money yesterday that was given to the men who blew up the safe house."

"Interesting indeed. I didn't think he'd be that careless." Parker said.

"It was from an off-shore account. He probably didn't think we'd be able to find it. We now believe that Davis also knew about the safehouse. He manipulated his testimony during the interrogation in hopes that we would have you stay there."

"Right, because if we left town in a rented vehicle as planned, they wouldn't have been able to find us. Now what?"

"No one knows you got out alive, so they won't be looking for you."

"Nice. It will be fun to see their faces when we all show up at the trial." Matt finally smiled, put on his glasses, and then used the crutches to hoist himself to his feet.

"Can someone give us a ride to the rental place?" Parker asked.

Captain Smith had come and was leaning against the door frame. "Of course."

Parker turned to face him. "We plan to continue our search for Melissa, so we're not going straight back to Philly. Can I keep the rental for a week, or should I see about replacing my Jeep today?"

"After all you've gone through and the help you've been to this city, I'll personally pay for the rental for as long as you need it," Smith said. "It's the least I can do."

"Oh sweet. Thanks."

The Captain laughed. "Come on, I'll escort you out."

"I have one last question before we leave," Matt said. "From what you know about the Stanton case, when we find Melissa, can we let her know she's finally safe?"

"We have a lot of physical evidence tied to Stanton. Trafficking children is a federal crime. Both Ryan and Allison are looking for plea deals and have turned on Stanton; not to mention Parker's abduction and the attempted murder at the safe house. I'm confident that he'll never hurt anyone else ever again."

"Great, because at this point, we want him to be put away as badly as Melissa does."

"I can't blame you there. Let me know if you find her and if I can help you in any way, don't hesitate to contact me."

"You got it." Parker reached to shake Captain Smith's hand.

"Rodrigues will take you to pick up your rental. I've called ahead and secured a blue Jeep Wrangler for you."

Parker grinned.

Chapter 24

LOUISVILLE

Rodrigues had already backed the car around and started to pull away from the precinct when Reade came running out.

"Hey, hold up," Matt said.

Rodrigues stopped and lowered his window. "What's wrong, sir?"

"Nothing." Reade hesitated to catch his breath. "I have a temporary driver's license for Parker. He can't get the rental without it."

"Oh right." Parker reached to take the paper. "That never crossed my mind."

"It's good for thirty days so you should be all set."

"Thanks."

❑ ❑ ❑

The paperwork was ready for Parker to sign when they got to the rental place. As they walked out to the Jeep, he said, "We should stop to see Joel before we leave town."

Matt agreed and called the hospital. Once he talked to the doctor, he relayed the information to Parker. "Joel's stable, but they still have him sedated. We'd have to wait until tomorrow before we can see him."

"That's going to be a problem because I don't care to spend another night in St. Louis."

"Neither do I! I think he'd understand, and we can call him tomorrow to see how he's doing."

"And who knows, maybe we'll have another lead by then." Parker adjusted his rearview mirror and pulled away from the rental place. "Do you mind if we stop at a mall? We don't even have a change of clothes."

"Yes, to new clothes. I'm glad I kept my wallet in my pants' pocket at the safe house. Now we at least have some money for our trip home."

"I'll be sure to reimburse you too."

"I wasn't worried about it, but thanks. I thought it was nice of Reade to give us these T-shirts from the precinct." Matt pulled on the front of his. "It will be a good reminder that I'm braver and more adventurous than I realized."

"You most certainly are." Parker nodded. "These events have stretched me too. My biggest adventure before this was climbing Mount Rainier. That seems small in comparison."

"Ha, I'd settle for a mountain. It's crazy how much traumatic events can change a person because even after all we've gone through, I'm more determined than ever to help find Melissa."

"Glad to hear it. And speaking of finding Melissa, have you heard from our guy?"

Matt grabbed his phone. "Huh, good thing I checked. This text came in seventeen minutes ago. It says, 'Head to Louisville.'"

"He couldn't say, *thanks*, for almost getting us killed?" Parker quipped.

Matt's phone immediately vibrated, and he busted out laughing. "Here, look." He held the phone so Parker could see.

'THANKS! ☺'

"Are you happy, now?"

Parker shook his head. "Well, I think it's safe to say he has a sense of humor."

"Yeah, this was pretty great!" Matt lowered the phone and keyed 'Louisville' into the GPS.

"Don't forget to find a mall."

"Okay, but I'll look for one out on Route 64. I'd rather get farther away from St. Louis before we stop."

"Me too!"

Neither spoke for a while.

After a bit, Matt asked, "Did you have any idea that we came here for Stanton?"

"No, but then I didn't expect to be abducted either." Rope burns were still visible on Parker's wrist. The black and blue around his eye and cheek were changing to a ghastly yellow.

"Or eerily close to being blown to pieces," Matt said. "I hope this is the last of our conflict for a while. It wasn't any fun."

"Yeah, I'm not a fan. Neither is my aching body." Parker glanced Matt's way.

"What?"

"Now it makes sense why our guy had me wait to come to St. Louis. He knew I'd need your help."

"Lucky me." Matt patted his injured leg.

"I'm serious. If you and Joel didn't risk your lives to rescue me, I'd be dead, and Stanton's people would continue to sell children. You're a hero in my book."

"Uh, no—I was scared half to death."

"Do you think I wasn't scared? Being scared comes with being human. I'm impressed that you didn't let it stop you."

"Yeah, well, desperation is a powerful motivator. I'm just glad we got there before they changed their mind about killing you."

"You and me both." Parker smiled. "I do find it interesting that our guy wanted the police to already have charges against Stanton before we find Melissa. Though I'm not sure why we had to go through these painful ordeals—"

"Well for one, we weren't *given* all the details. You discovered valuable information through your abduction. And for two, it added validity to our story when we went to the police. Even the safe house explosion will give the prosecution leverage to show how coldblooded Stanton is and that he belongs in prison." Matt raised his bandaged arms. "And though these wounds and burns hurt, they will heal. I hope we find Melissa soon so we can give her this wonderful news."

❑ ❑ ❑

Matt found a mall in Fairview Heights.

There was a kiosk near the entrance, so Parker got his phone first and then they went to buy clothes and some other necessities. This took a while and Matt's leg was throbbing.

"How about we get something to eat while I elevate my leg for a bit."

"That works. It will give me a chance to download my contacts onto my new phone. Then we still need to buy cameras and at least one laptop."

"Yes, to a laptop. It's hard to view our photos from the camera screen."

Forty-five minutes later, Parker was thrilled to see the store had the camera he wanted in stock. He also purchased a few different lenses to replace the ones he lost.

Matt bought a camera and a laptop. Then they decided it was time to get back on the road.

On their way out to the Jeep, Parker asked, "Are you up to driving? My back hurts worse when it rubs against the seat and this will give me a chance to check out my camera."

"My leg's going to hurt either way, so I'd love to drive. Here, throw me the keys."

No one spoke for the first half hour or so, but after Parker put his camera away, they started talking about everything that had happened since their mystery guy first called.

Once the conversation started to die down, Matt said, "Well, on a different note, I have news. While we waited for you yesterday, I looked for information about the building on Chestnut Street and came across an article written in July 1995. It was the feature story in the Philadelphia Business Journal that month. The building is two adjoining structures owned by the

Walsh Corporation. The bigger side was a thriving hotel and the tall, skinny building had an Irish Pub on the ground floor and the owner's personal residence on the second. The top two floors were a part of the hotel and housed their luxury suites. The hotel had a four-star rating and the pub was a popular hangout for tourists and young professionals."

"Sounds like solid info, but you're no closer to finding out what caused the business's demise, right? I bet it was something drastic—like maybe a death in the family."

"Possibly, but that doesn't seem like a reason not to sell. Especially after all these years."

"What's your boss want in the article?"

"He figures with a little digging we could find out what happened. Learning the owner's story and sharing it in the paper would at least help the community to understand the hold up."

"Or show steps are being taken to remedy the problem."

"Exactly. From what I could tell, the Walsh Corporation still owns it. Because the taxes have always been paid, the city can't legally make them sell. A committee that supervises the upkeep of the historic district is putting pressure on the city to force the owners to at least get the building looking respectable on the outside."

❑ ❑ ❑

It was late when they reached Louisville. As soon as they got to their hotel room, they were happy to call it a night.

Parker woke to the sound of a text.

'Take pictures at the Louisville Slugger Museum. Go now.'

"Hey, Matt, get up. We've got work to do."

"Huh, what's that?" Matt mumbled as he rolled over. "Did you get a text?"

"Yeah, and we're supposed to go now. I'll find the address while you get around."

Matt limped into the bathroom and splashed some cold water on his face before getting dressed. He was ready to leave within minutes.

"Whoa." Parker looked up from his phone. "What's gotten into you? I've never seen you move that fast and you even have a bum leg."

"Ha. Well, that's because I have a good feeling about this." Matt threw his camera bag over his shoulder and grabbed his crutches. "Where to?"

"The Louisville Slugger Museum."

"Cool, I've never been there."

They weren't surprised that the Museum was closed when they arrived and assumed their guy had a purpose for that. They were impressed with the gigantic baseball bat that leaned against the five-story brick building.

"That bat must be at least eight stories high," Parker said before crossing the street. He hoped from over there he would have enough room to get the whole bat in his first few pictures.

"They weren't kidding when they tout that it's the world's biggest bat. Like anyone else would need a bat that big." Matt laughed.

"True. But now, how about you get your camera out and start helping. This early morning light is causing some cool reflections in the windows."

When they finished their photo shoot, they went back to their hotel, eager to see what their new leads would be. Matt loaded the pictures from both cameras onto his laptop and started scanning through them. Like always, most of the photos had no extra details. Eventually, he came to an image that had changed. The large circular area of gray bricks under the bat became a large bowl and the bat became a giant wooden spoon.

"That's interesting." Parker tipped his head to see if there was any writing on the spoon. "Any ideas?"

"Sure, it's a giant bowl of soup, but let's see if we have any other clues before we start guessing."

Parker couldn't tell if Matt was kidding or serious, so he didn't reply.

The next picture showed more of the glass windows from the museum and, in the reflection, there was a line of people entering the building behind them.

"I thought this might happen," Matt said. He switched to his pictures. "I took a few of the building across the street because I knew there would be reflections. This way we can be sure if it's the same building or a likeness of somewhere else."

"You're getting good at this, thinking like a real detective. Maybe you should change careers." Parker pulled up a second chair so he could see better. Matt's pictures of the building across the street looked nothing like the reflection in Parker's picture. "Enlarge my photo with the people in it so we can see if there are any road signs or a name on the building."

"I don't see any words."

"Neither do I, but we both took more photos, so keep looking."

Matt scrolled until he found one with a girl standing in front of the bat. Zooming in on her face, they could see she looked like an older version of the healthy Melissa in the school yearbook.

"Is she here? Have we found her?" Matt asked.

"Maybe, but we still don't know where she is."

"Well, let's think about the clues. We have a bowl and spoon and a line of people in front of a building. Remember how we thought our guy had an obsession for missions, but it turned out that Melissa came to the one? This looks like a line to a soup kitchen." Matt spoke way too fast. "How can you not be excited when we're this close?"

"Probably because I've been here before. She could've come to this soup kitchen years ago and is long gone."

"But she's healthy and looks closer to the right age."

"True, but what if this is just another step? Another part of the story?"

Matt rolled his eyes. "I don't see any harm in being hopeful. If she's not here, we can cross that bridge when we get to it."

Parker gingerly sat back in his chair. "I appreciate your enthusiasm, especially after the traumatic experiences of the last two days, but if she's here and doing well why would she need to be at a soup kitchen?"

Matt turned back to the picture. He rolled his thumb over the touchpad while tapping his foot.

When Parker realized Matt wasn't going to answer, he did. "I get it. I want to find her too. I just think we need to be prepared for what we might find. So far we haven't had much good news on the Melissa front."

"But that can change," Matt said adamantly. He stopped tapping his foot and looked at Parker. "Even though it was hard, good things resulted from the last few days. I say we're on the upswing, so I wish you wouldn't spoil the moment."

Parker stood and leaned against the desk. "I'm not trying to spoil anything. I'm only suggesting that we save our excitement for when we're sure. How about we do a search of old buildings in Louisville and see if we can find one that matches our picture."

"Or it might be quicker if we look for soup kitchens," Matt suggested.

They both got out their phones. Parker punched in 'old buildings in Louisville' and clicked on images. While he scrolled through those, Matt looked for 'soup kitchens.'

He found four soup kitchens in the city and opened the first site. Their building looked nothing like the reflection in Parker's picture, so he went to the next site. "Hey, look, I found it."

Parker looked at his phone and then at the photo on the computer. "Nice work."

Matt saved the location on his phone and then used the desk to pull himself to his feet. "Are you ready?"

Chapter 25

SOUP KITCHEN

Matt was almost to the door before Parker said, "Hold up! We need to give this some thought." His words stopped Matt cold. "If we do find her today, what are you going to say?"

"What do you mean? We'll talk to her, of course." Matt looked surprised by the question and miffed at the delay. *What's his problem?*

"It's not that simple. Think about it. We know a lot about Melissa and her past, but she knows nothing about us."

"But we have good news for her."

"And why should she believe us? For all she knows, we could be making this story up to gain her trust. She'll probably accuse us of working for her dad."

"That's crazy."

"Is it? We know that's not the case, but she doesn't. Give me one good reason why she would even talk to us?"

Matt frowned. Slumping against the door, he let out an exaggerated sigh. This wasn't what he wanted to hear. He rested his hurt leg in front of the other and started drumming his fingers on his crutches. His mind raced as he searched for answers, but none came.

"Another thing to take into consideration," Parker said, "is that we don't even have all of the pieces yet. For example: who are her real parents? The only news we can give her is that her adoptive dad is in trouble with the law. At this point in her life, she probably doesn't care and wishes nothing more than to forget about her past. And, if she's still on the street, needing a soup kitchen, how's that going to help her?"

"Wow, that's heavy." Matt limped back and took a seat on the edge of his bed. "Why didn't you bring this up sooner?"

"I just thought of it. We've been so wrapped up in what we know that we never considered how Melissa would respond. I think we need to plan a few different ways to approach her, you know, depending on what we find."

Matt clasped his hands together over his knees and stared at the floor.

Parker walked to the window. Neither spoke.

Several minutes passed before Matt sat up and said, "I never gave her real parents a thought. I just hoped we could find her. We'd hear her story and she'd be happy to know her adoptive dad could no longer harm her. I guess I assumed by now that she'd be doing okay. What if she's not okay? What do we do then?"

"I have no idea." Parker came back to the desk. "But now that I've had time to think about it a little more, I don't expect our guy would have us finding her today if we can't be of some help to her."

"Well then, I say we go check out this lead. We won't know any more until we get there."

They exchanged a hopeful look and left to find the soup kitchen. When they arrived, people were gathering out front, some sat on benches and others on the curb. No one was going into the building.

Parker tried the door. It was locked.

A younger woman holding a child on her lap said, "They don't open for lunch until noon."

"Oh, okay. Thank you," Matt said.

"Will someone answer if we knock?" Parker asked.

The woman only shrugged.

Parker knocked. No one came. He looked at his watch and knocked again, louder this time.

An elderly, black man opened the door just a crack and said, "Lunch will be served in a half hour. Please be patient."

He started to close the door, but Parker stopped him. "Wait, sir. We need to ask you a question. Could you please give us a minute of your time?"

He gave Parker a quick scan and then said, "I suppose I have a minute. Come in."

As soon as Parker and Matt stepped inside, he closed and relocked the door.

They found themselves in a large, open room. The entire space was filled with tables and chairs. At the far end, there was a serving area where volunteers were setting up for lunch.

"Times-a-ticking. What can I help you with?"

"Hi, um, my name is Parker, and this is Matt. If you don't mind me asking, have you worked here long?"

"For over ten years. My name's Roy." He reached out to shake Parker's hand and added, "I started serving on a daily basis after I retired five years ago."

"Glad to hear it—maybe you can help me," Parker said. He held out his phone and showed Roy their most recent picture of Melissa. "Has this young woman ever been here?"

Roy took the phone and looked closer at the photo. He narrowed his eyes as his hands began to shake. "Ahem, uh, why do you want to know?"

Parker locked eyes with Roy. "We're trying to find her. Please, can you help us?"

Matt watched Roy, wondering what he was looking for. No one was sure how to proceed so he finally broke the silence. "We know about Melissa's past and why she ran away. We're not here to harm her."

"This is not Melissa," Roy said coldly as he handed the phone back to Parker. "So, I guess I can't help you."

Noticing some of the ladies looking their way, Parker whispered, "She goes by the name of Jordan, right?"

The man's head shot up as if startled by that name. One of the women, a heavy-set, middle-aged woman, must have overheard their conversation because she joined them.

"Roy, is there a problem?"

"No. These guys were just asking about a girl. But we can't help them."

Parker's phone was still open and seeing it, the woman asked, "Can I please look at the picture?" Then with bulging eyes, she snapped, "What's going on? How did you get this picture?"

Matt answered, "It's kind of a long story, ma'am. Is there somewhere we can talk?"

The woman didn't know how they acquired this personal information and felt threatened by their presence. Her first inclination was to demand that they leave, but she then realized it might be wiser to find out who they were and what they wanted.

"Does part of your story include those?" She pointed to their bandages.

"Yes, ma'am."

"Maybe later, but right now we have work to do. Can you guys stay to help us serve lunch and clean up? I'll have time to talk then."

"We sure can." Matt reached to shake her hand. "This is Parker Jackson and I'm Matt Howard. Just show us what to do."

"My name's Rita. Follow me." She introduced them to the others and then gave them jobs.

They gave Matt a stool and tipped a wash bucket upside-down so he could elevate his leg a little. For the next three hours, everyone worked well together. Parker and Matt cheerfully greeted and served those in the food line and helped wipe down the tables. They stayed until everything was done.

Rita had gone into the kitchen, so Matt said to Roy, "This is a great place. Thanks for allowing us to help."

"We never turn down help, young man. I told Rita I would stay with her while you talk."

Thankfully, his tone had softened. He even smiled.

Rita called from the kitchen door, "I put on a pot of coffee. Would either of you like some?"

"Yes, please," they said in unison and came to serve themselves.

"Are you guys trying to get brownie points? You're both charming. By the way, your help was a godsend. A few of my volunteers called in sick, so thank you." Once they all had their coffee, they sat at one of the tables nearest the kitchen. "Now, how did you get that picture and why are you asking about her?"

They had previously agreed that Parker would take the lead, so he answered. "You must know Jordan. Is she well?"

Rita nodded stiffly.

Parker wondered if she was second-guessing whether to trust them, so he was grateful for the nod. With a warm smile, he continued. "Finally, good news!"

"Thank God!" Matt pumped his fist.

"Yes. Until now, all we've learned about Jordan has been disheartening. Knowing she's alive and doing well makes our story easier to tell."

Their reactions seemed to set Rita at ease and they both noticed the glint in her eyes. She sipped her coffee and then said, "Please continue. We're all ears."

"I assume that you're people of faith, but even to you, this is going to sound crazy and impossible. Once you hear our story, I think you'll realize that you have nothing to fear from us."

It took Parker close to an hour, with Matt chiming in occasionally, to explain the pictures and their ordeal. They knew Rita and Roy didn't need every detail, but enough to gain their confidence.

"You're right, it's a good thing we have faith—otherwise this would be hard to believe. And yet, I do believe you," Rita said with a jovial laugh. "No one would even bother to make this kind of story up, let alone have that many actual details. Your account of Hope Mission House in Indianapolis is spot on. If Stanton hired you, he wouldn't have known those details. Do you feel there's a strong enough case against him that he won't be able to get off on a technicality?"

"Captain Smith in St. Louis believes they have enough evidence to put him and his team away for good."

"Right. None of them have been given bail due to the nature of their crimes and their attempt to murder us," Matt said. "Now, can you please tell us about Melissa—I mean, Jordan? How do you know her?" He leaned over his coffee mug and looked expectantly into Rita's eyes.

"Yes, I'll tell you, but first let me express my deepest gratitude for what you've suffered on behalf of a girl you've never met." Tears slipped from Rita's eyes. "What was it, Roy, almost five years ago that she showed up in the food line?"

"Yes, it was shortly after I started working here full time. She was one scared and messed-up teenager."

"I usually work in the kitchen and didn't hear about Jordan initially. Many of the people who come here are homeless, so she didn't stick out in the crowd, and she only came sporadically at first. But after a few weeks, she came and asked one of our volunteers if she could stay after and help clear and clean the tables in exchange for a place to wash up. She was so dirty. Her hair was a ratty, two-tone mess and she had dark bags under her bloodshot eyes. The volunteer got her a bucket of soapy water and she stayed until every table was clean. Then the same volunteer brought her to our staff bathroom and gave her some soap and a clean kitchen towel since we didn't have bath towels on hand. After a few days of this, I pulled her aside and asked her where she lived. At first, she wouldn't say much. I could tell it was more from a lack of trust than not wanting to. It took about two more weeks of staying to wash tables and my reaching out to her, before she began to open up. She had run away from home, was out of money, and living in a closet in an abandoned building. She said she'd lived there for months."

Matt shook his head. "Such a heartbreaking situation."

"It most certainly was. At that point, I didn't know the details you just gave me, but I was drawn to the girl and the next time she came, I asked her to stay. Jordan said she was scared and didn't know who to trust. I told her not to worry about that. We could talk later. I had brought a bath towel and some shampoo from home and invited her to the kitchen where she could use the big sink to wash her hair. She even let me help her brush it out. It was then that Jordan burst into tears, sobbing uncontrollably. Seeing her like that broke my heart and I held her for a long time. I also told her to bring her clothes, that I'd be happy to wash them for her.

"That night my husband, Frank, helped me look at the missing person's database and we found her picture—Melissa Stanton. She went missing in April and there was a number to call if anyone had information. Not knowing the details, we wanted to hear her side of the story before we did anything. We prayed that Jordan would be open and honest with us.

"She was back the next day with all her earthly possessions in a dirty duffel bag. She again stayed after to help wash tables and she said she was ready to tell me her story." Rita paused to sip her coffee and deliberately looked at each of them before continuing. "Her story is why we needed to make sure we could trust you. Anyway, that afternoon I brought her home with me. I washed her clothes and let her take a shower. While we waited for her things to dry, she told me the bone-chilling details of why she ran away and how she got to Louisville. She couldn't thank me enough for my kindness in reaching out to her and making her *feel human again.*"

Rita put her hand on her chest as tears again scurried down her cheeks. "I've worked at the soup kitchen for seventeen years and I've never met someone so exceedingly grateful for such a small amount of help. Here I am, overwhelmed by her story and she's asking me what she can do to repay my kindness. She even offered to rake the leaves in the front lawn. My heart melted and I invited her for dinner. I had her wait until after we ate for her to explain her situation to my husband. She'd been on the run for over six months and with winter coming she didn't know what to do. She was afraid of getting a job because she didn't want to leave a trace of her whereabouts so Stanton could find her. The poor girl was terrified of this man. Can you imagine? To be so terrified that it was better to live in a closet with no heat, water, or electricity in a dank cold and drafty building—than to go home."

Parker held up his bandaged arms. "We can. He tried to kill us, remember?"

"Oh right, sorry. Well, my husband was the one who spoke first and offered for her to live with us. He told her the only stipulation was that she had to finish high school. Though it was already the beginning of November, she was smart enough that she didn't need to be held back, and she graduated the following June."

"So is Melissa here?" Matt asked. He and Parker sat on the edge of their chairs and leaned over the table on their elbows. With eyes bright, both looked at Rita, eager for news.

"She still lives with us and goes by Jordan. She said her real name made her remember her past. We got a lawyer friend to help us with an official name change and he worked out the social security issue before she went to school.

"After graduation, she worked nights and weekends to pay her own way through community college. We love her like our own daughter and offered to pay, but she wouldn't let us. After she got her associates degree, we pressed, and she finally agreed to let us help her with her bachelor's degree. She graduated from Louisville University last May. She works . . . wait . . . let me talk with her and my husband tonight to see if she's willing to meet with you. It took her a long time to get over her fear of being discovered. When she learns that someone actually found her, I'm guessing it will cause some panic."

"We thought that might be her reaction," Matt said. "I'm glad we met you first. Now you can break the ice for us."

"I'm sure that after she hears your story, she'll want to meet you. Can you stop back tomorrow?"

"We sure can," Parker said. "We'll even come early to help again."

On their way back to the Jeep, Matt said, "That went well and Rita's a sweetheart. I am bummed, though, that we have to wait another day before we can meet Jordan."

"I think this is a good thing. It will give Jordan a chance to digest the reality that she's not only been found, but that she's finally free. Then she'll want to meet us, or she won't. Either way, I'm excited to learn that things eventually worked out for her and that she has people who truly care about her."

"So true. Now where to?"

"If you don't mind, I'd like to go back to the hotel," Parker said. "I'm exhausted and the pain meds have worn off."

"Me too. I hope we can actually unwind enough to sleep."

Chapter 26

THE CONNECTION

Two hours later, Matt's phone woke him. The autumn sky was already taking on hues of dusk. "Parker, time to rise and shine. We have a new message."

"Huh, I didn't expect to get a text about more pictures. Where to this time?"

"The Big Four Pedestrian Bridge in Louisville's Waterfront Park."

Neither man hurried and a good forty minutes passed before they reached the bridge. They parked as close as they could, which was still a half mile walk including the quarter mile ramp. Matt didn't mind; he had gotten pretty good with the cadence of the crutches and not putting any weight on his leg.

"Wow, that bridge is impressive," Parker said.

"It sure is, and I think it's cool that our guy uses area landmarks to get us our information."

It was almost dark and the multicolored LED lights that lined and crossed the steel girders of the footbridge and the spiral ramp leading up to it were already on. Parker took some pictures from the path along the Ohio River. As they got closer, he even got out his portable tripod, hoping to get some high-quality photos for his business.

Matt, on the other hand, only snapped a few shots before putting his camera away. It was easier to walk without it dangling from his neck.

Once they reached the bridge, they both took more pictures. Then Parker asked, "Are you up to walking to Indiana?"

"If we're not in a hurry, I should be okay."

"No hurry at all. I just thought I might be able to get a decent shot of the Louisville Skyline from over there."

"I'm game." As they continued across the bridge, Matt asked, "So what are we missing?"

"What do you mean?"

"Why did we need to find Melissa? Like you said this morning, except for her not having to worry about Stanton anymore, what do we have to offer?"

"But that alone is huge! You saw how nervous Rita and Roy were when we showed them the picture and knew her name. The fear of being found by Stanton still haunts them all these years later."

Matt nodded thoughtfully and then took a seat on an empty bench about halfway across the bridge. "How about you go on ahead and get the photos you want. I'll wait for you here."

Parker looked both directions. The bridge wasn't packed, but there were enough people to cause a moment of hesitation. "Um, I guess I'll pass. The last time we split up, it didn't work out so well."

"But—"

Parker held up a hand. "I don't need any more pictures."

They both sat in contemplative silence for a while. When they stood to head back, Matt asked Parker to take his picture. "We've been on this crazy adventure for weeks and taken dozens of photos, but we don't have any of us."

"Okay, stand right in the middle of the walkway, the colorful lights will make a cool backdrop."

After Parker got a few he was happy with, Matt offered to do the same. Then he grabbed his phone and took a selfie of them.

By the time they finished the photo shoot and got back to the Jeep, neither of them felt up to more sightseeing. It was hard to focus on anything else now that they had new photos.

❏ ❏ ❏

Parker got some amazing shots of the bridge that had no extra images. "Nice. I'm sure Bryce will be happy to sell some of these in his gallery."

"Or you can sell them online, but can we please focus on the clues?"

"Not anxious much, are you?"

Matt didn't answer, but his mouth dropped open when he saw the next picture. One of the photos Parker took of him on the bridge had Haley standing next to him with her arms wrapped around his waist. "What's this supposed to mean? I haven't talked to Haley since she dumped me and hadn't given her much thought since my flight to Indianapolis."

"Maybe our guy is giving you a heads-up that things didn't work out with what's-his-face."

"Oh, and I'm supposed to take her back as if nothing happened?"

"Not necessarily, but maybe you should give her a call. And don't pretend you don't want to talk to her. If you were over her, you wouldn't still have her picture on your lock screen." Parker nudged Matt's shoulder with a mischievous grin.

"Fine. What's in the next picture?" Matt wanted to change the subject. Yes, he still loved her, but he wasn't ready to forgive her. *I don't understand why our guy is bringing this up right now. We haven't even met Melissa yet.*

The next photo showed the colorful steel girders, but this time neither Matt nor Parker were in it. Instead, there was a woman with her child in the middle of the walkway. Suddenly the picture began to move like a video recording.

"This is incredible," Parker said. "Not because the picture's moving, but because it looks exactly like the vision I saw in Virginia Beach."

"You never mentioned a vision."

"That's because it freaked me out and I had already caused you enough pain. I didn't feel the need to let you know I was going crazy, too."

Matt waited for the video to stop before saying, "I don't understand."

"It happened the night I put you in the hospital. Once we knew you had to stay, I took Anna home, got my things and left. I didn't know where to go, so I drove around for a while before parking in front of the New Beginnings Mission. The mural of the children on the front window changed to this scene, but at the time it was animated. I supposed it was a hallucination brought on from hearing Anna's story and never gave it another thought."

"Will it play again?" Matt asked, captivated by the movement.

Parker closed and reopened the image and like the first time, it moved. This time neither of them spoke but focused on the details. Then Parker paused the video where the woman's face could be seen clearly. "Look," he touched the screen, "doesn't she look like Anna?"

"I suppose if we exchanged her bleached-blond hair for auburn, and pictured her twenty years younger, yeah this could be Anna." Matt leaned forward so he could get a better look. "There's no scar on her right cheek, but the dimple when she smiles is definitely hers."

"That's what I thought, and Nora is still with her, so she wouldn't have the scar yet. If this is Anna that means the child is Nora."

Matt crossed his arms. "So? We already know Anna's story. I don't see how that's relevant. Just like the picture of Haley, it's not relevant to anything we need to know right now."

"But it is! Think about it—we're seeing this video right now—the night before we meet Jordan." Parker's eyes widened with excitement. "Don't you get it? Nora *is* Jordan."

"You're crazy. There's no possible way there could be a connection."

"Why not?"

Matt threw his hands toward Parker and limped to the other end of the room. He couldn't believe Parker would even suggest such a thing. Disgusted, he snapped, "Is this some kind of game to you?"

Parker looked bewildered. "What are you talking about?"

"I'm talking about Anna and Jordan, of course." Matt glared. "It's like you've thrown logic out and jumped headlong into the realm of wishful thinking."

"How is this any less probable than everything else we've learned or gone through so far?" Not waiting for an answer Parker said, "Wow, it seems like you of all people would be thrilled if there was a connection between the two. You have a bond with Anna and have shared every detail of our adventure with her."

"Exactly," Matt said. "She has such a generous heart and expects nothing in return. I don't want to get her hopes up on a whim and then end up hurting her when there's no connection."

Parker looked again at the picture. "Come look. Can't you see the resemblance from Jordan's school picture and this younger version of Anna? It has to be her."

Matt came and took a seat at the desk. Parker enlarged Anna's face so they could look for similarities. Matt's expression softened. "According to Anna's story, Jordan would be the right age. But how do we get concrete proof?"

Parker thought for a minute. "I think I know a way." He started the video again and paused it right at a point where Nora looked straight forward. Then he took a screenshot of her face and emailed it to Captain Smith with an 'urgent' tag on it and a note that read, 'Can you have one of your tech specialists do a time-lapse of this picture? What would this child look like at the age of 16? If possible, we need results by 11:00 A.M. EST. Thanks, Parker Jackson'

"Why did you request sixteen and not twenty-two?"

"We have a good picture of Melissa from the yearbook at sixteen. I figured with fewer years to lapse, the more accurate it will be. I'll call the captain in the morning to make sure they can do it. If not, he should know who can."

"You could also ask about their investigation."

□ □ □

With an hour time difference, Parker waited until 9:00AM to call.

"Good Morning, Captain."

"Parker, I'm glad you felt you could take me up on my offer to help," Smith said. "We've already started the time-lapse."

"Thank you, sir. How are things going on the Stanton investigation?"

"We've confiscated a large volume of evidence."

Parker started to pace his hotel room. "Were many children sold?"

"Yes, but I can't give you any details right now."

"Sounds like you're making progress. That's great."

"It will be a long and drawn out process. Many of the stolen children won't ever be returned."

"Why not?"

"Because Allison said they didn't keep any records of when or where they took the children. Finding the *real* parents is the challenge."

Parker carefully sat in the chair by the window. "That sucks."

"Yet thanks to you guys, this group won't be stealing any more children."

"So you're positive Stanton will be convicted and put away for good?"

"Absolutely."

"That's great because we've found Melissa."

"So soon? Where are you?"

"I'd rather not say. We haven't seen her yet and the people we met yesterday thought at first that we worked for Stanton. It took some convincing for them to trust us and I don't want to betray that trust."

"I agree wholeheartedly," the Captain said. "So she's doing well then?"

"Very well; thanks for asking. Now, how much longer will it take to do the time-lapse?"

"Not long. We'll send it as soon as it's done."

By the time Parker filled Matt in on Captain Smith's update, the time-lapse was sent back. He opened it and put it beside Melissa's school photo.

Matt adjusted his glasses and leaned closer to the screen. "And to think I didn't want to rent a room at Anna's house."

"It's enough to blow your mind, right?"

"I'll say." Matt kept his eyes on the pictures. "Nothing we've gone through compares to this. I hope Jordan agreed to meet us."

Matt saved the pictures and brought the laptop with him to the soup kitchen. They were warmly greeted by the staff and offered to help as promised.

"Do you know why I trusted you guys yesterday?" Rita asked.

Both shook their heads.

"Your work ethic. I've learned you can tell a lot about people by their willingness to work and serve others."

"Oh," Parker grinned, "we thought it was because of our dashing good looks and charm."

Rita covered her mouth to stifle a laugh.

Preoccupied with the prospect of meeting Jordan, Matt offered only a small smile before asking, "Um, did Jordan agree to speak with us?"

"Yes, Matt. Once she heard your news, she was actually relieved. She said she'd meet us here later."

When the tables were washed and the dishes were done, Roy asked Rita, "Do you mind if I stay again today? I would like to hear more of this story."

"Of course, you can stay, Roy. You're like a grandfather to Jordan. I've got the coffee ready and Jordan helped me make cookies last night. She should be here soon."

Both Parker and Matt's hearts were racing with anticipation when the door from the kitchen slowly opened. Everyone stood and watched as a tall, redheaded woman entered. Roy immediately went to escort her.

"Thanks, Roy, you're a real sweetheart." She looped her arm through his and they made their way to the table.

"Hello, my name is Jordan."

Parker introduced himself first and reached out to shake her hand. To his surprise, she didn't let go. The rope burns were still visible on his wrist along with other bandages and burns on his arms from the explosion.

"Are these wounds from your recent abduction?"

"And from a fire, ma'am."

She blushed. "Please, call me Jordan. From what I hear, I owe you a great big thank you."

Parker turned three shades of red as their eyes met. "Oh, uh, you're welcome, but hey, this is Matt." He used his free hand to point. "He risked his life to save mine."

With a smile, she squeezed his hand before letting go to take Matt's. "It's a pleasure to meet you. Rita told me your story. It's quite remarkable."

"Please, come sit." Rita gestured and everyone followed her lead.

"So, Parker, you spoke with my friend Susie?"

"Yes. I met her last week."

"How is she?"

"She's doing great and has a good job in Memphis. She said if I ever found you to give you her love."

"Aww." Jordan placed a hand on her chest. "I miss her so much. She was my closest and dearest friend. Losing her has been my only regret."

"It was obvious to me that she felt your loss too. Given that no one has seen or heard from you since the day you ran away, everyone I talked with assumed you were dead."

"Well, it seemed to me that disappearing completely was the safest option. It broke my heart to cut everyone off, but my silence was the only way to be sure he couldn't find me . . . but then again, you found me."

Matt jumped in. "But we had help."

"Yeah, about that, do you have any of those miracle pictures with you? I'd like to see them." Jordan's greenish-gray eyes sparkled, and she was more at ease than either of them expected.

Parker had loaded all the relevant photos onto his phone and quickly opened it to that file.

Jordan took the phone and shuddered when she saw the pictures of herself at the mission. "I obviously never posed for a photo, but these capture the fear and desolation that I felt for months."

"We can't even imagine," Matt said, "but the pain emanating from your eyes was enough to grip our hearts."

"And I can't even imagine the risks you two took for me." She gave them both a sincere nod before scrolling to the next picture. "Oh my, you even have a photo of Susie and me in Virginia Beach." She stretched the image with her fingers. "That was one of my fondest memories growing up."

Parker shot Matt a look.

"Can I have this picture?"

"Of course."

Jordan punched her number into Parker's phone and texted the image to herself. Then she got out her own phone and stared at the picture.

Parker reached across the table to retrieve his phone. Two smiling girls met his gaze. He shook his head as he silently handed the phone to Matt.

Rita watched this exchange with knit brows. "What are we missing?"

"More miracles," Matt said with an expansive grin.

Jordan looked up from her phone. "What do you mean?"

"I mean this." Matt handed Parker's phone to Rita. "Susie wasn't in our original pictures, her mom was."

"Seriously?" Jordan's eyes widened as she looked again at her friend.

"Yeah, I'd say that was just for you. Oh, and Susie gave me her business card, but my abductors took my wallet."

"Is she married?"

"No."

"Then I'll be able to find her when the time is right. I want to be positive Stanton . . ." her voice faltered as her body visibly shook. "That he's no longer a threat."

"Hey, I totally get that." They locked eyes. "Mrs. Weber asked about you too."

She pinched her lips and nodded.

"Excuse me, Jordan." Matt interrupted their moment. "We've heard parts of your story, but we don't know how you ended up in Louisville. Would you be willing to tell us?"

"Well, if you talked to Susie, you know I took my mom's car as far as St. Louis. From there I walked to a gas station near the interstate and watched people from the shadows until I found a young woman traveling alone. She didn't ask questions and was happy to have the company. At that point, I didn't care where I ended up; I just knew I had to get further away. She was heading to Columbus, but we parted ways in Indianapolis."

"But why didn't you go with her to Columbus?" Parker asked.

Chapter 27

FED A LIE

"I felt uneasy to stay with this woman any longer," Jordan said. "She was incredibly kind and friendly, but if we were seen together on security cameras, they could identify her from her license plate, and I would be discovered. I begged her not to say where she dropped me off if the police contacted her.

"Well anyway, I stayed in Indianapolis for a few months, trying to figure out what I should do. Unfortunately, I didn't exactly have a plan. For a while I stayed in cheap motels, but then my money started to run out and I ended up homeless, sleeping wherever I could find a place that looked safe from street creeps. I think Rita told you why I didn't dare to get a job."

They nodded.

She continued, "I met a few girls in Indianapolis who said they could hook me up with their pimp. They said, 'He was good to them and would take care of me.' I freaked out and left immediately because that was the last thing I wanted to do. Here I am, living on the streets to get away from an abusive pervert. I wasn't going to willingly settle for, or be forced into, that kind of lifestyle. That's when I fled to the mission you visited. I thought they might be able to help, but their questions scared me. Not knowing if they were going to hand me over to

Child Protective Services, I panicked. Without thinking past that moment, I climbed out the bathroom window and fled."

"Yeah, about that," Parker interrupted, "I looked out the bathroom window. That was quite the drop. I even found a faded piece of cloth stuck in between the bricks. Were you hurt when you fell?"

"Some scratches on my stomach and a sprained ankle, but I was so overcome with fear that I ran despite the pain."

"As soon as John realized you fled, he, his staff, and even some of the men they were helping started looking for you. They couldn't believe you took off before they had time to come up with a legal plan. One that would protect you, but also one that wouldn't put their mission in jeopardy for concealing an under-aged fugitive."

Jordan nodded thoughtfully as if a light of understanding came to her.

"Shortly after that, they networked with another area mission that works with homeless women, and runaway and abused teenage girls. They wanted to be sure a situation like yours would never happen again."

"That's wonderful news. I should contact them."

"John asked me to let him know if we ever found you. I know it'd mean so much more if you were the one to call."

"Do you have the name of the place?"

"Yes. Hope Mission House. You can find the number on their website."

"Parker," Matt nudged his arm, "you cut Jordan off in the middle of her story."

"Oh, uh, right . . . sorry."

"No worries, I'm grateful to know good came from that experience and even though it didn't appear so at the time, I was moved by their kindness to me."

"They seemed like great people, so I'm not surprised. Now, what'd you do next?"

"I knew I couldn't stay in Indianapolis, so I ran as fast as I could to put distance between myself and anyone who might come looking for me. Thankfully, I came to some railroad tracks and followed them south. I didn't know where they went, nor did I care. I walked mostly at night and slept under trestles or in sluices if they were dry enough during the day. One morning I spotted an old barn not too far from the tracks. I stayed there for a few days to let my ankle heal up, but then had to keep moving so I could buy food."

"That whole ordeal must have been terrifying," Matt said.

"Pretty much, but it was better than being found. I wasn't surprised when Rita said Stanton hired goons to blow you up." She nodded toward their wounds.

Matt rolled his palms upward. "This is nothing compared to what you've been through. And anyway, they didn't succeed."

"And for that I'm grateful. I still can't believe you two risked your lives for me." The glint in her eyes brightened.

"Hey, Matt, who's interrupting Jordan's story now?"

"Touché."

Rita chuckled at their friendly banter. "You two are a trip. Jordan, go ahead and finish your story."

"Eventually, I made it to Louisville. I can't remember how long it took, and by the time I got here, I was out of money.

"Thank God I found this Soup Kitchen and met this amazing lady." Jordan patted Rita's hand. "She saved my life, and though I've endured my share of struggles and loss, things have worked out for me." Her smile could not have been more genuine. But then, as if bitten by reality, she asked, "Did Susie know anything about the evidence I left in my mom's car?"

Parker nodded. "She mentioned it, but without your DNA to confirm the evidence was yours, Stanton was able to get the case dismissed."

"Well, I'm not surprised. I knew he would get away with it."

"The trial did destroy his law practice in Memphis, though, and after the dust settled, Mrs. Stanton divorced him."

"Hmm, well that is something. More than I expected. She had a cushy life. I can't prove it, but I think she knew he was abusing me. But then she *was* recovering from cancer and I hoped it was more from her weakened state than from not caring."

"You know, Jordan," Matt hesitated, "if you gave the authorities your DNA now, you could have him convicted for his crimes against you."

"And risk giving up my location?" For the first time, Jordan soured. She abruptly pushed her chair back and yelled, "Not a chance!" Then she left the table and headed for the kitchen.

Rita followed as quickly as her short legs would take her. "Hold up, sweetie. No one's making you risk anything."

Roy glared at Matt, but he paid him no heed. Getting to his feet he said, "Rita's right, Jordan. We're not asking you to risk anything. I'm sorry I brought it up."

She stared at him, her voice now trembling, "But I thought you had a strong case against him already."

"We do . . . and it's ironclad." Matt motioned to their chairs. "Please, come sit and we'll explain."

The ladies retook their places at the table.

"Captain Smith is the one who offered to help you if you *wanted* your day in court. Sex crimes against minors are a pet peeve of his. He would never have suggested it if he thought you could be hurt again."

"Yeah, no one wants to put you back in harm's way. You can put your mind at ease because we haven't given him, or anyone else, your new name or location," Parker said.

Fear mixed with disgust emanated from Jordan's eyes. "The thought of being near that man ever again makes me sick and having to talk about it would be unbearable!"

"End of story, then." Parker reached across the table to squeeze her hand. "Stanton has committed too many crimes and there's too much evidence for him to finagle his way out of life-in-prison. He'll never be able to hurt you again."

The color of fear drained from Jordan's cheeks. She blew out a long, calming breath before saying, "Thank the Lord!"

As Parker released her hand, he added, "We do have one more piece of news that we'd like to share with you."

"Is it good news?"

"We think so. Matt, why don't you tell them."

He straightened his glasses and then motioned toward Jordan. "We've learned that you were fed a lie by Stanton. Susie said he told you that your teenage mom willingly gave you up for adoption because a baby cramped her style and she never wanted to see you again."

"A lie? I'm not following."

"We believe you were stolen from a loving family when you were a toddler."

Jordan gasped and covered her mouth.

Roy's eyes widened.

Rita patted her chest and gasped for air. "Oh, my."

"We're 98% sure that with our new information we know who your real mother is. To be positive beyond a doubt, we'd need to get both of your DNA tested to confirm a match."

Any color that was left in Jordan's face was now gone. She held out her hands as if to say, *enough*. Then she lowered her elbows to the table, bowed her head, and started massaging her temples.

Rita gently rubbed her back as she raised her other hand in question toward Matt. He didn't answer, giving Jordan a chance to process the news. The last six years of her life had hinged on a decision her mother apparently never made. And now she might have the chance to meet her.

When Jordan finally looked up, her hands pulled against her cheeks. She clasped them at her chin, looking first to Matt, then to Parker. "Um, sorry, this is just a lot to take in." She turned to Rita. "Why didn't you tell me?"

Parker answered before Rita could. "Because she didn't know. We only found out just before we came here today."

"Wow. Okay. I don't know what I'm supposed to think or how I should feel." Jordan looked thoughtfully at Rita for a moment before saying, "I mean, what about you and Frank?"

"Don't you worry about us, sweetie. To know you have a family, and that they didn't willingly throw you away, fills my heart with joy." Rita gave Jordan a sidelong hug. "This doesn't affect our relationship one bit." Then she turned to look at the others. "I saw no reason to mention this yesterday, but my husband and I lost our only child, Robert, to Sudden Infant Death Syndrome."

"Oh, Rita, I'm so sorry," Roy said, "I never knew you had a son."

"It's okay, Roy. I only brought it up now to say, Jordan, I think you should pursue this. I know what loss feels like, yet our situation is completely different. We know that Robert is with Jesus, but think of how devastating it was for your parents to lose you. To never know what happened to you, my heart breaks for them."

"But what if too much time has passed? What if she doesn't want to meet me?" Jordan anxiously tapped her fingers on the table.

"You're afraid that she won't want to meet you because of the lies you were fed, but I can tell you from experience that there is nothing a mother wouldn't give to have the chance to see her baby again."

Tears began to flow like a river and Jordan buried her face in Rita's chest. She couldn't stop crying—nor did she try. Rita held her close as Roy went to find a box of tissues. No one spoke; each knew these tears were the beginning of a cleansing process and a step toward healing.

When no more tears would come, Jordan took another tissue, wiped her eyes and blew her nose. "Does she know?"

Matt shook his head, "Not yet. Parker and I talked it over before we came today and thought it best to see if you'd be open to the possibility before we got her hopes up."

"But how in the world could you possibly know who my real mom is?"

"Remember our miracle pictures? Well, one of the photos changed to an ad with rooms for rent. We followed that lead and stayed for a few days with the woman we now believe to be your mother. Her name is Anna Collins and she lives in Virginia

Beach. While we were at her house, Parker asked about a black and white picture on her desk. It took some coaxing, but she finally told us the inconceivable story of the abduction of her child."

Again, Jordan covered her mouth to bite back a groan.

"Yeah, and we were at her house when we got our first clues about you and Memphis," Parker said. "It never crossed our minds that there could be a connection until last night. Now that we've met you, we can see the resemblance. You have her eyes and the same dimple when you smile."

"Anna is such a sweet lady," Matt added. "She's actually the one who encouraged us to find you and when we wanted to quit, she pushed us to continue. She never gave any indication that she thought we could possibly be searching for her own daughter, but she knew you were someone's daughter and her heart broke for you. We've kept her in the loop, so she knows as much about you and your story as we do—every painful detail. She's cried with us, prayed for us, and even started praying for you."

Then Parker jumped back in. "Anna will be expecting another update soon, but we don't want to mention the connection without being 100% sure. If you're willing to trust our leads, which have brought us miraculously to you both, we can get your DNA tested. Then without letting Anna know we found you, we'd work out a way to get hers. Once we're positive it's a match, we can come up with a plan to break the news."

Though Jordan's face was a blotchy mess, and her eyes now rimmed in red, a little laugh escaped her lips. "Wow, this is incredible. What new lead did you get to make the connection?"

"Our latest photo transformed into a video of Anna playing with you at the park before you were abducted."

"But how do you know it's me?"

"We had a professional time-lapse done of the child in the video and compared it with your high school picture. It's a match."

Matt grabbed his crutches and got to his feet. "Hang on, I brought my laptop. It's in the kitchen."

A minute later he returned, opened all three photos, and arranged them so they were side by side on the same screen. The one on the left was the screenshot of her as a toddler, the one on the right was her high school photo and in the middle was the time-lapse. He spun the computer and moved it in front of Jordan and Rita. Roy stepped behind them so he could see from over their shoulders. Jordan leaned closer, looking from one to the other, her gaze finally settling on the one in the middle.

Roy whistled. Rita squealed with delight.

Matt bent toward Parker and whispered, "This is better than Christmas morning." Then he asked Jordan if she would like to see the video.

"Absolutely. What button do I push?"

Matt showed her and they watched in silence. When the video stopped, Jordan hit the play button again and paused it at the same place Parker had the night before. She reached out to touch the screen. "My mom is beautiful."

Rita and Roy agreed.

Jordan watched the video three more times before noticing a boy in the background and paused it again. "Is this a random kid or do I have a brother?"

Parker and Matt both smiled and said in unison, "You have a brother." Then laughing, Matt let Parker explain. "His name is Owen. He's twenty-five, married, and has a little boy who's about two."

"Rita, I have a family!" Jordan clasped her hands together and brought them to her heart.

"Yes, sweetie, it appears you do. But before we get too excited, I think it would be good to have absolute proof."

"Oh, right. Are you sure you don't mind?"

"Of course not. The sooner we know the better."

Jordan's face glowed like an angel. "Okay, okay, I want to do it. But how do I go about getting my DNA tested?"

Both Parker and Matt got out their phones.

Once they had their answer and everything was settled, Roy said, "I need to get home to the Mrs. God bless you guys. I'll see you tomorrow, Rita." He kissed Jordan on the forehead and then excused himself.

"Another thing worth mentioning," Matt said after Roy left, "is that we experienced a mishap while staying with Anna. Because of this, we got to know her not just as a gracious host, but as a woman that will go the extra mile for strangers. She's become a dear friend to us, and we can't wait to get the results. It's going to be such a grand reunion." Matt couldn't stop smiling, his own reservations now distilled.

"So much for waiting to be 100% sure," Parker said.

"There have been too many miracles to doubt and look at her." Matt raised a hand toward Jordan. "She looks so much like Anna."

"So, we're throwing all caution to the wind then?"

Matt shrugged. "I didn't say we shouldn't test the DNA. It's just that we already know the answer, so I'm excited."

"Me too, but we should probably get going." Parker got to his feet and Matt joined him. "It's been such a pleasure to meet you, Jordan."

She came around the table to where they were standing. "This is definitely a lot to take in. At first, I wasn't sure if it was even safe to meet you guys and now, I find out my mother didn't abandon me. I don't know how I can ever repay you for all your troubles."

"There's no need." Parker smiled and reached to shake her hand. "Just to know that you're alive and doing well is huge."

"That's so true," Matt chimed in. "We're thrilled."

She took a step back. "I still can't believe you guys kept looking for me after that explosion."

"Yes, but to quit would be to let Stanton win. And even better, he doesn't know we lived. He'll be shocked when we show up to testify against him."

"Ah, now that I would like to see." Almost instantly, Jordan shuddered. "No, I take that back." Her head continued to shake. "To have him put away for good is more than enough for me. I never want to lay eyes on that man again!"

"We don't blame you there. I'm not too keen on seeing him either, but it has to be done," Parker affirmed. "You have my number. Be sure to let me know when you have the DNA results."

"I will."

Rita hurried to catch them at the back door. "With all this exciting news, I almost forgot to tell you, I put in a pot roast before coming to work today. We'd love to have you join us for dinner."

Parker looked at Matt who nodded approvingly. "We accept. A home-cooked meal sounds great."

Chapter 28

BREAKING NEWS

"Supper was fantastic, and we couldn't have asked for the day to go any better," Parker said as they left the comfort of Rita's home around 9:00 that evening.

"I agree, and who would've known Jordan likes baseball as much as Anna."

"Yeah," Parker laughed, "last I knew that's not in the genes."

"Speaking of Anna, I need to give her a call."

"Be sure not to mention Jordan."

"No worries. I'll let her know we're still following leads, but that our latest photos touched on personal issues."

"Ah, way to come up with a legitimate diversion. Maybe we should invite ourselves back to Anna's house on the grounds that it's not safe for us to go home to Philadelphia yet. Then we could get a DNA sample and have it analyzed without her suspecting anything."

"Perfect! I'll give her a call as soon as we get back to the hotel."

Anna did have rooms available, so Matt wasn't on the phone for long.

Parker looked up from the newspaper he was perusing. "Is there a problem?"

"Nope. Once Anna knew we were coming, she said that if I didn't have any *breaking news*, we could catch up tomorrow."

"Ha, breaking news, that's ironic."

"I know, right? It's truly incredible how everything is tied together." Matt bubbled with excitement.

"I think it might be fun to see if Jordan and Rita would meet us in Virginia Beach and have Jordan give Anna the news herself."

"I like it. Under normal circumstances, reconnecting with them without being warned first might be overwhelming. But because Anna has such an abundance of love and faith it will be fun to see how she reacts."

"And even though Jordan will have the advantage of already knowing, it will still be an amazing moment for her too." Parker smiled and then started to get ready for bed. "With a ten-hour drive ahead of us, I say we call it a night."

❑ ❑ ❑

They had been on the road for several hours when Matt said, "We've been so wrapped up in our own discoveries that we forgot to check on Joel."

"Ah, that was poor of us. We could call him now," Parker suggested.

"Good idea." Matt called Joel's phone, unsure if he was still at the hospital. It rang several times before he answered. "Hey Joel, how's it going? We were going to come see you before we left town, but they had you sedated."

"I'm on this side of the grave, so all is well," Joel said in his usual chipper tone.

"That's not exactly an answer," Parker said.

"Oh, hi Parker. To be honest, I don't remember the first two days. Yesterday was rough, but I feel a little better today."

"We're sorry you took the worst hit."

"Don't be. Lieutenant Reade came to see me last night and he said you guys didn't exactly go unscathed. He also mentioned that the more they go through the evidence, the more grateful they are to have Davis, Stanton, and their cohorts in custody."

"Hopefully that makes your pain a little more bearable," Matt said.

"It does because I was lying here feeling forgotten and wondering if this mission was a demotion for me."

"Not in our book," Parker said. "You helped save us twice—I'd call that a promotion and we're indebted to you."

"Thanks. Have you made any progress in your search for Melissa?"

"Yes! We found her."

"Wow. That's super cool!"

Matt and Parker proceeded to share all the details with Joel, knowing it would keep him entertained for a while.

"Hey, guys, a nurse just came in. I've got to go. Let's keep in touch."

"We will and we'll see you at the trial," Parker said.

"You got it."

❏ ❏ ❏

Anna was in the kitchen making supper when Parker and Matt knocked on the back door. She called for them to come in. "Whoa, what happened to you guys?"

"Hello to you, too." Parker smirked with a mischievous glint in his eyes.

Matt laughed at Anna's pert reaction. "Hey, we lived."

"Well, that's good. I have dinner ready; come in and get freshened up. You can tell me what happened while we eat."

Parker and Matt took turns telling the details of their stay at the safe house and how they had barely escaped the explosion.

"I thought last night you said you didn't have any breaking news." Anna held up her hands. "I'd call your near-death escape, news."

"We didn't want to worry you," Matt said. "I haven't even told my parents."

"Now you know why it wasn't safe for us to go home yet," Parker added.

"It sounds like that impish cat and the aggressive dog helped save your lives."

"Ha, good point."

"See, I told you, Anna always has a way to find the best in every situation."

She shook her head. "Well if nothing else, you two certainly know how to keep things interesting. Do you have any new information on Melissa?"

Matt answered, "Actually our leads have taken us in a different direction, though we're not sure why." He got out his phone to show Anna the photo of himself on the bridge with Haley.

"Oh my. I bet you didn't see that coming."

"That'd be putting it mildly." He sighed.

They were both relieved that Anna didn't press for an update about Melissa.

❑ ❑ ❑

The next morning, after Anna left for work, Matt snuck into her master bathroom and gathered some hair from her brush and put it into a zip lock bag. For reinforcement, they also brought her used coffee mug that was still on the table in the breakfast nook.

Matt handed over his samples and while he filled out the paperwork, an employee swabbed the cup and gave it back to him.

On their way out of the building, Parker asked, "Did Anna know of a place where we can get our wounds looked at?"

"Yeah, I have the address on my phone."

"Good, because my back is killing me."

"I'm sure our ten-hour drive yesterday didn't help any."

When they met back up in the waiting room, Parker said, "Wow, I'm glad we came. There wasn't any infection, but just

255

having everything cleaned and rebandaged has made a world of difference. How about you?"

"Because I lost a chunk of my calf muscle, it's going to take a while to heal. The doctor did say I could start adding some weight to that leg though."

"Does that mean you're up for doing something or would you rather go back to the house?"

"Let's do something. I thought I was going to have to work on my article about the building on Chestnut Street. But then my boss emailed this morning and said the purchase offer has been put on hold."

"Hmm, that's interesting." A text kept Parker from saying more. "Our guy wants us to take pictures of the King Neptune Statue on the boardwalk."

"I guess that settles it then. Let's go." Matt still used one crutch but found the pain was less than he expected after his first few steps. On their way to the statue, he suggested that they buy some steaks. "I think it would be nice to make Anna dinner and we could invite Owen and his family, too. I'd like to meet them."

"Works for me and I make a mean steak."

"I know. That's why I suggested it." Matt smacked his lips together and pulled out his phone to text Anna.

They had reached the statue and were already done taking pictures by the time Anna texted back. She gave a thumbs up, so they stopped by the market to get what they needed on their way back to the house.

Parker marinated the steaks and put them in the fridge.

While he was doing that, Matt got out his computer and loaded the photos from both cameras. Then he checked his email to keep himself from taking a sneak peek.

It wasn't long before Parker entered the room and spun the empty chair around where he could sit with his arms propped on the back. "It'll be interesting to see what clues we get today."

"There's only one way to find out." Matt grinned and opened the first photo. It showed a boy and his mother standing in front of King Neptune. Matt magnified the faces. Parker's eyes widened. It was a picture of him and his mom when he was about twelve.

"Well, that's a blast from the past. We never came to Virginia Beach together, so what's with that?" Parker asked aloud, not expecting an answer.

Matt replied anyway. "I trust this is a real event. Where were you when this picture was taken?"

Parker looked at the picture for a minute. "Ah, now I remember. We were standing in front of a fighter jet at an Airshow on base. We spent the day with my uncle's family before she left me with them for the summer."

"Well, think. What was significant about that day?"

Parker frowned. "Hanging out with her that day was the last *fun* thing we ever did together. When I got home that fall, she was preoccupied with work and boyfriends. By my junior year, she had a steady guy, but you already know about the abuse. I took off right after graduation and I haven't seen or talked to my mom since."

"Now you at least have a picture of her that's attached to a good memory."

"True, but I assume it's about more than that. Anna thinks I should get ahold of her and make things right. There's a slight problem though, I have no way of contacting her. I don't even know where she lives or if she's still with that loser, Mike."

Matt scrolled to the next photo. This time King Neptune had what looked to be a piece of parchment attached to his trident. Seeing nothing else of interest, Parker asked Matt to zoom in on the parchment. At the top was his mom's name: Cindy Jackson. Underneath the name were an address and a phone number.

"No offense, man, but I'd say that excuse is off the table." Matt handed Parker a pen and a notepad.

"Are you trying to be funny? Because you're not."

Matt rolled his eyes. "Here we go again—you can dish it, but you can't take it. What did you tell me when Haley showed up in one of my pictures the night before last? Something about not being over her and that I should give her a call? Well, the shoe's on your foot now, so what are you going to do about it?"

"That was painfully blunt. It looks like *he* wants us both to deal with some personal issues while we wait for the DNA results." Parker wrote down the info and then said, "Next photo please."

Matt's phone rang. "It's my boss. I have to take this." He answered it as he left the room.

Parker looked at the rest of his pictures and saw things he didn't want to see. Discouraged, he closed the computer and wandered out to the back deck. *It doesn't look like anything's changed as far as my mom is concerned and seeing her again is not going to magically fix things between us.*

Matt looked bummed when he found Parker a few minutes later. "My boss said we have breaking news in the business district and if I want to keep my job, I better be on the first train back to Philadelphia in the morning. I already bought my ticket."

"Well, it looks like we're being pulled in different directions. I need to leave in the morning, too. I'm going to find my mom. Let's not mention any of this to Anna until after dinner. There's no reason to spoil a festive occasion."

◻ ◻ ◻

Parker grilled the steaks to perfection and, with the weather still warm, they ate outside. Owen and his wife, Shannon, joined in the conversation with ease and after dinner, Anna occupied little Devin so the others could continue to talk.

It started to get dark before Shannon said, "Oh wow, look how the time has flown. We should get going. Thanks for dinner; the food was great, and it was nice to finally meet you guys."

"We're glad you could make it." Parker stood to join them.

"Us, too," Owen said. He reached to shake Parker's hand. "We plan to be in Philadelphia next weekend to catch a game. Do you guys want to join us?"

"That'd be great," Parker said.

Matt gave a thumbs up. "Let me take care of getting the tickets. My boss has connections and I'm sure he could hook me up with some decent seats."

Owen shook Matt's hand. "Even better. The Saturday afternoon game works the best for us because of Devin. If you can't get us close, don't worry about it. Anywhere works; we just like the atmosphere of being at the game."

After their goodbyes, Parker and Matt helped Anna clear the table and bring everything back inside.

Matt set the few glasses he was carrying by the sink and then said, "Anna, we didn't want to tell you before dinner, but our plans have changed again. I'm catching the train to Philly in the morning. I have a one o'clock meeting that I can't miss."

"Will it be safe for you in Philly?"

He nodded. "Yes, and duty calls."

"Captain Smith told me that I can go home, too," Parker said. "He believes from the evidence they've collected, the perps are all in custody—"

"Not to mention, they think we're dead."

"That too."

Neither man smiled, knowing how close Stanton actually came to killing them.

Anna shuddered before saying, "Thank the Lord for not allowing that to happen."

"For sure. And by the way, I'm *not* going home. I have new information which includes an address for my mom. I'll take Matt to the train in the morning and then head to Pittsburgh."

"Oh, how wonderful." Anna clasped her hands together with a priceless smile.

Parker grimaced. "But Anna, what am I to do? Some of the pictures still showed her all black and blue. I don't see how there can be reconciliation if nothing's changed."

"I'm guessing she knows she's made some bad choices, but maybe she doesn't have the strength to get out of it by herself." Anna stepped forward and patted Parker on the chest. "You could be her link to a better life."

"When I saw those pictures, it broke my heart. I still can't bear to see her like that." He leaned against the counter and crossed his arms. "I left her and never looked back. I doubt she'll even be happy to see me."

"She's your mom. Of course, she'll be thrilled to see you."

Anna's assurance didn't do much to bolster Parker's confidence. "I hope you're right."

"I'll be praying for you both." Anna took a seat at the island and changed the subject. "But with your jobs and the clues taking you in different directions, does that mean the leads about Melissa have stopped?"

There was a moment of silence. Neither man wanted to lie, but they didn't want to spoil the truth either.

Matt spoke first. "Maybe our part in this story was to help the police catch Stanton and shut down this criminal enterprise."

"That is truly wonderful. Having been subjected to losing a child in this heartless fashion, I couldn't be happier." She paused. "It just seems like you wouldn't have needed to know Melissa's story if you weren't supposed to find her."

"That's what we thought too."

Parker quickly held up a hand to get their attention. "Who's to say we won't get other leads? If we do, you'll be the first to know."

Chapter 29

CRITICAL CHOICES

Once they reached the office, Parker said, "Good answer, and quite believable."

"That's what I thought. Having Anna know Stanton and his cohorts are in custody is huge and it legitimately buys us some time. Now, can I see the pictures of your mom?"

"Go for it." Parker lay on the couch. "I don't care to see them again."

"That bad, huh? Could you tell if the pictures looked up to date? They might be old like the first ones we got of Melissa."

"They made me so angry that I didn't look real close."

Matt took a seat at the desk and scrolled through the pictures he hadn't seen yet. There were three photos of Parker's mom. He zoomed in and found a timestamp on each one. The first date was 6.28.2011, the second 3.17.2014, the third 9.30.2017.

"Not that this helps, but the last picture is from a few years ago." Matt spun his chair toward Parker. "Things could have changed by now."

"I suppose. But how can I help her when I still have so much anger in me? It makes me no better than her abuser."

"Well, you do have a long drive ahead of you; I'm sure you'll have time to work out some of your frustrations before you get there," Matt said. "On a different note, what are we to do about getting Anna and Jordan together?"

"To be honest, since I saw the pictures of my mom and got her address, I haven't thought of much else."

Both of their phones vibrated at the same time. `Look at Matt's King Neptune pictures.'

Parker joined Matt at the desk and pulled up a second chair. Together they looked at the photos. Not one had extra images.

"This doesn't make any sense," Matt snapped as he pushed the laptop away. "Why were we told to look at the pictures of the statue? They don't even have any new information."

"Hold up, maybe we're not looking for the right details. Let's look again."

Parker pulled the laptop in front of him and reopened the first picture. They both looked, hoping something would jump out at them. After a few seconds, he scrolled to the next picture.

"Nothing," Matt yelled.

"Hey, keep it down. What's gotten into you?"

Matt shook his head and lowered his voice to a whisper. "With us going in opposite directions in the morning, none of this makes sense. What? Don't we get to be a part of the grand reunion?"

"Who's to say these pictures have anything to do with that? And anyway, we don't even have the test results yet and a lot can happen between now and then. Let's keep looking." Parker opened the next picture . . . and the next . . .

"This is pointless. Why was I so gullible to think we would get some guidance from these photos?"

Parker leaned back in his chair, crossed his arms and gave Matt a pointed look. "Seriously? We've received countless clues and experienced several miracles, including escaping from the safe house. Are you going to give up this easily? I wasn't raised in the church and don't fully understand what it means to have faith, but after all we've gone through and the help we've received, I'm starting to get it. We've seen Anna's faith in action. Her life wasn't instantly made perfect just because she believes in Jesus, yet she's cheerful and puts others before herself. We also got to hear how Jordan's horrific story turned into a story of redemption because of Rita and Frank. Not to mention your eye. How can we not believe?"

Matt squirmed as his face reddened.

When he didn't answer, Parker took a deep breath and said, "Matt, look at me." He uncrossed his arms and moved to the front of his chair. "I need to tell you something." He waited for their eyes to meet before he continued. "When I was strung up at the factory, I was seriously afraid I was going to die. But then, with pain coursing through my every muscle and the darkness overwhelming me, I heard a child crying. That changed everything and I prayed. For the first time in my life, I prayed to God and He delivered us both." Parker's voice began to tremble. He rested his elbows on his knees and clasped his hands together. "I need to hang on to this faith for tomorrow when I see my mom. It's been nine lost years. We need to hang onto this faith for Jordan and Anna. For them, it's been twenty lost years. If we don't have our answer right this minute, that doesn't mean it won't work out."

By the time Parker finished, the crease in Matt's brow was gone. He leaned back in his chair and said, "I knew something was different about you, but I couldn't put my finger on it. Yes, we've undeniably experienced the miraculous. And yet I must admit—it seems easier to trust in these pictures because I can *see* them, more than believing in God, whom I can't see."

"But we do see Him! In the life of every one of these people and through each of these experiences. Now, do you want to finish looking at the pictures with me?"

Matt nodded as he took off his glasses and wiped them on his shirt. "You're right. We've come too far to doubt now. Thanks for setting me straight."

They scrolled to the next picture and then to the last. Matt pumped his fists. "What a fantastic idea!"

Parker laughed. "Yes, it is."

The next morning, Parker dropped Matt off at the train station and reached the outskirts of Pittsburgh around 6:00 that evening. He found his mom's three-story, brick apartment building without a problem. Going in wasn't going to be so easy. Parker sat in his Jeep on the opposite side of the street for a long time trying to get up the nerve to say hello. He even got out his phone to call but couldn't bring himself to hit her number.

Twilight was approaching and the streetlights came on. This seemed to be Parker's cue. He got out of his vehicle and started to cross the street at the same time a woman with dark, shoulder-length hair and glasses came from the building. She was wearing sporty sneakers, tight jeans, and a low-cut top. As he reached the sidewalk, he realized she was his mother and quickly said hello.

To his surprise, she tucked her purse tighter under her arm and said, "I'm not interested." Then as she hurried past him, she added, "And anyway, I'm old enough to be your mother."

What? Parker clenched his teeth to keep himself from going into a tirade. Of all the greetings he expected, this was *not* one of them. His shock and disgust would have to wait though if he wanted to salvage any hope to be reunited. "But you *are* my mother!" His tone was far from pleasant.

She stopped in her tracks and spun toward him. "Parker, is that you? Step into the light." She approached him as he moved to the closest lamppost, where she stared at him in disbelief. "I haven't heard from you in like ten years. Why? Why did you abandon me?"

"Wait just a minute—that's not fair. You chose Mike over me, remember? You even shipped me off to your brother's house every summer so I wouldn't be in your way."

"I was trying to keep my head above water. I did the best I could, but apparently, it wasn't good enough for you. You left without a word. I didn't even know if you were safe."

Parker knew that getting upset wasn't going to help, but her words stung. "And I didn't even think you cared. What did you expect me to do? Stay and keep getting my face smashed in? Or sit by and watch Mike beat you every time he wasn't happy about something?"

"Well, at least he helped pay the bills. What'd you ever do?"

"This is incredible. I just drove ten hours to see you and you can't even be civil for five minutes?" Parker turned and headed for his Jeep.

"Yeah, walk away. That's real big of you," she yelled after him.

Parker didn't bother to look back. He jumped into his Jeep, slammed the door, and sped away. *What a waste! She won't even give me a chance.* Several blocks later, he pulled over and hit the steering wheel. *What am I supposed to do now?*

Parker's phone vibrated.

'You're The Photographer. Take Pictures.'

He read the message and tossed his phone on the passenger seat. "I'm through with taking pictures. I tried reaching out to my mom at your bidding and see how she treats me? Nothing's changed."

A second text came: 'TAKE PICTURES!'

"Are you deaf? I said I was done. We found Melissa and solved your cold case. Mission accomplished." Weary and dejected, Parker leaned his head onto the steering wheel, closed his eyes, and wept. After he quit feeling sorry for himself, the pep talk he gave Matt about having faith came to mind. *Ugh, I'm such a fool.*

It was completely dark by the time Parker decided to look for a place to take pictures. After doing a search of area landmarks, he chose to photograph the city skyline from the Upper Platform of the Duquesne Incline. From there he had a great view of the rivers, bridges, and city. He was able to get some impressive photos, which momentarily helped to squelch the pain. When he was done, he sat on the hood of his Jeep and tried to enjoy the view, but thoughts of his encounter with his mom came flooding back in. He gasped for air. He had assumed she'd be happy to see him. Her rejection hit him hard.

Wanting nothing more than to subdue the ache, he got a hotel room and buried his head under a pillow.

❏ ❏ ❏

He woke to the sound of his phone. After a poor night's sleep, he was too emotionally beaten down to put up a fight. All he said was, "Yeah?"

"Good morning, Parker. It's time to look at the pictures."

"But what good will it do? These pictures aren't going to give my mom a change of heart." Parker wasn't argumentative; he just couldn't see the point.

"No, but they will give *you* a change of heart. You recently put all of your time and energy into finding Melissa, a girl whom you knew nothing about two weeks ago. How is it that you care about a stranger—who at this point is healthy and happy—but you won't fight for your own mother who still needs your help?"

"She's made her choice."

"True, but it's not the life she wanted. She's been hurt so many times that she's become cold and calloused. You need to show her love and not give up on her at the first sign of rejection."

"But—"

"Look at the pictures." The call ended.

Fine. Because Parker didn't have a laptop, he tried to use his camera, but the screen was too small even when he zoomed in. *Maybe the hotel has computers.* He called the front desk and received directions to their business center.

Within minutes he found an empty computer, inserted his SD card, and loaded his pictures.

A wave of anxiety flooded over him as he scrolled the mouse over the tab that would open his first picture. *Ugh. This is stupid. It's not like waiting is going to change anything.*

One quick tap revealed a photo of his mom's apartment building. The second picture was of the same building, but there was a woman sitting on the front stoop all battered and bruised. In the third, a woman lay sprawled on her apartment floor . . .

her lifeless eyes stared at him. *Wait, is my mother dead?* Because he knew his photos represented real events, he began hyperventilating. Parker grabbed a fistful of his shirt and put pressure on his chest as he tried to stop the pounding.

Focus, there are more pictures.

In the next picture, the skyline had changed to Philadelphia's. Next was a picture of Parker and his mom sitting at the Cafe on Chestnut Street. She looked healthy and they both looked happy. The third split into two pictures. On the left, Parker had his arm around a woman and his mom held a baby. On the right was the same picture, except his mom wasn't in it and the woman held the baby. Parker zoomed in, but her face was obscured. His heart quit pounding. *Hmm, looks like a family is in my future.* He briefly smiled but then realized his mom was not in the second picture of his family. *So what happens?* He opened the last picture. It was the first photo he ever took at his mystery guy's bidding, the abandoned building on Chestnut Street. It looked pretty much the same except for the message spray-painted across the building. 'The choice is yours.'

Parker scrolled through the pictures again. *The first three are a progression of things getting worse for my mom and the second three are a progression of things getting better. The choice is mine.*

"The choice is mine. I don't have a moment to lose." Parker got his SD card out of the computer and ran up the four flights of stairs to his room. He grabbed his keys and sped to his mom's apartment. He knocked loudly on her door, but no one answered. He knocked again and again. "Mom, open up!" *Maybe she spent the night somewhere else.*

Suddenly the door across the hallway opened and an elderly man spoke. "What's all the racket, sonny?"

"My mom lives here in 2B, and I need to speak with her."

"Have you tried the handle?"

Parker turned the knob and the door opened. "Mom, are you here?"

Still no answer, so he hurried in with the neighbor hard on his heels. They split up and Parker hurried towards her bedroom.

"Oh, God, no! She's in here," the neighbor yelled. Cindy lay unconscious on the kitchen floor. The man was feeling for a pulse when Parker ran in and knelt beside them. "She's barely breathing. Quick, give me your phone. I'll call 9-1-1 for you."

Parker handed it to him and then hurried to the living room, where he grabbed an afghan off the couch. When he returned, he carefully turned her over and caught a whiff of alcohol on her breath. A bottle of Hydrocodone lay empty on the floor not far from her left hand. *That can't be good. Please God, don't let her die.* Not knowing what else to do, he covered her and sat on the floor with her head on his lap.

The man finished the call and put Parker's phone on the counter. "The EMTs will be here shortly."

"Thank you, sir. Do you know my mom well?"

"Well enough. We've been neighbors for a few years now." The man wet a dish towel and placed it on Cindy's head. "I'm surprised she would try to take her life. Let's hope we're not too late." He headed for the door. "I'll go wait for the ambulance."

A few minutes later, two medics came in.

"What happened?" one of the men asked as he took her vitals.

"I don't know. We just got here and called 9-1-1."

They moved Cindy onto a stretcher. "And who are you?"

"I'm her son, Parker. Here." He held out the empty script. "I'm guessing it's a overdose."

The man took the container and winced. "It's a good thing you showed up when you did."

The other man put an oxygen mask on her, and they whisked her away.

Parker thanked the neighbor, grabbed his phone, and followed the ambulance to the hospital.

Chapter 30

LOVE BREAKS THROUGH

Time passed slowly as Parker alternately sat and paced in the waiting room. Receiving a text from Anna seemed to loosen the knot in his stomach.

'How are things going with you and your mom?'

He checked the time. *Oh wow, it's noon already.* Parker figured it would be best to get an update before he replied. The woman at the window let him know his mom had been admitted but that she wasn't ready for visitors yet.

Parker thanked her and then went outside to call Anna. "Hey, do you have a minute to talk?"

"Of course, but what's going on? You sound dejected, much like you did the night we were at the ER with Matt."

"It's not good. My mom's in the hospital from a drug overdose. She tried to take her own life early this morning. If I didn't show up when I did, she'd be dead by now."

"Oh no, Parker, that's awful. What a blessing that you got there in time."

"Well, not exactly. I saw her last night, but her words were so harsh, I left without getting a chance to talk with her. Then this happened. It's all my fault." He started pacing again and the more he talked, the more agitated he became.

"Parker, snap out of it. Your mom's *not* dead because you were there to save her. Now you need to get a grip so that when

269

she comes to, you don't walk out on her again, no matter what she says."

"But she's so selfish and condescending."

"No, she's desperate and crying out for help. She needs someone to look past her faults and see her brokenness. I understand how she feels because, though I wasn't suicidal, in my darkest hours I didn't care much about living. After Nora, I fell into a deep depression; I locked myself in her room for days at a time. I didn't take care of Owen and I wouldn't let Quinn comfort me. He was grieving, too, but I was too selfish to notice. It was my poor attitude that pushed him away. He was no more hurtful to me than I was to him. I'm telling you this because I needed help. Thankfully, I got it. Give your mom a chance. Though her situation is different from mine, and arguably her fault, she lost a child, too."

"But what about me?" Parker retorted. "As far as I see it, she threw me away. She has it all backwards."

"Maybe, but think about it. All you can see is her choosing an abuser over you. You wear your rejection like a badge of honor. You don't see her for who she is. And she's doing the exact same thing. Someone must yield and, right now, you're in a better position to do that. Being right doesn't matter if the outcome is death."

"But—"

"Parker, take a step back and look. Your life has turned out pretty well, despite the road you traveled to get here. Right now, your mom needs you; whether you think she deserves you or not. You can be proud and walk away or you can be the son she never realized she had. If you can do that, then one day you will have gained a mother who loves and adores you. And eventually, she'll become a mother that you can love and adore back. The choice is yours."

"Why can you get away with speaking to me like this and I don't hang up?"

"I don't know, Parker, but I hope you'll make sure you're there for her when she wakes. Respect her as your mother, nothing less. She loves you; it might just take her a while to figure out how to show you."

"Okay, I'll try, but I can't make any promises."

□ □ □

Back in the waiting room, another half hour passed before a nurse came to get Parker. "The doctor would like to speak with you before he leaves. Please follow me." They took the elevator to the third floor and found him at the main desk. He looked up from his clipboard when they approached. "Doctor, this is Parker, Cindy Jackson's son."

Parker spoke first. "Hi, uh, is my mom going to be okay?" He sounded more nervous than he wanted to, but that didn't keep him from looking intently into the doctor's eyes.

"She'll live. They almost lost her in the ambulance, and it was touch and go in the ER, but we pumped her stomach and she began to stabilize. We've also administered activated charcoal to reduce the amount of narcotics absorbed into her blood. Do you happen to know why she emptied that bottle of Hydrocodone?"

Parker pursed his lips and started to shake his head but then realized he needed to be honest. "I hadn't seen or talked to my mom in close to a decade. When I showed up last night we argued, and I ended up leaving." He shoved his hands into his pockets. "I'm most likely the reason."

"Well, I can't help you there, but I strongly suggest Cindy check out our counseling options. Pain medicines of this strength are extremely addictive. If an overdose happens again, she might not be so lucky."

"Yes, sir. I'll be sure she gets help."

"We've given her a mild sedative, but you can go sit with her if you'd like."

Parker nodded. "I'd like that. Thank you."

The nurse took him to the dimly lit room where he found his mom hooked up to all kinds of monitors and IVs. He stood over her bed for a while, gazing at her thin, frail frame. A tear

271

slid down his cheek as a prayer rolled off his tongue. "I know this situation is different than being tied up at a factory, afraid of dying, but I need your strength and wisdom now more than ever. Please give my mom the hope that you gave Anna."

He pulled up a chair, reached through the bed rail, and gently held her hand.

About a half-hour later, a nurse came in to check on her. Parker rose and whispered, "Um, excuse me. How much longer do you think she'll sleep?"

"At least a couple more hours, but it could be longer. If you're interested, there's a cafeteria on the first floor."

"Okay, thanks, but I'm good. I want to make sure I'm here when she wakes."

It was close to 4:00 before Cindy woke. It took her a few minutes to realize she was in a hospital. Parker stood to lean over her bed. She squinted, straining to see.

"Parker, is that you?"

He took her hand and leaned over to kiss her forehead. "Yes, mom, it's me."

"Why'd you come back?"

"Because I love you."

She stared, trying to summon words. Anger salted her reply. "But you took off and I never heard another thing from you." She pulled her hand away. "How is that love?"

Parker cringed as heat flushed his face. He knew he had one chance to get this right, but she wasn't making it easy for him. "Ahem, well, for one, I'm not eighteen anymore. And for two, I didn't know how to find you until earlier this week. I came as soon as I had an address."

"But you just vanished." The pain emanating from her eyes faded behind a flood of tears.

Parker was at a loss and didn't know what to say. To cover, he scanned the room to find a box of tissues and handed it to her.

Once her nose was blown, she asked, "Can you guess why I had that script for Hydrocodone?"

He had an idea, but nine years had passed so he wasn't sure if Mike was still in the picture. The wrong answer could trigger a negative response. He cautiously shook his head.

"Mike pushed me down the stairs a few years ago and I broke two vertebrae in my back. When I got out of the hospital, he promised to change, but he'd promised that many times before and I had finally had enough. I not only moved out; I left the area. I'm in constant pain and, after seeing you last night just long enough to watch you walk away again, I drank more than usual." Her voice trailed off as she turned away. "I woke alone and with a splitting headache and I saw no purpose for living. I wanted my wretched life to be over."

"I'm sorry, I truly am. I was hurt and frustrated and didn't know any better back then, but I'm here now. Doesn't that count for something?"

She turned to face him. "Yeah, until you disappear again."

"I didn't come here to fight with you, Mom." He straightened her pillow and wiped her forehead with a damp cloth. "I came because I was hoping I could be a part of your life again and that you would want to be a part of mine." The hard line that creased her brow worried him, so he quickly added, "How about you get some rest. I'll be back in a bit."

Parker waited until she fell asleep before leaving to get something to eat and returned about an hour later with a cup of coffee and a newspaper.

He didn't realize that he had dozed off until the vibrating of his phone stirred him. When he opened it, he saw the picture of his mom with him at the café. Straightening in his chair, he looked thoughtfully from the picture to his mom.

To bring her to Philly seems like a huge step, especially when she can't even speak peaceably to me. There's no way she'll be able to get on her feet without help and if things don't work out, it will be worse than not trying. Parker was at a crossroads and didn't know what to do. In the picture, his mom was happy and full of life. The choice is yours, echoed in his ears. *Honestly though, what other option do I have?*

By the time she woke, it was late. "You're still here?" Her voice was stronger, yet her tone had softened. She found the control for her bed and raised the head. "I thought for sure I was dreaming."

"You're not dreaming." Parker pulled his chair closer. "How are you feeling?"

"Nauseous and I have a pounding headache, but I'll live . . . or so they say." And for the first time, a slight smile crept into the corners of her lips.

"Well, that's good." Parker winked and returned the smile. "The doctor told me you might get to go home tomorrow. Right now, we can visit if you're feeling up to it. We need to make a plan."

"A plan for what?"

"I'd like you to move back to Philadelphia with me. I have an extra bedroom and we can forge a new path together."

"You can't be serious." Her voice hardened. "Don't make promises you won't keep."

"It's a promise I plan on keeping." Then Parker realized that must have sounded a bit drastic and he didn't even know if she'd be up for it. "I say we talk about that later. Right now, we have some catching up to do. Where would you like to begin?"

❏ ❏ ❏

Cindy woke the next morning feeling much better and, once the physician knew Parker planned to stay with her, he said she could go home that afternoon. During their conversation, Parker asked if his mom would be able to make a trip to Philadelphia soon. The Doctor suggested waiting at least one more day but then said she'd be strong enough to travel as long as she kept hydrated and didn't take her pain medication without food.

❏ ❏ ❏

As soon as they were home, Cindy started packing.

"Whoa, Mom, slow down. We're going to take it easy this evening. Doctor's orders. I'll help you pack tomorrow."

She dropped into her recliner and looked thoughtfully at Parker. "I don't want to be a burden to you and keep you from your plans."

"But you *are* my plans. Now, do you have any coffee in the house?"

"Yes. K-cups are in the cupboard next to the fridge."

"Great. Want some?"

She nodded. "I drink mine black."

"Me too." Parker grinned as he got to his feet. "Oh, and you should probably call your boss to let him know why you won't be coming back." He stayed in the kitchen until the call ended. When he returned, he asked, "What's with that ridiculous grin?"

"My boss gave me the number of a business owner in Philly and said when I was ready to start working again to give her a call. He also said he would put a good word in for me."

"That's fantastic." He handed her one of the mugs and then took a seat on the leather sofa.

"Thanks." She sipped her coffee before adding, "Knowing that I'll have a job will make this move easier because I don't want to be a burden to you or get in your way."

"There's no hurry on my end, but I also agree that a job will be good for you . . . not because I want you out of my way, but so you can make friends and feel productive. I think you'd be happy to know that I've used the strong work ethic you instilled in me to my advantage."

"Huh. So, I actually did something right?"

Parker fought the urge to wince as a shot of pain pierced him.

She covered her mouth and whispered, "Sorry."

"No, don't be. I suppose I deserved that."

"Your disappearance has tormented me all these years. To be honest, it's hard not to resent you for that. And even harder to believe that you actually want me to come to Philadelphia. As you saw yesterday, I'd rather not try than to lose you again."

"Mom, we both need to realize this is going to take some time. Not only for our hearts to heal, but also to get to know each other again. Not as the people we were, but as the people we are now."

She nodded as her eyes glazed over.

"What's wrong?"

"You've grown into such a fine young man. I'm truly sorry I didn't put you first."

"Hey, stop with the tears. Neither of us can change the past. I say we focus on the present, okay?"

"Okay. Um, you said you wanted to be home by this weekend. What are we going to do about my things here?"

"If you don't mind, I say we pack the necessities and as much as we can fit into my Jeep. We'll leave Friday morning. We can come back in a few weeks, after you're feeling stronger, to get the rest and clean out the apartment."

"That should work . . . and Parker?"

"Hmm?"

"Thanks for coming back the other day. You've given me a reason to live."

Chapter 31

GRAND REUNION

Matt was able to secure good seats for the baseball game, which included a ticket for Parker's mom. It was a beautiful mid-September day. Anna, Owen, and his family were already at the designated gate when they arrived.

"Well hello to my two favorite houseguests," Anna said with a huge grin. She gave them both a hug.

"Hi, Anna. It's great to see you. I would like to introduce you to my mom, Cindy."

Cindy reached to shake her hand, but Anna hugged her instead. "It's such a pleasure to meet you."

"Thanks." Then gaining courage from Anna's warm welcome, she added, "I've heard a lot about you. Maybe we could talk sometime."

"I would love nothing better! We're not leaving until tomorrow, so we can talk after the game, okay?"

"I'd like that."

Matt led the way into the ballpark.

"Oh wow, these seats are great," Shannon said.

"You can thank the Phillies for that. They're horrible this year."

Owen laughed. "Horrible is a bit strong, don't you think?"

"Not really." Matt grinned.

"Okay, fine. But hey, Devin's going to love being so close to their crazy 'Phanatic' mascot and we're going to enjoy being this close to the players."

The Phillies were behind most of the game with a few scoring opportunities that fell short. Finally, in the eighth inning, they got a three-run homerun and high-fives were given to everyone, even to those sitting around them. It wasn't enough to win the game, but for the diehard fans, it was a moment worth sharing.

When the game was over and they had made their way out of the stadium, Parker said, "I made reservations at a nice restaurant in town." He handed Owen a piece of paper. "Here's the address. If you want to head back to your hotel and get changed, we'll meet you there at 7:00."

❑ ❑ ❑

Once everyone had congregated in the foyer, they were led to a private dining room where a big, round table was set with a linen tablecloth and napkins, crystal glassware, and elegant china. Candelabras lined the walls and big comfortable chairs were set on each side of a lit fireplace.

Those chairs were already occupied by a man and two women. They immediately rose and came forward to greet the newcomers.

"You beat us here. Nice." Parker winked and then turned to the others. "We invited some good friends to join us."

Before he had the chance to introduce them, Anna spoke. "Wait, you sat in the row behind us at the game. I gave you all high-fives."

"Yes, my hand still tingles," the younger woman said.

"Oh, I'm so sorry. I get a little carried away sometimes. My name's Anna."

"I didn't say it hurt. I'm Nora."

"Pleased to meet you, Nora. That's one of my favorite names," she said in her usual cheerful tone as she reached to shake her hand.

"I know. You gave it to me." With eyes sparkling and a priceless smile, she reached to take Anna's other hand. "It's me, Nora."

Time abruptly stood still.

Owen's mouth dropped open in disbelief.

Anna only stared, trying to process the sound of her voice and absorb the meaning of her words. She shook her head and looked toward Parker and Matt. "Can it be?"

Both men nodded with huge grins plastered on their faces. Matt waved a hand toward Nora. "Yes, Anna, your daughter's been found."

Overwhelmed by the news, Anna's world went dark. Her hands fell limp and she collapsed. Parker was close enough to break her fall. For a moment, the room was filled with confusion.

Nora gasped, immediately kneeling by her mother. "This wasn't right. We should've forewarned her."

Owen quickly joined them and put his arm around her shoulders. "Hey, it's okay. We just had no idea you were even alive, so yeah, this is quite a shock for all of us."

"Sorry."

"Don't be, we couldn't be more thrilled! By the way, I'm your brother, Owen."

"Nice to meet you, Owen." She leaned into his embrace. "I only found out that I was stolen from a loving family a little over a week ago. But for you and Anna, you've lived with the pain of my disappearance for the last twenty years."

"And that's exactly why we're in shock. We never expected to see you again."

Rita handed Nora a napkin from the table that she had dipped into a glass of ice water. Nora took it and started caressing Anna's forehead.

Anna blinked a few times and tried to sit up. Her head swam and she fell back to the floor. "Whoa . . . what happened?"

"You blacked out." Owen slipped an arm under her back and helped her to a sitting position. "Here, put your head between your knees for a minute."

Several seconds passed before she looked up. Her eyes met Nora's. "Is it really you, my dear child?"

She nodded cheerfully. "Yes, it's really me."

"Unbelievable." She reached a hand to Owen and he and Parker helped her to her feet. Once she had her footing, she immediately engulfed Nora in her arms and wouldn't let go. Owen joined them. The three cried and held their embrace for a long time.

Devin pulled on Shannon's leg. "Mommy, why are Daddy and Mimi crying?"

His little voice brought Anna back to the park twenty years earlier when Owen asked, 'Mommy, why are you crying? Mommy, where is Nora?'

She's right here. Anna again burst into tears. "She's right here!" After a bit, Rita handed out tissues and Anna began to laugh as she dried her eyes. "This is incredible." She took Nora's hands again. "How did you find us?"

"You have Parker and Matt to thank for that. We'll explain over dinner, but first, let me introduce you to Rita and Frank. They're the angels God sent to rescue me."

Anna gave them big hugs and introduced Owen, Shannon, and Devin.

Owen shook his head. "It's hard to believe you're alive and well."

"And here." Anna still looked a bit dazed as she covered her heart.

A waitress came in, got them seated, and took their orders.

While they waited for dinner to arrive, Anna asked, "What do you mean, your angels? Aren't Rita and Frank your adoptive parents?"

"If you don't mind, Rita, I'd like to answer," Matt said. She nodded approvingly and he began. "Anna, you were the one to encourage us to follow the leads to find Melissa. And when it got hard, you wouldn't let us quit. Well, your love and care for a stranger kept us in pursuit. As you know, our leads brought us to Stanton and his crimes have been uncovered. We thought we had accomplished our mission. Well, we've kept you in the loop every step of the way . . . until recently."

"No way!" She shook her head and raised a hand to cover her mouth.

"Yes. Nora is Melissa."

Anna looked at a loss for words.

"Except I hate that name, so can we please stop using it? I've been going by the name of Jordan ever since I fled that awful situation."

"Sorry, Jordan, but Anna needed to be clear who we were talking about," Parker said as he continued with their story. "When we reached Louisville, our new leads brought us to Rita where we heard her account of what happened next. That night we took more pictures and received new information, which made us believe Jordan was your daughter. It wasn't until the next day that we finally met her. With the miraculous way our information led us to you both, Jordan agreed to get her DNA tested. Then we came back to your house in Virginia Beach so we could get yours without you knowing."

"Yeah, we didn't want to get your hopes up, in case we were wrong," Matt added. "But we were pretty sure what the DNA would show."

"Well, aren't you two clever. And here I thought you came back because you missed me." Anna chuckled.

"You are too cute, Anna." Jordan's cheeks immediately reddened. "I mean, Mom."

"No worries. I don't mind if you call me Anna and we'll gladly call you Jordan." She squeezed her hand.

"Thanks. And these 'clever guys', as you call them, weren't wrong when they said you were amazing." She beamed as she picked up where Parker left off. "Well, anyway, Matt told us about how your child was stolen. After they received an image of you with a toddler, the night before they were to meet me, they realized I could be that child. Captain Smith had one of his techs do a time-lapse of the toddler which looked incredibly close to an older picture they had of me. Just to know that my mother didn't willingly cast me off as an inconvenience caused a dead part of me to live again. At first, I didn't know what to do because God had given me Rita and Frank. I would never want to hurt them or betray their trust—"

"Nor should you!" Anna turned to Rita and Frank. "Words cannot rightly express our gratitude for your kindness in not only rescuing . . ." She placed a hand above her quivering lips, "but also in caring for our girl."

"Amen to that." The sincerity in Owen's voice surpassed his twenty-five years. "Just to know Jordan is alive and well is more than enough for us."

Frank nodded. "You're both very welcome." His eyes began to glaze. "Jordan has filled our lives with joy."

"That's so very true," Rita added. "But we also see God's hand in this. There was no way we would ever choose to keep Jordan from finding her *real* family."

"Right. Rita even went with me to get my DNA tested and as you've realized by now, the lab work came back as a perfect match. I was so excited about meeting you, but then Matt got called back to Philadelphia on business and Parker to Pittsburgh to see his mom. Suddenly, we weren't sure what to do. I didn't want to wait and yet, after their hard work and even risking their lives for me, I wanted them to be a part of this reunion. Matt suggested the baseball game because he knew you loved baseball as much as I do. But Parker suggested I wait to meet you in a more private setting.

"We all agreed and came up with this dinner plan, but I still wanted to come to the game. You don't know how much I enjoyed listening to your conversations and seeing how you interacted with each other. I clearly had the advantage and when you gave me that high-five, it took all that was in me not to give you a big hug and tell you right then."

"Waiting until now is perfect. Sorry I ruined the moment by passing out."

"Nothing was ruined. You did have us scared for a minute, though." Jordan playfully nudged her shoulder.

Anna smiled and nudged her back. "Well, it's still hard to believe that you're here. To be honest, I lost all hope years ago of ever seeing you again." She moved a hand to her heart and looked from face to face. "Thanks to all of you for making this happen. Especially, since I know what it took for you all to get here."

Their food arrived and the room quickly filled with joyful chatter. Partway through their meal, Anna said, "Jordan, I only know your story as far as Indianapolis. Can you tell us how you got to Louisville and met Rita and Frank?"

Over the course of dinner, everyone listened as Jordan and Rita told their stories. Occasionally, Frank would chime in with some fun facts.

After dessert, Parker suggested they continue their conversation over by the fireplace. "I've rented the room until closing so we still have a few hours."

Matt and Owen helped Parker move a few chairs, so everyone had a place to sit and more coffee was served.

Once everyone settled, Parker said, "I want you all to know that I received a call from Captain Smith yesterday. The court date in St. Louis is set for November 14th. He's confident that, with all the evidence they've collected and our testimonies, the people involved with the child abductions and bogus adoption ring will spend the rest of their lives in prison. They've also found and returned the last two children to their parents, who are eager to testify as well."

"That's wonderful news!" Anna said.

"Yeah, except the Captain wasn't sure if any of the other children could be restored to their families because, even if they find the adoptive parents, they won't necessarily be able to find the real parents."

"That, on the other hand, is very sad," Rita said. "Hopefully the new parents will treat the children well."

"I was treated well until I turned sixteen." An uncontrolled shudder shook Jordan. "Are you still confident *he* won't get off on a technicality?"

"More confident than ever; he wasn't even released on bail."

Jordan blew out a long breath. Tears again welled in her eyes. "Ugh. Sorry I'm so emotional about this, but it's like the weight of the world has rolled off my shoulders." Overwhelmed with emotion, she could no longer hold back the flood of tears. Through her sobs, she struggled to speak. "Even though I've been out of that awful situation for over five years, the fear of him still haunts me."

There wasn't a dry eye in the room. Cindy handed out tissues.

Eventually, Jordan wiped her face and turned to Parker and Matt. "I don't even know how to begin to thank you."

"We're just the messengers," Parker said. "I believe God is the one we should be thanking."

"So true, but if you didn't follow the leads, this grand reunion would never have happened."

Thanksgiving and joy again filled the room. Gradually the conversation turned to lighter things and more coffee was served.

"So Matt, what's the latest word on Haley?" Anna asked. "Here we are rejoicing in our good fortune. Do you have news?"

"Not yet; as far as I know she's still with what's-his-face."

"I'm sorry to hear that."

"Don't be. If everything had worked out with Haley, I would be getting married soon, but I wouldn't have been a part of this phenomenal adventure. And I wouldn't have met this amazing group of people. I'm truly blessed and if Haley ever wants to give *us* another shot, she's worth it to me."

"Aww, that's so cute," Shannon said.

"And *big* of you," Owen added. "You must really love her, to forgive such a selfish act."

"Yeah, I still love her and yet, I've also grown as a person since this all began. So even if Haley never comes back, I know I'll be okay."

"We're glad to hear it, Matt." Anna smiled and turned to Parker. "What about you? We never had the chance to talk about personal stuff, except for a few minutes at the hospital. Do you have a girlfriend?"

"Not at the moment. I travel a lot for work, which isn't real conducive to dating. And, to be honest, for a long time I didn't dare to date because I had a temper. After seeing what my mom went through because of Mike's unchecked anger, I made up my mind that I wasn't going to be *that guy*. No woman deserves to be treated like that."

Cindy flinched at his answer. "Oh, Parker, I'm so sorry. Just because I wasn't strong enough to get out from under him, doesn't mean you should have to go through life alone."

"Cindy's right, don't keep that door closed forever," Anna added in her usual optimistic tone.

Parker grinned and pulled out his phone. "Here, Anna. Look at this." There was the picture with Parker, his wife, and child. "I don't know who she is yet, and it's only fitting that her face is obscured, but I'm guessing things work out for me."

"Yes, I'm sure they will."

"And what about you, Anna?" Jordan asked. "Did you ever date after things fell apart with you and my father?"

"Yes, a few times, but nothing ever became serious. Your dad was my high school sweetheart and I struggled with opening my heart up to anyone else. We both handled your disappearance and our grief in different ways and ended up hurting each other. Under different circumstances, we'd be celebrating our twenty-eighth anniversary this year."

Cindy stared at Anna with a confused look on her face. "So you're telling us that you spent the last twenty years alone because of love?"

Anna shrugged. "I guess that'd be one way to look at it."

Cindy shook her head. "I don't get that. I stayed with the wrong guy all those years because I didn't want to be alone. Do you even know if he still loves you? What if he's moved on and is remarried or living with someone?"

"I don't know the answer to those questions, Cindy. I never said it was easy and yes, I often wished things were different. I didn't *enjoy* waking up alone and, in the early years, I would cry myself to sleep. But, hey, life goes on, right? And look, I have all the love I need right here in this room."

"Parker said you were an amazing woman. I might not agree with, or even understand, your choice to be alone, but I've watched how you treat people—even strangers like me—and I agree: you're pretty amazing."

Anna blushed. "Stop. It's only by the grace of God. Now, more coffee anyone?"

Frank answered first. "It's getting late. Rita and I need to be going, but we're staying at the same hotel. Jordan, if you want to stay, I'm sure Owen will be happy to give you a ride."

Devin had been asleep for hours, but Shannon thought they should get him to bed. "How about we have breakfast together in the morning before we head home?"

"Good idea, Shannon. We still have lots of catching up to do," Anna said as they all stood. "Parker, Matt, like Jordan said, there aren't enough words to thank you for all that you've done for us. Let's keep in touch. You're family now."

"We will, and let's make it a tradition to catch at least one Phillies game a year together," Matt said, his eyes still bright though the hour was late.

Jordan approached Parker and Matt last. She took each of their hands and said, "After Rita and Frank took me in, Frank encouraged me not to blame God for what I'd gone through. He said, 'We live in a fallen world where evil exists. People have free wills and some allow the evil to rule over them. That does not change who God is.' I understand that now and, though heartache has touched each one of our lives, God has not forsaken us. You two have proven that good still exists and that God walks among us through his people. I know there are still a few emotional hurdles in my way, but I'm a lot closer to being whole because of you. Thank you." Then she gave each of them a kiss on the cheek before saying goodnight.

Chapter 32

ON THE ROAD AGAIN

It was midnight by the time they reached the parking lot.

"Don't hurry on my account," Cindy said. "I just need to rest my back." She climbed into the Jeep, lowered the seat, and closed her eyes.

Matt spun his keys around his index finger while he waited for Parker to join him on the driver's side. "What an amazing day, and tomorrow we'll be back to real life, right?"

"I would guess so." Parker leaned against the hood and crossed his arms. "Jordan's been reunited with her mom and brother. Stanton is no longer a threat. So yes, I would say mission accomplished. Oh, do you think your mom would be willing to take my mom shopping on Monday? I was hoping that would be an excuse for them to meet. Your mom is strong and outgoing, and my mom could use some positive influences in her life."

"I'll ask her tomorrow. If she doesn't already have plans, I'm sure she'd be happy to."

"Great, thanks. And you know, now that I've gotten to spend some time with my mom, I see she has a lot of good qualities under that tough skin of hers. I think if they spend time together, our moms could become good friends."

"That'd be cool. I'll let you know."

Parker stepped forward and gave Matt a robust handshake. "I can't tell you how appreciative I am that you didn't give up on me after I landed you in the hospital. Your friendship means a lot to me and I'm glad things worked out for you to be a part of finding Jordan."

"Thanks. And in retrospect, the night terror incident wasn't even the hardest part of this experience, but it's taught me a lot about myself."

"You're certainly more daring and adventurous than you realized. If Haley can't see what a great guy you are, then she doesn't deserve you."

Matt nodded thoughtfully and then headed for his own car.

❏ ❏ ❏

The next morning, Matt woke earlier than planned, but because he was still riding high from everything that had happened, he decided to go to the coffee shop and then head to church. He hadn't been since the breakup.

Upon exiting his apartment building, he didn't notice the woman who sat cross-legged on the stone wall to the left of the entrance and walked right past her.

"Matt, wait!" She uncrossed her legs and jumped to her feet.

He recognized the voice and in a muddled haze turned to face Haley. *Wow, I didn't see this coming.* His remarks from last night echoed in his ears. *Am I really willing to give her a second chance?* His smile vanished as he stared blankly through the predawn mist.

Haley spoke first. "Hi . . . Um . . ." She nervously tucked her long, strawberry blond hair behind her ears and shoved her hands into the pockets of her leather jacket. "I'm so sorry, Matt."

Her eyes were red and swollen. Though this clawed at his heart, he chose to remain stoic and took a step back, putting a greater distance between them.

His reaction caused fresh tears to run down her cheeks. Instead of brushing them away, she locked her eyes on his. "I know my actions have been reprehensible, but could you find it in your heart to forgive me?"

"What? Did what's-his-face dump you?" Matt crossed his arms so she couldn't see his hands tremble. And even though he knew his words were harsh, things had changed. He had changed. He was no longer *blinded* by his love for her and had no intentions of being her rebound.

"Truthfully, I'm the one who broke it off over a week ago, but I couldn't bring myself to contact you."

"I can't blame you there. Your betrayal, by an email nonetheless, was devastating."

"And heartless . . . and shameful . . . and cruel . . . I know. And, I guess it's silly for me to hope that you could forgive me when I can't even forgive myself." She wiped her eyes with the backs of her hands, which smudged her mascara even more. With a heavy sigh, she sat on the steps and pulled her knees to her chest. "I don't expect you to take me back as if nothing happened, but maybe—"

Matt finally came forward. "But maybe we could start by trying to make sense of what went wrong, so it won't happen again?" He took a seat on the stone ledge adjacent the steps, clasped his hands together in front of him, and said, "You first."

❑ ❑ ❑

Monday morning Bryce called from the Village Gallery. "Hey, Parker. What's my favorite photographer been up to? I haven't heard from you in like a month."

"I've taken a road trip and have lots of new photos."

"So, you haven't bailed on me for a different gallery then?"

This amused Parker. *He has no idea.* "You have nothing to worry about, Bryce. I only got home a few days ago. I'm going to look through my pictures this morning and I'll get you some new prints by week's end."

"Ah, thanks, man. Business just isn't the same without your work on display."

When Parker opened his cloud account, he was pleased to find that several of his photos were of gallery quality. His favorite was the shot he took in Nashville of the old couple who were walking arm in arm toward the Ryman Theater.

Then he remembered that the man in the picture gave him his business card. As he pulled his wallet from his back pocket, the feel of the new leather reminded him that he had lost his old one along with the card. *Oh well. I can still get this one framed and take it to Bryce.*

After a few hours of sorting and editing photos, Parker took a break. It was overcast, but not raining, so he walked to the end of the street to retrieve his mail. Mixed in with the rest was a business-sized envelope with only his name on it. *Hmm, this is odd.* He looked to see if anyone was out and about that might have seen who put the envelope in his mailbox. There wasn't, so he opened it and found a handwritten letter that read:

'I would like to thank you and Matt for following my leads. You both did a commendable job and didn't quit when it got hard. I would like to show my appreciation by sending you on a little vacation. Below is the flight itinerary for your trip to Ireland along with reservations for a weekend stay at Delaney's Bed & Breakfast. Again, my sincerest thanks.' The letter was not signed.

Parker couldn't help but smile as he pulled out the flight info and saw a business card that looked like the one the old man had given him. His words echoed in Parker's ears: *'Thank you, young man, and if you ever visit Ireland, be sure to look us up . . .'*

It started to sprinkle, so he quickly stuffed the papers back into the envelope and ran back to the house. As soon as he got inside, he flipped off his shoes and called Matt. "Hey, I hope you don't have plans for this weekend because we're going to Ireland."

"You got a new lead, already?"

"Nope, just a complimentary trip, courtesy of our mystery guy! We're on the red-eye flight that leaves at 7:00 Thursday evening."

"That's so cool," Matt said, "but unfortunately I'll have to clear it with my boss first. Apparently, the owners of the Chestnut Street building have decided *not* to sell."

"Still? What's their problem?"

"That's what I'm supposed to find out. I'll see what I can do."

❑ ❑ ❑

Matt was able to get a few days off and they arrived in Dublin Friday morning. To their surprise, among the many people waiting for passengers was a man holding up a sign with their names on it. They approached him and asked how he knew they were coming.

"Hello. Mr. Delaney always sends a wagon for his guests. Please, follow me." It took them about ten minutes to reach the vehicle and when they climbed into the back seat, they found a breakfast sandwich and a hot mug of coffee for each of them. "The food is compliments of Delaney's. My boss wants to make sure you enjoy your visit to our fine country." He put their bags in the trunk and drove away. "The Bed & Breakfast is just over an hour from here. The countryside is beautiful, so if you see anything you would like to take pictures of, ask me to stop."

"Thanks. I'm a photographer by trade, so if you know of any extra good spots, please let us know," Parker said.

About forty minutes later, they came upon a quaint village and the driver told them it was one of his favorite places. Parker and Matt got out their cameras and took their time walking through the shops, as well as taking lots of pictures of the buildings and the locals.

"This feels a little too familiar," Parker said reluctantly. "I'm half expecting extra images to appear in these photos."

"Yeah, but I miss getting clues. Maybe someday they'll start again with a different quest."

"I'm game, but after the adventures of the last month, I sincerely hope nothing shows up in these."

Close to an hour passed before they were back on the road and neither of them cared to stop again, even though Parker did take some pictures from the vehicle.

The Bed & Breakfast sat on a hill back away from the main road. As they drove up the winding driveway, the lake came into view. "Oh wow, look at that," Parker said. "Is there access to the water from this property?"

"Yes, they've made a nice trail. It's a bit of a hike down to the lake, but well worth the effort. There's a nice big dock with built-in seating and kayaks available if you want to get out on the water."

"Sweet. We'll have to check that out."

Because of the time of year, most of the flower gardens were past their prime, but the grounds were still pristinely maintained. Rock walks led to wooden benches situated for the best views of the lake. The building itself was a large two-story stone structure, with a terracotta roof. Windows lined both floors and the end wall was draped in ivy.

"What a great place and the views are fantastic," Matt said as he jumped out of the wagon.

"It sure is," the driver agreed. He got out their bags and set them on the stone bench by the entrance. "*Slán Agat.* It's been a pleasure."

"It certainly has." Matt reached to shake his hand.

Parker handed him a tip. "And thanks for showing us the sights." The driver gladly took the cash and nodded his appreciation before driving away.

Matt shouldered his bag. "Well, we couldn't ask for a better start to a relaxing weekend."

Parker agreed. He grabbed his suitcase and they went inside.

Antique vases filled with chrysanthemums graced both sides of the entrance. The lobby was a decent sized room with a tiled floor and rustic wood beams that crossed the vaulted ceiling. To their left, a large impressionist painting hung on the wall behind the camel-backed sofa. Tall square tables sat at each end; each holding a lamp and a few well-worn books. To their right was an ornate, mahogany desk with a welcome sign, brochures of tourist destinations, and a vase of fresh-cut flowers. To complete the ambiance, a vintage chandelier hung above the desk.

A tall, middle-aged man came from the next room to greet them. He was clean-shaven, with short, graying hair and deep-set eyes. "Welcome. I trust you had a pleasant flight and an enjoyable ride here?"

"We sure did," Matt said, "but we didn't expect a chauffeur and breakfast."

"We aim to please. My uncle started supplying transportation about three years ago. It's amazing how much our business has grown since then."

"Is this the same uncle that came to the States about a month ago?"

"He is, but how do you know that?"

"I happened to be at the Ryman Theater in Nashville and your uncle asked me to take a picture of him with his wife. When I gave his camera back, he gave me his business card."

"Ha, that's not surprising. My uncle has business on the brain."

"Are they here? I took a picture of them with my own camera as they walked away. I was hoping to give them a copy."

"Yes. My aunt takes a turn at the desk in about an hour. You can greet her then. I'll let my uncle know you took him up on his offer to come for a visit. He'll get a kick out of that and want to say hello."

"That's great, thanks."

"So you boys are from Nashville, then?"

"No, we live in Philadelphia," Matt said.

"Oh yeah? I grew up in Philadelphia."

"Ah, no wonder your Irish accent isn't as strong," Parker said. "How long have you lived here?"

"It's been a while." He opened his guest book and jotted something down. "Philadelphia is a big city. Are you guys familiar with Chestnut Street?"

"We sure are. My favorite café is on the east end of that street!" Matt said. "Why did you leave?"

"My parents immigrated to the States when I was three. But years later, we ran into some personal problems, so we came back to Ireland."

"Oh, we're sorry to hear that," Parker said.

He shrugged. "It's not your fault, so there's no need to be sorry. My parents still own a building on Chestnut Street. Funny this should be brought up because recently we received a purchase offer for that property."

"Wait! Are you talking about the abandoned building that used to be a thriving Hotel and Irish Pub?" Matt asked in a flurry.

"The very one." He smiled at Matt's exuberance.

"This is unbelievable. I'm a reporter and my boss asked me a few weeks ago to write a story about that property. At the time, we thought the building was going to be sold and because it sat empty for so long, we wanted to add some historical details to the article. When we found out the purchase offer was turned down, my boss still wanted me to write the story so the people who live in the area could at least understand the holdup. Would you be willing to explain why you won't sell?"

"I'll tell you what, let me show you to your rooms and when my aunt comes, we can talk then."

Chapter 33

FULL CIRCLE

"Do you realize our mystery guy just orchestrated a complete circle of events?" Parker asked after they dropped off their bags and checked out their rooms. "Even taking that random photo in Nashville wasn't by chance. What are the odds?"

"A gazillion-to-one." Matt looked more dazed than happy. "I thought nothing could surprise me by now, but this? It blows my mind. My boss will be thrilled to get the news—and who knows, maybe we can talk them into selling."

"Now that would definitely be a cool ending to our story. You might even get a raise."

"Well, that's not my reason for wanting to do the interview, but I am curious to see what Mr. Delaney has to say."

"Me, too. In the meantime, he told me where to find the path to the lake and said he'd meet us there in about forty-five minutes."

It wasn't long before they were weaving their way down the winding path. Treated lumber stairs were built in the places where it was too steep to maneuver safely, making it an enjoyable descent to the water.

They walked in silence for a bit, but then Parker asked, "Do you have a list of questions or will you just see how it goes?"

"Both. I have some questions ready, but I'm hoping he's in the mood to tell us the story without too much prodding."

"Just be careful not to scare him off. Since he mentioned personal problems, we don't want him to feel like he's being interrogated."

"True, but it would be nice to at least get to the root of why they won't sell. They must have relinquished over a hundred thousand dollars in taxes alone, not to mention lost revenue."

"That's a great point and it certainly adds to the intrigue."

When they reached the water, they both walked to the end of the dock and stood there for a while in silence, just taking in the views. Hills rose on both sides of the elongated lake with a hint of fall colors tinging the trees. It was simply beautiful.

Parker had already taken several pictures when he noticed a path along the water. He looked at his watch. "We still have about twenty minutes before Mr. Delaney comes. I'm going to see what's beyond that next bend. Want to come?"

"No, I'll stay. I need to write down some questions. There are a few specific details that I still need for my article, and I don't want to forget to ask."

"Okay, suit yourself." Camera in tow, Parker took off down the path.

❏ ❏ ❏

Matt sat on one of the wood benches and got out his notebook. As he started to write down questions, he realized that the answers his boss wanted were no longer the questions he felt to ask. *I'm guessing whatever happened all those years ago is something they don't want to make public.*

A gust of wind tussled Matt's hair. Lost in thought, he turned his gaze toward the water and mindlessly weaved his pen between his fingers. A few ducks landed on the lake and then took off again.

Parker returned about fifteen minutes later and joined Matt. "I spotted Mr. Delaney on the path a few minutes ago. He'll be here soon."

"Oh, good," Matt said, as he stood to join Parker.

"Are you ready?"

"I'm actually kind of nervous, though I don't know why."

"You've done hundreds of interviews; this one is no different."

"I know, it's just—"

"Hey guys, isn't it beautiful here?" the man called from the shore.

"It sure is," Parker said. "I've taken close to thirty photos already."

He waited until he had joined them on the dock before saying, "Well, that looks like quite the camera you have there. Maybe later you could show them to me? We're always looking for new pictures to use on our website and in our brochures."

"Sure thing. Maybe later today, I could even take some of the building, foyer, and anything else you might want."

"That would be fantastic, but I don't want to interfere with your vacation."

Parker held up his camera with a big grin on his face. "It's obviously a passion of mine, so I certainly wouldn't mind."

"Great. But now that I'm here, Matt, you said you had some questions about the building on Chestnut Street?"

"It might be easier if we take a seat first." Matt motioned to the benches and he and Parker sat across from him.

"So what is it that you want to know?"

"What everyone in Philadelphia wants to know. Why has the building sat empty all these years and why won't your parents sell it?"

"Well, that's about as direct as you can get," he said, his eyes taking on the blue-green hue of the lake. He crossed his legs and rested his left arm on the back of the bench. "My father and I just got back from Philadelphia last weekend. It was the first time either of us had returned since he locked the doors. We met with the prospective buyers and heard their plans for the property. We also walked through the building and were pleased to see things just as we left them—along with decades of dust and cobwebs, of course." He grinned.

"So you didn't like the offer or what?" Matt asked.

"We haven't said we *won't* sell, but on the flight home, my father made me an offer. He said we could sell the building, and the profits would be my inheritance, or he would give me the building if I was interested in returning to the States. Because this offer was just made to me, I wanted to take a few weeks to weigh my options.

"At first, I told him that I couldn't accept his offer because it was my fault they walked away from a prosperous business and gave up their American dream. He told me it wasn't my fault and that I was worth more to them than their success. My parents refused to sit by and watch me throw my life away."

Parker leaned forward and put his elbows on his knees.

Matt straightened his glasses and wrote something in his notebook before asking, "If you don't mind, can you tell us what happened?"

"I had everything—a family, money, success. We were living the dream, but over time, everything changed. I ran the pub and had unlimited access to the liquor." His eyes dropped as he shook his head. Then he shifted his position to look at the lake and clasped his hands together. He squeezed them so tightly that his knuckles turned white. "I . . . I threw the dream away. I started to drink . . . and became condescending and abusive. Finally, I lost my family which caused me to drink even more. One day, not long after this, my mom found me passed out on the floor in my office with a note telling them I'd lost everything that mattered to me, and how sorry I was that I'd become a black spot on their business and their good name."

Parker didn't move.

Matt stopped writing and looked over his glasses. He waited for a minute before asking, "So what happened?"

He loosened his grip and watched as color rushed back into his hands. "Obviously, I lived. But while I was in the hospital, my parents hired a company to cover everything in every single room with thick white blankets. They boarded over all the windows and locked the doors. When we left the hospital, we went straight to the airport and flew to Dublin. Both my parents found work, but I was so messed up, I wasn't able to keep a job. I saw shrinks and went to AA meetings, but nothing helped. My parents were beside themselves; they didn't know how to bring me back from the abyss. Finally, they asked my aunt and uncle if I could move in with them and become their groundskeeper. They figured it would keep me busy and, more importantly, away from the abundance of pubs in Dublin."

He turned back to face Parker and Matt.

Neither of them spoke, so he continued, "Spending most of my time outside and working with my hands to make things look beautiful was just what I needed. As you can tell, I'm good at it." For the first time in his story, he smiled. "Eventually, I got better, but it took years and by then, it seemed pointless to go back to Philadelphia. When we first left the States, the plan was to return. That's why we never sold the building.

"I was finally healthy and doing well, and I didn't want to risk changing that by going back to where our lives became hell. My parents agreed with me, but I'm not sure why they never sold the property. Maybe they hoped I would change my mind because my mom inherited the building from her great uncle.

"The funny thing about time is that it can get away from you rather quickly. The building sat empty all these years because of me."

"Okay, you're manning up and taking the blame, but I don't get it," Parker said. "What happened? You don't become an alcoholic overnight. What changed?"

His eyes glossed over, turning to a cold misty gray. The memory of lost things and destroyed lives haunted him. He abruptly stood and started to leave the dock.

Without a moment to lose, Matt jumped to his feet and followed him. "Please, Mr. Delaney, please help us to understand. I promise I won't put it in the article, but something awful must have happened. Can you tell us what?"

Parker joined Matt and pulled on his arm. "Give him some space."

The man stopped as abruptly as he had stood, but only turned enough to look down at the water. He shoved his hands deep into his pockets and with a tear now running down his cheek, he said, "One day my little girl went missing and was never found. From that moment, our lives fell apart."

Parker shot a look toward Matt in time to see him do a double take.

His expression was one of shock mixed with wonder. *It can't be . . . can it?* Matt shook his head hard; once he regained his composure, he asked, "What was your daughter's name?"

"Nora."

Matt, now wild with excitement, blurted out, "And is your name, Quinn?"

His eyes darted Matt's way. "Yes, but I never said my name, so how do you know that?"

"Because we recently met Anna, and she told us her story. She mentioned you, but she never said anything about the building on Chestnut Street, so we didn't make the connection. Especially when your last names didn't match."

"So, she's remarried?"

"No, her last name is Collins; same as Owen's."

He smiled a little. "Delaney is my uncle's surname. My name is Quinn Collins."

Matt momentarily cupped his hands behind his head. "This is incredible." Then he stepped closer to Quinn, "Man, have we got some fantastic news for you. Nora's alive! We found her a few weeks ago."

Stunned, Quinn's lips began to quiver as he seized Matt's arms. "How do you know she's *our* Nora?"

"We had both Nora's and Anna's DNA tested. The results were a match."

Quinn fell to his knees and buried his face in his hands on the dock. He heaved uncontrollably, rocking back and forth.

Parker took a step back. Matt, on the other hand, knelt next to Quinn and put his arm around his shoulders. "She's not only alive, she's beautiful. Would you like to see a picture of her?"

Another minute passed before he pulled himself together. He leaned back on his heels and looked at Matt. "But how? How did you find her?"

"It's kind of a long story," Matt said. "But if you have time, we'd be happy to share it with you."

Quinn nodded. "But I don't understand. How do you know Anna?"

"Ha, that will be a part of our story." Matt reached out a hand and helped Quinn to his feet.

Parker had already gotten out his phone and opened a picture of Nora. "Last weekend, when you were in Philadelphia, so were they. We arranged an opportunity for Nora to be reunited with Anna. Owen and his family were there too." He handed Quinn his phone. "The reunion was simply beautiful—except for when Nora asked where her dad was, and no one knew the answer."

"But now we know!" Matt said enthusiastically.

Fresh tears ran down Quinn's face as he stared at the picture. "This is unbelievable." Eventually, he walked back and sat on the bench and stretched the photo so he could see her face better. "I still can't believe Nora is alive. It's crazy how much she looks like Anna at that age."

"There are more," Parker said, nodding toward the phone.

Quinn took his time looking at each picture before going to the next. Finally, he stopped at one that was just of Anna. He whispered, "God she's beautiful." Then he looked at Parker and Matt. "Anna emailed my mom and invited us to Owen's wedding. But we'd been out of his life for so long, we felt like it wouldn't be fair to show up at such an important event and distract from his special day. Anna sent pictures of the wedding and has been good about sending pictures of Devin. But she never sent pictures of herself. So, I guess she still hates me."

"From what she told us, she's never stopped loving you. But back at the time of Nora's disappearance, she said she was broken. That she couldn't even help herself, let alone help you," Parker said. "I'm guessing she never sent personal photos because she didn't want to remind you of her failure to protect Nora."

"It wasn't her fault. I know that now. Unfortunately, that day destroyed us. It took over a decade before I started to heal and could function without alcohol."

"You seem to be doing fine now," Matt said.

"Yeah, I'm good, but I admit, I keep myself busier than I should—mostly so I won't feel the pain of my loss." Quinn zoomed in on Anna's face. Then he turned to Matt, "You say she never remarried?"

"Nope."

"Huh . . . Me neither. Anna's the only woman I've ever loved." He looked back at the phone as another tear rolled down his cheek. He brushed it off with his shoulder. "I was so cruel to her. How could she ever forgive me?"

"Do you see those eyes?" Parker said. "She holds no animosity."

"But our good times together were a lifetime ago. There's been too much water under the bridge to even broach that subject now."

"I wouldn't be so sure about that," Matt said. "Anna never remarried because of her love for you. So . . ." He paused to grin. "What do you say to a visit to Virginia Beach?"

THE END

Whether simple or grand, all novels are birthed from an idea. Mine originated with this photo and a question: "What caused the building to die?"

Now renovated, this building is located on Chestnut Street in Philadelphia's Historic District.

Photo Credit: Bridget Dowling

Also available is Arleen's debut novel,

The Painter

Their lives were all but destroyed . . .
Her paintings are about to change everything.

While painting, Claire jumps at the sound of a loud crash, which causes her to drop a loaded brush of paint onto the watercolor paper. She manages to spill the jar of water too. The painting is ruined. Or is it? To her astonishment, three perfectly painted teenage boys fill the paper. But how? Once she realizes others can see the boys too, she's at a loss. Not knowing what else to do, she turns her attention from *how* it happened to *why*.

Weeks later, Claire is stunned when she meets a woman at Frontier Days who recognizes the boys in the painting. Though her account is heartbreaking, the details spur Claire to ask for permission to come see where the boys grew up. There she meets Chase, a strong yet broken rancher.

As their friendship deepens, more of Claire's paintings change and she is determined to find their purpose. An unlikely cast of characters weave their way into her heart and turn this unbelievable tale into a real-life adventure of love, loss, and the need for forgiveness.

Acknowledgments

I love that the Lord Jesus put this story into my heart and then helped me in my efforts to let it spill out onto these pages. I am forever grateful.

The Photographer was the first full-length novel I wrote, and in the early stages, it needed a lot of work. My deepest appreciation and thanks go to Chris Gallmann. You not only scrutinized every part of this manuscript, you also offered constructive advice and pushed me to become a better writer. I'm glad you saw the potential in this story and were willing to give of your own time to help me bring it to completion.

Thank you, Colleen Frasier. You encouraged me to turn this *short story* into a full-length novel. From the first draft to final edits to the internal design, you played an invaluable part in improving this book.

To my team of beta readers and early draft editors: Colleen, Jay Jennings, and Stephanie Dean. Each of you found different elements that needed work. Your attention to detail, including the removal of character inconsistencies, strengthened the story. You were all fantastic and deserve praise. Thank you!

Many thanks to Brenda Riehle and Debra Benedict. You both played special parts, not only with the editing but also with affirmation I needed at critical points in the process.

To Karen Buell for helping me with the business end of things. It's not my forte, but so very important when it comes to getting the book into the hands of readers. Thank You!

To my beloved, Ron. Because you know me so well, you were able to help me improve my writing without changing my style. Your support and input, from beta reading to editing to publishing, have been a great blessing. Thank you so much!

www.arleenjennings.com

Made in the USA
Lexington, KY
16 November 2019